Praise for *House of Hollow*

'Stepping nimbly among the liminal spaces and eerie real-world haunts of our heroine's cipher-sister, this haunting modern fairy tale will wrap you up like a glittering fog, before going for your throat.'
Melissa Albert, author of *The Hazel Wood*

'This dark, deliciously twisted novel has everything you could hope for as a reader – a brilliant concept, glamorous characters with secrets to hide, immersive world building, and some of the finest writing I've seen in YA fiction. I'll put it like this – I am obsessed with the House of Hollow.'
Louise O'Neill, author of *After the Silence*

'Dark and delicious, *House of Hollow* hums with malice and mystery. I devoured it whole.'
Kiran Millwood Hargrave, author of *The Mercies*

'In *House of Hollow*, Krystal Sutherland turns her razor-sharp imagination to new horizons and proves, once again, that words blossom at her command. This story will steal up your spine, slip beneath your skin, and stick to you like honey.'
Samantha Shannon, author of *The Bone Season*

'Alive with lush language and a dark fairy tale feel, this is a compelling readalike for lovers of Holly Black's many wonderful fair folk standalones and series.'
School Library Journal

'Iris' smart and assured narration easily carries a fast-paced story entwining themes of grief and loss with elements of folklore and some very inventive body horror. The pervasive feeling of dread builds to a shocking twist. A lush and darkly twisted modern fairy tale.'
Kirkus

'House of Hollow is a horrifyingly beautiful story that will stick with you. This fairy tale turned horror is [. . .] gorgeously written and enchantin[g] into this beautifully terrifying w[ ] each word kept me tumbling dee[ ] fairy tale that is the Hollow sister[ ]

D0488826

KRYSTAL SUTHERLAND

HOUSE OF HOLLOW

HOT
KEY
BOOKS

First published in Great Britain in 2021 by
HOT KEY BOOKS
80–81 Wimpole St, London W1G 9RE
Owned by Bonnier Books
Sveavägen 56, Stockholm, Sweden
www.hotkeybooks.com

A CIP catalogue record for this book is available from the British Library.

ISBN: 978-1-4714-0989-9
Also available as an ebook and audio

2

Design by Suki Boynton
Printed and bound in Great Britain by Clays Ltd, Elcograf S.p.A.

Hot Key Books is an imprint of Bonnier Books UK
www.bonnierbooks.co.uk

For Martin,
my lover of stories

PROLOGUE

I WAS TEN years old the first time I realized I was strange.

Around midnight, a woman dressed in white slipped through my bedroom window and cut off a lock of my hair with sewing scissors. I was awake the whole time, tracking her in the dark, so frozen by fear that I couldn't move, couldn't scream.

I watched as she held the curl of my hair to her nose and inhaled. I watched as she put it on her tongue and closed her mouth and savored the taste for a few moments before swallowing. I watched as she bent over me and ran a fingertip along the hook-shaped scar at the base of my throat.

It was only when she opened my door—bound for the bedrooms of my older sisters, with the scissors still held at her side—that I finally screamed.

My mother tackled her in the hall. My sisters helped hold her down. The woman was rough and rabid, thrashing against the three of them with a strength we'd later learn was fueled by amphetamines. She bit my mother. She headbutted my middle sister, Vivi, so hard in the face that her nose was crushed and both of her eye sockets were bruised for weeks.

It was Grey, my eldest sister, who finally subdued her. When she thought my mother wasn't looking, she bent low over the wild woman's face and pressed her lips against her mouth. It was a soft kiss right out of a fairy tale, made gruesome by the fact that the woman's chin was slick with our mother's blood.

For a moment, the air smelled sweet and wrong, a mixture of honey and something else, something rotten. Grey pulled back and held the woman's head in her hands, and then watched her, intently, waiting. My sister's eyes were so black, they looked like polished river stones. She was fourteen then, and already the most beautiful creature I could imagine. I wanted to peel the skin from her body and wear it draped over mine.

The woman shuddered beneath Grey's touch and then just . . . stopped.

By the time the police arrived, the woman's eyes were wide and faraway, her limbs so liquid she could no longer stand and had to be carried out, limp as a drunk, by three officers.

I wonder if Grey already knew then what we were.

☾

The woman, the police would later tell us, had read about us on the internet and stalked us for several weeks before the break-in.

We were famous for a bizarre thing that had happened to us three years earlier, when I was seven, a thing I couldn't remember and never thought about but that apparently intrigued many other people a great deal.

I was keyed into our strangeness after that. I watched for it in the years that followed, saw it bloom around us in unexpected ways. There was the man who tried to pull Vivi into his car when she was fifteen because he thought she was an angel; she broke his jaw and knocked out two of his teeth. There was the teacher, the one Grey hated, who was fired after he pressed her against a wall and kissed her neck in front of her whole class. There was the pretty, popular girl who had bullied me, who stood in front of the entire school at assembly and silently began to shave her own head, tears streaming down her face as her dark locks fell in spools at her feet.

When I found Grey's eyes through the sea of faces that day, she was staring at me. The bullying had been going on for months, but I'd only told my sisters about it the night before. Grey winked, then returned to the book she was reading, uninterested in the show. Vivi, always less subtle, had her feet up on the back of the chair in front of her and was grinning from ear to ear, her crooked nose wrinkled in delight.

Dark, dangerous things happened around the Hollow sisters.

We each had black eyes and hair as white as milk. We each had enchanting four-letter names: Grey, Vivi, Iris. We walked to school together. We ate lunch together. We walked home together. We didn't have friends, because we didn't need them. We moved through the corridors like sharks, the other little fish parting around us, whispering behind our backs.

Everyone knew who we were. Everyone had heard our story. Everyone had their own theory about what had happened to us. My sisters used this to their advantage. They were very good at cultivating their own mystery like gardeners, coaxing the heady intrigue that ripened around them into the shape of their choosing. I simply followed in their wake, quiet and studious, always embarrassed by the attention. Strangeness only bred strangeness, and it felt dangerous to tempt fate, to invite in the darkness that seemed already naturally drawn to us.

It didn't occur to me that my sisters would leave school long before I did, until it actually happened. School hadn't suited either of them. Grey was blisteringly smart but never found anything in the curriculum particularly to her liking. If a class called for her to read and analyze *Jane Eyre*, she might instead decide Dante's *Inferno* was more interesting and write her essay on that. If an art class called for her to sketch a realistic self-portrait, she might instead draw a sunken-eyed monster with blood on its hands. Some teachers loved this; most did not, and before she dropped out, Grey only ever managed mediocre grades. If this bothered her, she never showed it, drifting through classes with the sureness of a person who had been told her future by a clairvoyant and had liked what she'd heard.

Vivi preferred to cut school as frequently as possible, which relieved the administration, since she was a handful when she did show up. She back-talked teachers, cut slashes in her uniforms to make them more punk, spray-painted graffiti in the toilets, and refused to remove her many piercings. The few assignments she handed in during her last year all scored easy As—there just weren't enough of them to keep her enrolled. Which suited Vivi just fine. Every rock star needed an origin story, and getting kicked out of your £30,000-per-year high school was as good a place to start as any.

They were both like that even then, both already in possession of an alchemical self-confidence that belonged to much older humans. They didn't care what other people thought of them. They didn't care what other people thought was cool (which, of course, made them *unbearably* cool).

They left school—and home—within weeks of each other. Grey was seventeen; Vivi was fifteen. They set off into the world, both bound for the glamorous, exotic futures they'd always known they were destined for. Which is how I found myself alone, the only Hollow left, still struggling to thrive in the long shadows they left behind. The quiet, bright one who loved science and geography and had a natural flair for mathematics. The one who wanted desperately, above all else, to be unremarkable.

Slowly, month by month, year by year, the strangeness that swelled around my sisters began to recede, and for a good long while, my life was what I'd craved ever since I'd seen Grey sedate an intruder with a simple kiss: normal.

It was, of course, not to last.

1

MY BREATH SNAGGED when I saw my sister's face staring up at me from the floor.

Grey's fine, hook-shaped scar was still the first thing you noticed about her, followed by how achingly beautiful she was. The *Vogue* magazine—her third US cover in as many years—must have arrived in the post and landed faceup on the hall rug, smack bang, which is where I found it in the silver ghost light of the morning. The words *The Secret Keeper* hovered in mossy green text beneath her. Her body was angled toward the photographer, her lips parted in a sigh, her black eyes staring at the camera. A pair of antlers emerged from her white hair as though they were her own.

For a short, watching moment, I'd thought she was actually there, in the flesh. The infamous Grey Hollow.

In the four years since she'd left home, my eldest sister had grown into a gossamer slip of a woman with hair like spun sugar and a face out of Greek mythology. Even in still pictures there was something vaporous and hyaline about her, like she might ascend into the ether at any moment. It was perhaps why journalists were forever describing her as ethereal, though I'd always thought of Grey as more earthy. No articles ever mentioned that she felt most at home in the woods, or how good she was at making things grow. Plants loved her. The wisteria outside her childhood bedroom had often snaked in through the open window and coiled around her fingers in the night.

I picked up the magazine and flicked to the cover story.

Grey Hollow wears her secrets like silk.

When I meet her in the lobby of the Lanesborough (Hollow never allows journalists near her apartment, nor, it's rumored, does she host parties or entertain guests), she's dressed in one of her hallmark enigmatic creations. Think heavy embroidery, hundreds of beads, thread spun from actual gold, and tulle so light it drifts like smoke. Hollow's couture has been described as a fairy tale meeting a nightmare inside a fever dream. Gowns drip with leaves and decaying petals, her catwalk models wear antlers scavenged from deer carcasses and the pelts of skinned mice, and she insists on wood-smoking her fabric before it's cut so her fashion shows smell like forest fires.

Hollow's creations are beautiful and decadent and strange, but it's the clandestine nature of her pieces that has made them so famous so quickly. There are secret messages hand-stitched into the lining of each of her gowns—but that's not all. Celebrities have reported finding scraps of rolled-up paper sewn into the boning of their bodices, or shards of engraved animal bone affixed alongside precious gems, or runic symbols painted in invisible ink, or minuscule vials of perfume that crack like glow sticks when the wearer moves, releasing Hollow's heady eponymous scent. The imagery that features in her embroidery is alien, sometimes disturbingly so. Think gene-spliced flowers and skeletal Minotaurs, their faces stripped of flesh.

Much like their creator, each piece is a puzzle box, begging to be solved.

I stopped reading there, because I knew what the rest of the article would say. I knew it would talk about the thing that happened to us as children, the thing none of us could remember. I knew it would talk about my father, the way he'd died.

I touched my fingertips to the scar at my throat. The same half-moon scar I shared with Grey, with Vivi. The scar none of us could remember getting.

I took the magazine up to my bedroom and slipped it under my pillow so my mother wouldn't find it, wouldn't burn it in the kitchen sink like the last one.

Before I left, I opened my Find Friends app and checked that it was turned on and transmitting my location. It was a requirement of my daily morning runs that my mother could track my little orange avatar as it bobbed around Hampstead Heath. Actually, it was a requirement if I wanted to leave the house *at all* that my mother could track my little orange avatar as it bobbed around . . . wherever. Cate's own avatar still hovered south, at the Royal Free Hospital, her nursing shift in A&E dragging—as per usual—into overtime.

Leaving now, I messaged her.

Okay, I will watch you, she pinged back immediately. **Message me when you're home safe.**

I set off into the predawn winter cold.

We lived in a tall, pointed house, covered in white stucco and wrapped with leadlight windows that reminded me of dragonfly wings. Remnants of night still clung to the eaves and collected in pools beneath the tree in our front yard. It was not the kind of place a single mother on a nurse's salary could usually afford, but it had once belonged to my mother's parents, who both died in a car accident when she was pregnant with Grey. They'd bought it at the start of their marriage, during World War II, when property prices in London had crashed because of the Blitz. They were teenagers then, barely older than I was now. The house had been grand once, though it had sagged and sunken with time.

In my favourite old photograph of the place, taken in the kitchen sometime in the sixties, the room was fat with lazy sunlight, the kind that lingers for hours in the summer months, sticking to the tops of trees in golden halos. My grandmother was squinting at the camera, a kaleidoscope of glittering green cast across her skin from a stained glass window that had since been broken. My grandfather stood with his arm around her, a cigar in his mouth, his trousers belted high and a pair of Coke-bottle glasses on his nose. The air looked warm and smoky, and my grandparents were both smiling. They were cool, relaxed. If you didn't know their story, you might think they were happy.

From the four pregnancies she'd carried to term, my grandmother had given birth to only one living child, quite late in her life: my mother, Cate. The rooms of this house that had been earmarked for children had been left empty, and my grandparents had not lived long enough to see any of their grandchildren born. There are things in every family that are not talked about. Stories you know without really knowing how you know them, tales of terrible things that cast long shadows over generations. Adelaide Fairlight's three stillborn babies was one of those stories.

Another was the thing that had happened to us when I was seven.

Vivi called before I'd even reached the end of the street. I took the call on my AirPods, knowing without even looking at my screen that it was her.

"Hey," I said. "You're up early. It can't even be lunchtime in Budapest."

"Ha ha." Vivi's voice sounded muffled, distracted. "What are you doing?"

"I'm out for a run. You know, the thing I do every morning." I turned left and ran along the footpath, past empty sports fields and the carcasses of trees that stood tall and stripped in the cold. It was a gray morning, the sun yawning sluggishly into the sky behind a pall of clouds. The chill needled my exposed skin, drawing tears from my eyes and making my ears ache with each heartbeat.

"Ew," Vivi said. I heard an airline announcement in the background. "Why would you do that to yourself?"

"It's the latest rage for cardiovascular health. Are you at an airport?"

"I'm flying in for a gig tonight, remember? I just landed in London."

"No, I do not remember. Because you definitely didn't tell me."

"I'm *sure* I told you."

"That would be a negative."

"Anyway, I'm here, and Grey's flying in from Paris for some

10

photo shoot today, and we're all hanging out in Camden before the gig. I'll pick you up when I get out of this god-awful airport."

"Vivi, it's a school day."

"You're still at that soul-destroying institution? Wait, hang on, I'm going through immigration."

My usual path took me through the green fields of Golders Hill Park, the grass sprinkled with a confetti bomb of yellow daffodils and white-and-purple crocuses. It had been a mild winter and spring was breaking already, rolling across the city in mid-February.

Minutes dragged by. I heard more airline announcements in the background as I ran along the western border of Hampstead Heath, then into the park, past the blanched milkstone of Kenwood House. I headed deeper into the twisting wildwood warrens of the heath, so tight and green and old in places it was hard to believe you were still in London. I gravitated to the untamed parts, where the trails were muddy and thick fairy-tale trees grew over them in archways. The leaves would soon begin to return, but this morning I moved beneath a thicket of stark branches, my path bordered on both sides by a carpet of fallen detritus. The air here smelled sodden, bloated with damp. The mud was thin from recent rain and flicked up the back of my calves as I pushed on. The sun was rising now, but the early-morning light was suffused with a drop of ink. It made the shadows deep, hungry-looking.

My sister's garbled voice on the phone: "You still there?"

"Yes," I replied. "Much to my chagrin. Your phone manners are appalling."

"As I was saying, school is thoroughly boring and I am very exciting. I demand you cut class and hang out with me."

"I can't—"

11

"Don't make me call the administration and tell them you need the day off for an STD test or something."

"You wouldn't—"

"Okay, good chat, see you soon!"

"Vivi—"

The line went quiet at the same time a pigeon shot out of the undergrowth and into my face. I yelped and fell backward into the muck, my hands instinctively coming up to protect my head even though the bird had already fluttered away. And then—a small movement on the path far ahead. There was a figure, obscured by trees and overgrown grass. A man, pale and shirtless despite the cold, far enough away that I couldn't tell if he was even looking in my direction.

From this distance, in the gunmetal light, it appeared as though he was wearing a horned skull over his head. I thought of my sister on the cover of *Vogue*, of the antlers her models wore on the catwalk, of the beasts she embroidered on her silk gowns.

I took a few deep breaths and lingered where I sat in the mud, unsure if the man had seen me or not, but he didn't move. A breeze cooled my forehead, carrying with it the smell of woodsmoke and the wild wet stench of something feral.

I knew that smell, even if I couldn't remember what it meant.

I scrambled to my feet and ran hard in the direction I'd come from, my blood hot and quick, my feet slipping, visions of a monster snagging my ponytail playing on repeat in my head. I kept checking behind me until I passed Kenwood House and stumbled out onto the road, but no one followed.

The world outside the green bubble of Hampstead Heath was busy, normal. London was waking up. When I caught my breath, my fear was replaced by embarrassment that a wet brown stain had spread over the back of my leggings. I stayed alert while I ran home, the way women do, one AirPod out, a sharp slice of adrenaline carving up the line of my spine. A passing cabdriver laughed at me, and a man out for his first cigarette of the day told me I was beautiful, told me to smile.

Both left a prickle of fright and anger in my gut, but I kept running, and they faded back into the white noise of the city.

That's the way it was with Vivi and Grey. All it took was one phone call from them for the strangeness to start seeping in again.

At the end of my street, I messaged my middle sister:

DO NOT come to my school.

2

At home, I found my mother's red Mini Cooper in the driveway and the front door ajar. It keened open and closed on its hinges, breathing with the wind. Wet footprints tracked inside. Our ancient demon of a cat, Sasha, was sitting on the doormat, licking her paw. The cat was older than me, and so threadbare and crooked she was beginning to look like a bad taxidermy job. She hissed when I picked her up—Sasha had never liked me or Vivi or Grey, and she made her feelings known with her claws— but she was too decrepit these days to put up much of a fight.

Something was off. The cat hadn't been allowed outside for probably ten years.

"Cate?" I called quietly as I pushed the door open and stepped inside. I couldn't remember when or why we'd stopped calling our mother *Mum*, but Cate preferred it this way, and it had stuck.

There was no answer. I put Sasha down and scuffed off my muddy shoes. Soft voices echoed down the stairs from the floor above, snippets of an odd conversation.

"That's the best you can do?" my mother asked. "You can't even tell me where they went? How it happened?"

A tinny speakerphone voice responded: a man with an American accent. "Listen, lady, you don't need a PI, you need a psychiatric intervention."

I followed the voices, my footfalls quiet. Cate was pacing by her bed, still in her A&E scrubs, the top drawer of her nightstand open. The room was dark, lit only by a dim honey lamp. Night shift at the hospital called for blackout curtains, so the space always had a slightly sour smell to it from the constant lack of sunlight. In one hand, Cate held her phone. In the other, a photograph of herself with a man and three children. This happened every winter, in the weeks following the anniversary: My mother hired a PI to try and solve the mystery the police were no closer to unraveling. Inevitably, the PI always failed.

"So that's it, then?" Cate asked.

"Jesus, why don't you ask your *daughters*," the man on the phone answered. "If anyone knows, it's them."

"Fuck you," she said sharply. My mother rarely swore. The wrongness of it sent a prickle into my fingertips.

Cate hung up. A glottal sound escaped her throat. It was not the kind of noise you'd make in the presence of others. I was immediately embarrassed to have stumbled on something so private. I went to turn away, but the floorboards creaked like old bones beneath my weight.

"Iris?" Cate said, startled. There was a prick of something odd in her expression when she looked up at me—anger? fear?—but it was quickly replaced with concern when she spotted my muddy leggings. "What happened? Are you hurt?"

"No, I was mauled by a rabid pigeon."

15

"And you were so scared that you shat your pants?"

I threw her a *very funny* pout. Cate laughed and perched on the edge of her bed and beckoned me with both hands. I went and sat cross-legged on the floor in front of her so she could fix my long blond hair into two braids, as she had done most mornings since I was little.

"Everything okay?" I asked as she ran her fingers through my hair. I caught the prickly chemical scent of hospital soap, overlaid with sweat and bad breath and other telltale hints of a fifteen-hour shift in A&E. Some people thought of their mothers when they smelled the perfume she wore when they were children, but for me, my mother would always be this: the cornstarch powder of latex gloves, the coppery tang of other people's blood. "You left the front door open."

"No, I didn't. Did I? It was a long shift. I spent a long time with a guy who was convinced his family was controlling him with anal probes."

"Does that count as a medical emergency?"

"I think I'd want some pretty rapid intervention if that was happening to me."

"Fair point." I sucked my bottom lip and exhaled through my nose. It was better to ask now, in person, than over text later. "Is it okay if I go out tonight? Vivi's in town for a gig and Grey is flying in from Paris. I want to spend time with them."

My mother said nothing, but her fingers slipped in my hair and tugged hard enough to make me gasp. She didn't apologize.

"They're my sisters," I said quietly. Sometimes, asking to see them—but especially asking to see Grey—felt like asking for permission to take up shooting heroin as an extracurricular activity. "They aren't going to let anything bad happen to me."

Cate gave a short, complicated laugh and started braiding again.

The picture she'd been looking at was facedown on the blanket, like she hoped I wouldn't notice it. I turned it over and studied it. It was of my mother and my father, Gabe, and the three of us girls when we were younger. Vivi wore a green tweed duffle coat. Grey was dressed in a Bordeaux faux-fur jacket. I was in a little red tartan coat with gold buttons. Around each of our necks hung matching gold heart pendants with our names pressed into the metal: IRIS, VIVI, GREY. Christmas presents from the grandparents we had been in Scotland to visit when the photo was taken.

The police had never found these items of clothing or jewelry, despite extensive searches for them.

"It's from that day," I said quietly. I hadn't seen any photographs from that day before. I hadn't even known there were any. "We all look so different."

"You can . . ." Cate's voice split, fell back down her throat. She let out a thin breath. "You can go to Vivi's gig."

"Thank you, thank you!"

"But I want you home before midnight."

"Deal."

"I should make us something to eat before you go to school, and you should definitely have a shower." She finished my braids and kissed me on the crown of my head before she left.

When she was gone, I looked at the photograph again, at her face, at my father's face, only a handful of hours before the worst thing that would ever happen to them happened. It had carved something out of my mother, shaved the apples from her cheeks and left her thinner and grayer than before. For much of my life, she had been a watercolor of a woman, sapped of vibrancy.

It had carved even more out of Gabe.

Yet it was the three of us girls who'd changed the most. I hardly recognized the dark-haired, blue-eyed children who stared back at me.

I've been told we were more secretive after it happened. That we didn't speak to anyone but each other for months. That we refused to sleep in separate rooms, or even separate beds. Sometimes, in the middle of the night, our parents would wake to check on us and find us huddled together in our pyjamas, our heads pressed together like witches bent over a cauldron, whispering.

Our eyes turned black. Our hair turned white. Our skin began to smell like milk and the earth after rain. We were always hungry, but never seemed to gain weight. We ate and ate and ate. We even chewed in our sleep, grinding down our baby teeth and sometimes biting our tongues and cheeks, so we woke with bloodstained lips.

Doctors diagnosed us with everything from PTSD to ADHD. We collected an alphabet of acronyms, but no treatment or therapy ever seemed to be able to reset us to how we'd been before it happened. We weren't ill, it was decided: We were just strange.

People always found it hard to believe now that Grey and Vivi and I had come from our parents.

Everything about Gabe Hollow had been gentle, except for his hands, which were rough from his work as a carpenter and his weekend hobby of throwing mugs on a potter's wheel. He'd worn cosy clothing from charity stores. His fingers were long and felt like sandpaper when he held your hand. He never watched sports or raised his voice. He caught spiders in plastic containers and carried them out to the garden. He talked to his kitchen herbs when he watered them.

Our mother was an equally soft woman. She drank everything—tea, juice, wine—only from the mugs my father had made for her. She owned three pairs of shoes and wore muddy Wellingtons as often as she could. After it rained, she picked up snails from the sidewalk and moved them to safety. She loved honey—honey on toast, honey on cheese, honey stirred into her hot drinks. She sewed her own summer dresses from patterns handed down to her by her grandmother.

Together, they'd worn waxed Barbour jackets and preferred walking in the English countryside to traveling overseas. They'd owned wooden hiking poles and hand reels for fishing in streams. They'd both loved to wrap themselves in wool blankets and read on rainy days. They both had light blue eyes, dark hair, and sweet, heart-shaped faces.

They were gentle people. Warm people.

Somehow, combined, they'd produced . . . us. We were each five eleven, a full ten inches taller than our tiny mother. We were each angular, elongated, sharp. We were each inconveniently beautiful, with high cheekbones and eyes like does. People told us as children, told our parents, how exquisite we were. The way they said it, it sounded like a warning—which, I supposed, it was.

We all knew the impact of our beauty and we all dealt with it in different ways.

Grey knew her power and brandished it forcefully, in a way I had seen few girls do. In a way I was afraid to mirror myself, because I had witnessed the repercussions of being beautiful, of being pretty, of being cute, of being sexy, and of attracting the wrong kind of attention, not only from boys and men but other girls, other women. Grey was an enchantress who looked like sex and smelled like a field of wildflowers, the human embodiment of late-summer evenings in the South of France. She accentuated her natural beauty wherever possible. She wore high heels and delicate lace bras and soft smoky eye makeup. She always knew the right amount of skin to show to achieve that cool-sexy look.

More than anything else, this is how I knew my eldest sister was different from me: She walked home alone at night, always beautiful, sometimes drunk, frequently in short skirts or low-cut tops. She walked through dark parks and down empty streets and along graffiti-smeared canals where itinerants clustered to drink and do drugs and sleep in piles. She did this without fear. She went to the places and wore the things that—if anything happened to her—would later prompt people to say she was asking for it.

She moved through the world like no other woman I knew.

"What you don't understand," she said to me once when I told her how dangerous it was, "is that *I* am the thing in the dark."

Vivi was the opposite. She tried to banish her beauty. She shaved her head, pierced her skin, inked the words FUCK OFF! across her fingers, a spell to try and ward off unwanted desire from unwanted men. Even with these enchantments, even with a zigzag nose and a wicked tongue and unshaved body hair and the dark grooves beneath her eyes carved out by drink and drugs and sleepless nights, she was achingly beautiful, and ached after accordingly. She collected each wolf whistle, each smacked butt cheek, each groped breast, kept them all beneath her skin where they boiled in a cauldron of rage that she let out onstage on the strings of her bass guitar.

I fell somewhere between my sisters. I didn't actively try to wield or waste my beauty. I kept my hair washed and wore no scent but deodorant. I smelled clean but not intoxicating, not sweet, not tempting. I wore no makeup and only loose-fitting clothing. I didn't take up the hem of my uniform. I didn't walk alone at night.

I went to put the photograph back in Cate's open drawer. A manila folder, distended with paper, sat beneath her socks and underwear. I pulled it out, flicked it open. It was filled with photocopies of police files, their edges curled with age. I saw my name, my sisters' names, caught snippets of our story as I riffled through, unable to look away.

```
The children claim to have no memory of
where they have been or what happened
to them.

Officer ████████ and Officer ██████ refuse
to be in the same room as the children,
citing shared nightmares after taking
their statements.

The flowers found in the children's
hair are unidentifiable hybrids—possible
pyrophytes.

The cadaver dogs continue to react to the
children even days after their return.

Gabe Hollow insists that all three chil-
dren's eyes have changed, and that baby
teeth have grown back in places where they
were already lost.
```

My stomach pressed against my throat. I snapped the folder shut and tried to shove it back into the drawer, but it snagged on the wood and split open, heaving paper onto the floor. I knelt and gathered the sheets into a pile with shaking hands, trying not to look at its contents. Pictures, witness statements, pieces of evidence. My mouth was dry. The paper felt corrupted and wrong in my fingers. I wanted to burn it, the way you'd burn a blighted crop so the rot couldn't spread.

And there, at the top of the stack of documents, I found a photograph of Grey at eleven years old, two white flowers—real, living flowers—growing out of the paper as if they were bursting from her eyes.

3

I WAS HUNGRY when I arrived at school, even after Cate had cooked me breakfast. Even now, years after whatever trauma had first sparked my unusual appetite, I was *still* always hungry. Just last week I'd gotten home ravenous and laid waste to the kitchen. The fridge and pantry had been stocked with food after Cate's fortnightly grocery shopping: two loaves of fresh sourdough bread, a tub of marinated olives, two dozen eggs, four cans of chickpeas, a bag of carrots, crisps and salsa, four avocadoes . . . The list goes on. Enough food for two people for two weeks. I ate it all, every bite. I ate and ate and ate. I ate until my mouth bled and my jaw ached from chewing. Even when all the new groceries were devoured, I downed an old can of beans, a box of stale cereal, and a tin of shortbread.

Afterwards, my hunger finally sated, I stood in front of my bedroom mirror and turned this way and that, wondering where the hell the food went. I was still skinny, not so much as bump.

At school, I felt high-strung and jumpy. When a car door slammed in the drop-off line, I smacked my hand to my chest so hard, the skin was still stinging. I straightened my uniform tie and tried to center my thoughts. My fingers felt grimy and smelled of something putrid, even though I'd washed them three times at home. The smell came from the flowers on the photo. I'd plucked one from my sister's eye before I left. It was an odd bloom, with waxy petals and roots that threaded into the paper like stitches. I'd recognized it. It was the same flower Grey had turned into a pattern and embroidered on many of her designs.

I'd held it close to my nose and inhaled, expecting a sweet scent like gardenia, but the stench of raw meat and garbage had made me dry heave. I'd left the files and fetid bloom in my mother's drawer and slammed her bedroom door shut behind me.

I breathed a little easier at school, felt like I was coming back to myself—or at least to the carefully curated version of myself I was at Highgate Wood School for Girls. My backpack, groaning at the seams with books on Python and A-level study guides, cut hot tracks into my shoulders. The rules and structure here made sense. The weirdness that lurked in old, empty houses and the wildwood thickets of ancient heaths found it hard to permeate the monotony of uniforms and fluorescent lighting. It had become my sanctuary away from the baseline strangeness of my life, even if I didn't belong here with the children of some of London's richest families.

I hurried through the busy corridors, bound for the library.

"You're five minutes *late*," said Paisley, one of the dozen students I tutored before and after school. Paisley was a pint-size twelve-year-old who somehow managed to make the school uniform look boho chic. Her parents had been paying me decent money for weeks to try and teach her basic coding. The annoying thing was, Paisley was a natural. When she paid attention, she picked up Python with an easy elegance that reminded me of Grey.

"Oh, I'm deeply sorry, Paisley. I'll give you a free extra hour after school to make up for it." She glared at me. "That's what I thought. Where's your laptop?"

"I heard you're a witch," she said as she returned to tapping away at her phone, curls of mousy hair falling into her eyes. "I heard your sisters were expelled for sacrificing a teacher to the devil in the auditorium." Wow. The rumors had gotten out of control in the last four years, but honestly, I was more surprised that it had taken this long for one to reach her.

"I'm not a witch. I'm a mermaid," I said as I set up my laptop and opened the textbook to where we left off. "Now show me the homework I set for you last week."

"Why is your hair white if you're not a witch?"

"I bleach it that way," I lied. In fact, the week after Grey and Vivi left, I'd tried to dye it darker. I'd bought three boxes of dye and spent a rainy summer evening drinking apple cider while I painted my hair. I'd waited the forty-five minutes the instructions recommended, then a little longer just to be sure, before rinsing it out. I was excited to see the new me. It felt like the transformative scene in a spy movie when the protagonist is on the run, forced to change their appearance in a service station toilet after they go rogue.

When I wiped away the fog of condensation on the mirror, I shrieked. My hair was its usual milky blond, entirely untouched by the dye.

"*Homework*," I ordered again.

Paisley rolled her little eyes and dug her laptop out of her

Fjällräven bag. "There." She turned her screen toward me. "Well?" she demanded as I scrolled through her code.

"It's good. Despite your best efforts, you're picking this up."

"What a terrible shame this will be our last session."

God, what kind of twelve-year-old talked like that?

I tsked her. "Not so fast. Unfortunately for both of us, your parents have paid through the rest of the term."

"That was until they found out who your sisters are." Paisley handed me an envelope. My name was written on the front in her mother's loopy handwriting. "They're super into Jesus. They won't even let me read Harry Potter. Suddenly they don't seem to think you're such a good influence on me." She packed her things, stood to leave. "Bye, Sabrina," she called sweetly on her way out.

"Wow," came a disembodied voice. "Some people are *so* *rude*."

"Oh," I said as a small bottle-blond figure made her way out of the stacks and pulled up the chair across from me. "Hello, Jennifer."

In the months after Grey and Vivi had left school, when the loneliness of being without them sank so deeply into my body that every heartbeat ached, I'd desperately wanted to make friends with some of my peers. I'd never needed friends before, but without my sisters, I had no one to eat with at lunchtime and no one but my mother to spend time with on the weekends.

When Jennifer Weir had invited me to her sleepover birthday party (reluctantly, I suspected—our mothers worked together at the Royal Free), I'd cautiously accepted. It was an appropriately posh affair: Each girl had her own mini tipi set up in the Weirs' vast living room, each frosted with fairy lights and set among a floating sea of blush and gold balloons. We watched three of the *Conjuring* movies into the early hours of the morning and ate so much birthday cake and so many delicate baked goods that I thought someone might vomit. We talked about the boys who attended nearby schools and how cute they were. We snuck into Jennifer's parents' drinks cabinet and did two shots of tequila each. Even Justine Khan, the girl who'd bullied me and subsequently shaved her head in front of the school, seemed not to mind my presence. For a handful of pink, sugary, alcohol-softened hours, I dared to allow myself to imagine a future that looked like this—and it might have been possible, if not for the now-infamous game of spin the bottle that had landed both Justine and me in A&E.

Jennifer Weir hadn't spoken to me since that night, when I left her house with blood dripping from my lips.

"Did you want something?" I asked her.

"Well, *actually*," Jennifer said with a smile, "I bought tickets to the gig at Camden Jazz Café tonight. I heard your sister was going to be there."

"Of course she's going to be there," I said, confused. "She's in the band."

"Oh, no, silly, I meant your other sister. *Grey*. I was wondering . . . I mean, I would totally *love* to meet her. Maybe you could introduce me?"

I stared at her for a long time. Jennifer Weir and Justine Khan (together, they called themselves JJ), had been making my life a living hell for the better part of four years. Where Jennifer outright ignored me, Justine made up the difference: *witch* scrawled across my locker in blood, dead birds slipped into my backpack, and—one time—broken glass sprinkled over my lunch.

"Anyway," Jennifer continued, her saccharine smile beginning to go sour, "think about it. It wouldn't be the worst thing that could happen to you, you know—being my friend. I'll see you tonight."

When she was gone, I read Paisley's note, in which her parents explained they'd heard some "concerning accusations" and asked for their advance back. I tore it up and dumped it in the bin, then checked the countdown timer on my phone to see how many days were left until graduation: hundreds. Forever. The school had a long memory when it came to the Hollow girls, and it had been my burden to bear since the month both of my sisters had skipped town.

My first class of the day was English. I took my usual seat at the front of the classroom, by the window, my annotated copy of *Frankenstein* open on my desk, its pages frilled with a rainbow of multicolored sticky notes. I'd read it twice in preparation for this class, carefully underlining passages and making notes, trying to find the pattern, the key. My English teacher, Mrs. Thistle, was deeply conflicted by this behavior: On the one hand, a student who did the assigned readings—*all* of them, always, frequently more than once—was something of a phenomenon. On the other hand, a student who wanted the *right answer* for a work of literature sent her half-mad.

It was drizzling outside. A flicker of strange movement caught my eye as I set up my things, and I looked through the glass over the wet gulch of grass between buildings.

There, in the distance, was the man in the bull skull, watching me.

4

I STOOD SO suddenly and with such force that my desk toppled forwards, my books and pens spilling across the floor. The entire class, startled by the sudden violent intrusion on the tedium of the school day, went silent and turned to stare at me.

I was wide-eyed, dragging breaths, my heart punching inside my chest.

"Iris," said Mrs. Thistle, alarmed, "are you okay?"

"Don't get too close to her," Justine Khan said to our teacher. I had once thought she was beautiful—and she probably still was, if you couldn't see past the veneer of her skin to the pool of venom stagnating beneath. She now wore her curtain of dark hair long and straight, and carried a brush in her backpack to groom it at recess. It was so shiny and so well cared for that it was almost embarrassing. It also served the double purpose of concealing the scars my fingernails had left on either side of her neck when she'd kissed me. "Everyone knows she bites."

There were some titters of laughter, but most people seemed too rattled to know how to react.

"Uh . . ." I needed an excuse, a cover to get out of there. "I'm going to be sick," I said as I knelt to shove my things into my bag. I left my desk and chair where they lay.

"Go to the sick bay," Mrs. Thistle instructed, but I was already halfway out the door.

Another good thing about being a shameless teacher's pet: They never doubted you if you said you were sick.

Once clear of the classroom, I slung my backpack over my shoulder and bolted for the spot outside where I'd seen the man, in the shadowy slip of space between two buildings. The day was gray, grim: typical London. Muddy water flicked up the back of my socks as I ran. I could already see from afar that there was no one there now, but I kept running until I stood where he had stood. The air around me was dank with the smell of smoke and wet animal. I could see into my classroom through the mist of rain.

I called Grey. I needed to hear her voice. She'd always been good at calming me down.

It went to voicemail; she must be on the plane from Paris already. I left a message. "Hey. Uh. Call me back when you land. I'm kind of freaking out. I think someone is following me. Okay. Bye."

Reluctantly, I called Vivi. "I knew you'd change your mind!" she said after one ring.

"I haven't."

"Oh. Well, this is awkward. Turn around."

I turned. In the distance, in the car park, I could see her waving.

"Ugh," I said. "I've got to go. Some weird woman is stalking me."

At nineteen, my middle sister was a tattooed, pierced,

clove-cigarette-smoking bass player with a blond buzz cut, a zig-zag nose, and a smirk so sharp it could cut right through you. When I reached her in the school car park, she was lounging on the hood of some teacher's red midlife crisis car, unbothered by the rain. Despite just landing from Budapest, she carried no luggage but a small leather backpack. She was dressed like that old Cake song, in a short skirt and a long jacket. Two years ago, when Grey's scar had become the season's hottest fashion accessory and teenage girls had started carving half-moons into their necks, Vivi had covered hers with a wisteria tattoo that unfurled across her collarbones, her back, halfway down her arms. Her tongue was pierced, her nose was pierced, and her ears probably contained enough metal to melt into a bullet.

Grey was high fashion, but Vivi was pure rock 'n' roll.

I looked her up and down. "Lose your way to the *Mad Max* set, Furiosa?"

She let her black eyes linger on me while she took a draw of her cigarette. Few people could pull off a shaved head and a gross smoking habit and still manage to look like a siren, but Vivi could. "Like you can talk, Hermione." I thought of the Cake song again: *A voice that is dark like tinted glass.*

"Oh, sick burn," I said, shaking my head. "Your mind is slipping in your old age."

We both laughed then. Vivi slid off the car and pulled me into a bear hug. I could feel the tensile strength of her muscles beneath the heavy curtain of her coat; she could handle herself. She'd been serious about self-defense classes ever since that guy had tried to pull her into his car. "It's good to see you, kid," she said.

"God, you smell terrible. What *is* that?"

"Ah." Vivi wafted air from under her armpits in my direction. "That noxious stench would be Grey's perfume."

Hollow by Grey Hollow, her eponymous scent, the one she stitched in little vials into her couture. For Christmas two years ago, she'd sent me a bottle of perfume that smelled like smoke and forest, with something wild and rotten scratching beneath it. One sniff made me drop to my knees, gagging.

Like everything that Grey Hollow made, it became a bestseller. Fashion magazines called it heady and cryptic. Grey sent a carton of the vile stuff to my school, a fuck-you-look-at-me-now gift for every teacher who'd ever given her grief. They wore it like drug-store perfume. It clung to their hair and clothing, a damp green aura. It seemed to sweep other scents into its orbit and take them hostage, hints of curdled milk and wood rot tugging at the edges of the perfume whenever the heating climbed too high. Classrooms stank of it. Nobody else seemed to mind the smell.

"How many of your friends said no to meeting you today before you called me?" I asked, though we both knew that, much like me, Vivi had no friends in London.

"Like, five, six max," Vivi said. "Everyone's getting *jobs*. It's disgusting. So are you coming or not?"

"I can't just *leave* school."

"You can. I should know. I did it every day."

"Yes, well, some of us want to go to university. Besides, Cate will freak out if I cut. It was hard enough getting permission to come to your gig. You know what she's like."

"Cate's codependence on you and your respect for authority are equally repulsive. Give me your phone." Vivi guessed my passcode—16 for Grey's birthday, 29 for Vivi's birthday, 11 for my birthday—then called our mother, who picked up immediately.

"No, Cate, nothing's wrong." Vivi rolled her eyes. "I'm kidnapping Iris for the day." We locked eyes on the word *kidnapping*. I shook my head. "She's not going to be at school, so don't flip when you check your creepy, privacy-invading tracker, okay? . . . Yes, I know. No, Grey isn't here. It's just Iris and me, I promise . . . I will . . . I know . . . Yes, Cate, I *know*. She's safe with me, okay? . . . Yeah, I'm going to crash at home after the show. I'm looking forward to seeing you too. Love you." Vivi hung up and threw my phone back to me. "Done. Easy."

I wondered what Cate's reaction would be if Grey showed up at my school unannounced and tried to pull me out of classes for the day. There would probably already be police sirens screaming in the distance.

"*Kidnapping*?" I said. "Really? Stellar word choice."

"It was an accident. Oh shit, incoming."

Mrs. Thistle was hurrying toward us. "Iris," she said, "I was on my way to check on you. Are you feeling better?"

"Oh," I said. "No. I think I need to go home." I pointed at Vivi.

Mrs. Thistle's gaze slid to my sister. "Hello, Vivienne," she said flatly.

"Hello, *Thistle*," Vivi replied with a wave . . . which she then turned around into the middle finger. Mrs. Thistle pursed her lips and went back the way she came, shaking her head. Vivi hadn't been the easiest student. I smacked her in the stomach with the back of my hand.

"*Vivi*," I said.

"What? No matter how many times I tell that old hag my name is *just Vivi*, she insists on calling me *Vivienne*. Plus, she failed me in English."

"Yeah, because you never, ever went to English."

"*Allegedly.*"

I rolled my eyes. "Have you heard from Grey today?"

"No. Not for a few days. I tried calling her when I landed, but her phone must be out of juice. She knows the plan, though. Come on. Let's go get food and wait for our *terribly* busy and important sister to grace us with her presence."

☾

Vivi slammed through the day, chain-smoking clove cigarettes and drinking spiked Earl Grey tea from a flask. I forgot how much *fun* she could be. After lunch at a kebab shop, we spent the afternoon crashing her favourite London haunts: guitar shops on Denmark Street, vintage shops in Camden, Flamin' Eight Tattoo Studio in Kentish Town, where she spent a good fifteen minutes trying to convince me to get a full sleeve. We snacked on croissants and slices of sourdough pizza, and Vivi told me all about the six months since I'd last seen her: the European tour through Germany and Hungary and the Czech Republic, the gigs in ruin bars and abandoned warehouses and empty swimming pools, the beautiful European women she'd bedded along the way, in more detail than I cared to hear.

The time Grey was supposed to meet us came and went. It felt almost strange to spend time alone with my middle sister, just the two of us. All our lives, even after Vivi and Grey had moved out, whenever we met up, it was almost always the three of us together. Always a set, never a pair. Without Grey, I felt unanchored somehow, like the internal hierarchy of our sisterhood had collapsed into chaos. We all knew our roles: Grey was the boss, the leader, the captain, the one who took charge and made decisions and forged ahead. Vivi was the fun assistant, the suggester of mischief, the teller of jokes, the wild one—but even with her penchant for anarchy and dislike of authority, she always fell in line behind Grey. I half suspected the reason Vivi had set off on her own at fifteen was to escape Grey's iron rule. My role was to be the youngest, the baby, a thing to be protected. My sisters were kinder and gentler to me than they were to each other. Grey rarely pulled me into line the way she did Vivi. Vivi rarely snapped and yelled at me the way she did Grey.

As afternoon turned into evening, we sent her pictures on WhatsApp of us hanging out without her, of all the fun she was missing. It was a special kind of sisterly punishment: Grey hated being left out, hated us embarking on plans that had not been sanctioned by her in advance. She was a general and we were her small but fiercely loyal army. "If Grey jumped off a bridge, would you?" my mother had asked me once as she splinted my broken pinkie finger. Grey had broken her pinkie hours before, so I had found a hammer in my father's pottery shed and used it to shatter my own.

It was a question without answer. It was not a question at all.

I didn't follow my sister. I *was* my sister. I breathed when she breathed. I blinked when she blinked. I felt pain when she felt pain. If Grey was going to jump off a bridge, I was going to be there with her, holding her hand.

Of course, of course, of course.

In the evening, we met up with Vivi's bandmates for dinner before the gig: Candace, a hard-drinking German with a voice like Janis Joplin, and Laura, the Danish drummer, who looked like a pixie and played drums like a banshee. I'd had something of a crush on her since I'd first seen her play, on a weekend trip to Prague six months ago. Grey had met us there and we'd spent two nights wandering the labyrinthine stone alleys of the Old Town, eating nothing but trdelník and drinking nothing but absinthe.

When we'd watched the band play at a red-lit basement bar, Grey had mouthed the words to each of their songs. It was one of the things I loved most about her: you might not see her for months, and then she'd show up and know every word to every song you'd written and recite them back to you like they were Shakespearean poetry. Grey didn't just *know* I got good grades; she contacted my teachers and requested to read every essay I handed in, then commented on their merits the next time we met up.

So where was she now?

For dinner, we ate bowls of spicy chicken karaage at Vivi's favourite pub, the Lady Hamilton, named after the famous eighteenth-century muse and mistress Emma Hart. Vivi's first ever tattoo had been George Romney's painting *Emma Hart as Circe*, a soft beauty with round eyes, pouting lips, and hair whipped around by the wind. I wasn't sure if Vivi had discovered the pub or the woman first, but either way, whenever she came to London, we inevitably ended up eating here. Inside, the pub was warm and cosy, the walls and furniture all dark wood, the roof a lattice of Bordeaux cornice and ceiling roses. Candles dripped white wax onto our table as we ate. Vivi slipped me a sneaky glass of house red wine. Another difference between my sisters: the budgets. If Grey were here, we'd likely be eating the tasting menu at Sketch and knocking back twenty-pound cocktails like they were candy.

I thought about the classes I had the next day, all the prep work I was missing out on by taking a night off. I thought about the skin of Laura's neck, what it might taste like if I kissed her. I thought about how young I looked in my uniform. I thought about the horned man, and how Vivi couldn't be in town for ten minutes before weird shit started happening.

After dinner, we wandered down Kentish Town Road toward Camden, past convenience stores and late-night barbers and the hot-oil smell that lingered around the doorways of chicken shops. Even on a weeknight in winter, the streets around Camden Town Station were humming with people: a punk in a leather jacket and a fluorescent-orange Mohawk was charging tourists a pound for photographs; a vape company handed out free tester kits to the crowds coming home from work or heading to the nearby market for food; revelers spilled out of honey-lit bars; couples held hands on their way to the Odeon cinema; shoppers carried bags of groceries from M&S and Sainsbury's and Whole Foods.

Vivi's band, Sisters of the Sacred, had been booked to play at the Jazz Café, which, contrary to what its name would suggest, was not actually a jazz café but rather a nightclub/live music venue in an old Barclays Bank. Its white columns and arched windows gave it a faux Grecian vibe, and blue neon letters loudly declared it LONDONS FAMOUS JAZZ VENUE. There was a line out the front already, despite the cold, which made Vivi and her bandmates stop.

"Oh my," Laura said. "Are we famous now?"

Sisters of the Sacred was semi well known in the underground scenes of Europe's coolest, grungiest cities, but they certainly weren't famous. Not in the way that Grey was famous.

Vivi stared at the line and lit a cigarette. "I may have told the venue manager that my sister and a gaggle of scantily dressed supermodels would come and watch our show if they booked us."

"This is the correct term for a multitude of supermodels?" Candace asked. "Gaggle?"

"It is indeed, Candace."

"Pimping out your own sister for exposure is a bit morally bankrupt," I said.

"Supermodels were *invented* to sell shit to people," Vivi said. "What's the point of being a direct blood relative of one if I don't occasionally utilize her for profit?"

"Oh my God, Iris!" A hand waved frantically from the line. "Here!"

Jennifer Weir and Justine Khan were standing close to the front. Jennifer was the one waving at me. Justine had her arms crossed and was staring straight ahead, her jaw set tight.

"Friends of yours?" Vivi muttered as Jennifer ducked out of the line and tugged Justine after her.

"Mortal enemies, actually," I muttered back.

"Oh my God, I hoped we'd run into you!" Jennifer said. "We got here early and have been waiting in line for, like, an hour."

"Big fans of the band?" Vivi asked.

"Oh, sure, yeah," Jennifer said.

Vivi's gaze slid to Justine. "You look familiar." My sister clicked her fingers and pointed at her. "I know! You're the girl who shaved her head in front of the whole school! That was so metal." Vivi reached out and curled a lock of Justine's long hair around her finger. "It's a shame you let it grow out. I much preferred it short."

"Don't fucking touch me, witch," Justine snapped. She turned and stormed toward an Italian restaurant across the road.

"Justine! Justine!" Jennifer called. "Sorry about her. I don't know what her problem is." Jennifer turned back to me. "Is your sister here? Is she still coming?"

"I'm her sister," Vivi offered.

"I think she's coming," I said. "We haven't heard from her today."

"Do you think you'll go to Cuckoo afterwards?" Jennifer asked. "Oh my God, do you think Tyler Yang will be there?"

"Cuckoo?"

"Only the coolest and most ultra-exclusive nightclub in London. *Duh*. It's impossible for regular humans to get in, but Grey and Tyler go *all* the time when she's here."

A slow, sharp smile spread across Vivi's face. She despised when people talked about our sister like they knew her. Grey was ours. She belonged to us. "We'll be sure to let you know," she said, maintaining the smile. "See you later."

Jennifer was apparently unaware that she'd been dismissed. "Oh, actually, I kind of lost my place in line. Do you think I could come in with you? I would *love* to see backstage."

Vivi took one long last drag on her cigarette and let the clove-scented smoke bloom in Jennifer's face. "Do you know any of our music—or are you just here to starfuck Grey? Can you name one song?"

Jennifer stumbled over her words. "I . . . I don't think . . . That's not fair."

"Actually," Vivi said as she stubbed out her cigarette with her boot, "what's our band called?"

Again, Jennifer made gasping fish sounds.

"Yeah, that's what I thought," Vivi said. "Back in line."

"Ah. Classic Vivi. Making friends wherever she goes," Laura mused as the bouncers opened the doors for us and we made our way inside.

Vivi threw her arms around her bandmates' shoulders and

swaggered into the club like the rock star she was. "Starfuckers never change," she said, oblivious to the fact that I would be the one who'd have to face said starfucker—now glaring at me with her arms crossed—and her henchwomen at school tomorrow.

☾

We hung out backstage while the support act warmed up the crowd. Then, when Sisters of the Sacred took the stage and Grey was still MIA, I messaged her again:

They're starting. WHERE. ARE. YOU?

It was weird for her not to have seen my previous messages. Vivi could go weeks without checking social media, but Grey was chained to it. I opened Instagram. My account was set to private, but I had thousands of message requests. Everybody wants a piece of you when your sister is famous. Or rather, they want a piece of your sister, and they want you to deliver it to them. Ghouls haunted my Instagram, my Facebook, hungry for a filtered taste of her.

> You go to school with my cousin. I think you're so hot. Send me a pic of you naked, beautiful. (Or your sister if you're too shy!)

> Tell Grey that if she breaks Tyler's heart I will literally kill her. Literally.

> Hey, I have a theory about what happened to you as a kid. Have you considered the possibility that you were abducted by aliens? My best friend's great-uncle works at Area 51 and she says he has proof. I can share the details for a low price. Message me back!

I know you will probably never read this but I feel like I am DESTINED to become a catwalk model and I would REALLY appreciate you passing my headshots on to your sister.

I checked Grey's page to see if she'd posted recently. Grey Hollow, supermodel, had ninety-eight million followers. NINETY-EIGHT MILLION. There were pictures of her with other super-models, pictures of her on magazine covers, pictures of her backstage at concerts with pop stars, pictures of her on yachts, pictures of her with her model boyfriend, Tyler Yang, at some pink-lit club—Cuckoo, I guessed—in Mayfair.

Grey had first told me about Tyler six months ago on our trip to Prague, after we'd each drunk a few shots of absinthe from delicate glasses. We sat close together at a booth in a nightclub, warm and glittery on the inside from the alcohol and the wormwood, her head resting on my shoulder as we watched Vivi move on the dance floor with a girl she'd met at the bar. Grey held up her left hand and I held up my right and we pressed our fingertips together in an arch. I felt her heart-beat in my skin, in my chest, felt the strong thread that bound us together.

"I think I'm in love with him," she'd said quietly, her breath carrying a trace of sugar and anise. I could hear the smile in her voice. I already knew she loved him. I'd known it since the day before, when we'd met at Václav Havel Airport and I'd hugged her for the first time in months. She'd smelled different. She'd smelled . . . softer, somehow. It suited her. Being in love made her even more intoxicating.

I was surprised and unsurprised in equal measure. Unsurprised

41

because I already knew they were together. I'd seen paparazzi shots of them holding hands on the front of tabloid magazines, and Tyler had started to appear more and more frequently in her Instagram stories. Surprised because Grey had never had a real boyfriend before, only lovers who interested her for a short time, and—unlike Vivi, who frequently offered the details of her love and sex life—Grey was a locked box. She shared no more than morsels.

"Tyler Yang?" I'd asked her, and she'd nodded sleepily.

"He's quite special," she'd continued. "You'll know what I mean when you meet him."

The meeting had yet to happen, but maybe it would tonight—if she bothered showing up.

Grey's last post was from five days ago, an image of her in a green tulle gown lounging against a red banister with a glass of champagne in her hand, her skin saturated in fluorescent pink light, her blond head wreathed in baby's breath. #TBT London Fashion Week, the caption read. The location was tagged as the Cuckoo Club. Just over fifteen million people had liked it.

There were two levels inside Jazz Café: the lower level with the stage, the audience pressed up close to it, the band soaked in orange light and laser beams. Overhead, a mezzanine restaurant and bar wrapped around the space for those who preferred sipping wine to getting doused with beer in the mosh pit. I spotted JJ sitting at a round table, both looking sullen.

Grey wasn't there for the first song, or the second, or the third. Candace moved across the stage with Mick Jagger swagger, sex on legs, but I watched Laura, a thimble of a woman with Bambi eyes transformed into a she-beast as she attacked her drums. Hair in her face, sweat and spit flying, her T-shirt riding up to reveal a soft slip of stomach.

The crowd was loving the band, but by the fourth song I was distracted, worried. I kept looking around for my eldest sister, sure she would sneak up behind me and put her hands over my eyes at any moment, but she didn't show.

Then, somewhere toward the end of the gig, something happened.

Onstage, Vivi stopped playing her bass and let her arms fall slack to her sides. She was staring at someone or something in the crowd behind me, a veil over her eyes. I turned to look at what she was fixated on, but the room was dark and crowded. Laura and Candace exchanged confused glances and tried to catch Vivi's attention, without any luck. Vivi was frozen, wide-eyed, drawing quick, shallow breaths through her shuddering mouth. Candace moved across the stage as she sang and nudged Vivi, who blinked furiously and shook her head. She found my eyes in the crowd. A tear slipped down her cheek.

I knew then that something was very wrong.

Vivi swallowed and picked up her instrument again. The band played two more songs, but Vivi's heart wasn't in it, and she kept making mistakes. When the crowd called for an encore after the last song, only Candace and Laura came onstage to do an acoustic cover. I made my way through the crowd and slipped backstage. Vivi was sucking on a cigarette like it was hooked up to an oxygen tank, her head between her knees.

"Jesus," I said. I ran to the sink and wet a cloth, then draped it over the peach-fuzz crown of her skull. "What the hell happened out there? Are you okay?"

"I don't know. I don't know." A necklace of saliva sagged from her open mouth and drooped to the floor between her feet. "I think I had a panic attack."

"You saw something," I said.

Vivi shook her head.

"Yes, you did," I pushed. "What did you see?"

She sat up straight. Her lips were tinted faint blue and her skin was clammy with sweat. "A man. Except not a man. A . . . dude with a bull's skull over his head."

I stood up and took out my phone. "I'm calling the cops."

"What? No. Iris, seriously, it was dark and I was probably hallucin—"

"I saw him today too. *Twice.* He was at my school. Tall shirtless dude cosplaying a decomposing demon Minotaur."

"*What?*"

"Yeah. So, no, you weren't hallucinating. Some freak stalker from the internet has decided to try and scare us like that woman who broke in when we were kids, and I'm not putting up with that."

Vivi frowned. "Iris . . . you know this is not that, right?"

I hesitated. "Uh. No?"

"I recognized . . . the way he smelled. I can't explain it. It felt . . . familiar."

I stared at my sister for a long time, then at my phone, which still showed no notification from our eldest sister. "Where's Grey, Vivi? Why isn't she here?"

"I don't know."

"Grey doesn't miss these things. If she says she's going to do something, she does it. If she's not going to come to us, we're going to go to her."

5

WE SLIPPED OUT the back entrance of Jazz Café while Laura and Candace were still onstage, then hurried toward the crowded mouth of Camden Town Station, checking over our shoulders the whole way that we weren't being followed by whoever—or whatever—was stalking us.

Vivi was still rattled. On the train, she breathed into her cupped hands to settle her stomach. It took a few stops before the color started returning to her cheeks and dots of sweat stopped rising from her forehead.

We emerged from the Underground at Leicester Square, into a world in which Vivi no longer belonged. In Camden, her tattoos and piercings didn't look out of place, but here, as we hurried past crowds of tourists and chain restaurants and kiosks selling tickets for *Matilda* and *Magic Mike*, she was an oddity.

We let ourselves into Grey's apartment building with the key-codes she'd sent us when she bought the flat a year ago, though she was so infrequently in London that neither Vivi nor I had ever actually visited yet. Horrible images slotted into my thoughts as we caught the lift up to the penthouse, one after another, like an old-fashioned slide projector: Grey, OD'ed on her bathroom floor; Grey, murdered by the man in the bull skull. When we opened the front door, though, we found the place neat and vast and impersonal. City lights seeped through floor-to-ceiling windows that looked out over the Thames. The London Eye turned slowly in the distance.

There were no signs of anything weird. In fact, there were very few signs that anyone lived here at all. A couple of coffee table books about fashion but no bookshelves stuffed to bursting with the dark fairy tales Grey had loved most as a teenager. A sleek galley kitchen of gloss white and marble with floors of polished concrete, but no wood, no warmth, no food. The air tasted bitter, the smack of bleach and ammonia. All the furniture looked as though it had been chosen by an interior designer, then styled and lit for a *Vogue* photo shoot about bland celebrity homes.

It didn't feel like Grey. Grey's brain was chaotic. When she was a teenager, her room had never been clean. Her socks had never matched. She was always at least fifteen minutes late to everything. Nothing in her life had ever been neat or ordered. She slammed through the world, a tornado in the form of a girl, and left a trail of destruction behind her. That's what she'd been like at seventeen, anyway. Maybe becoming a supermodel and fashion designer had changed that, but it seemed as impossible as switching out the bones of your skeleton.

Vivi and I moved through the apartment in eerie silence, trailing our fingertips over Grey's possessions. The couches, the mirrors, the clocks and cabinets. It felt clandestine to be in someone else's personal space like this. Like I could open any drawer or door or cupboard and there find my sister's bare-naked soul, neatly folded. A thrill settled over me.

Suddenly I was ten years old again and obsessed with my big sister. Back then, Grey's bedroom had been a temple in wartime, a place of worship I had to sneak into when its guardian was unawares. Whenever I knew she'd be out of the house for a couple of hours, I'd push open the door and start exploring. I only did it when I knew I could take my time, savor the experience. Her makeup bag was a favourite, a seemingly bottomless chest of treasure filled with glosses and glitters that left my skin sticky and shellacked. I wanted to live in her skin, to know what it was like to be as beautiful and mysterious as Grey Hollow.

But the apartment was not the home of the sister I knew. When Grey daydreamed about running away, it hadn't been to a place like this. It had been to some rich, dark hidey-hole in Budapest or Prague, a place swaddled in velvet and brass. Vivi's request to Grey was that the place have a library. All I wanted was black-and-white chessboard floors in the kitchen and bathrooms, like I had in all my houses in *Sims 4* whenever I played. At thirteen, I'd considered it the height of opulence.

We found neither of those things here.

"It's like an interior designer masturbated in here," Vivi said, tapping her fingernails against a vase, "and came on everything."

"Gross."

"But true. None of this is Grey. She must've paid someone to do it. Either that or a reptilian shape-shifter is wearing her skin."

"I didn't know reptilian shape-shifters were renowned for their interior decorating skills."

"And that's why you'll never be part of the Illuminati."

The master bedroom was something out of a luxury hotel—

chic, modern, soulless. The bed was made with neat hospital corners and there were no personal items on display, not so much as a hairbrush or photograph. I opened the walk-in wardrobe. Here, too, it was painstakingly ordered. Rows and rows of unworn heels, bright as beetle backs. I ran my fingers over the clothes. Sequins and braided velvet and silk, all heavy and expensive. Oscar de la Renta, Vivienne Westwood, Elie Saab, Grey Hollow.

Vivi held up a pair of snakeskin trousers. "The reptilian shape-shifter theory is starting to check out."

"It doesn't look like anyone has been here for weeks," I said.

"It doesn't look like anyone has been here *ever*."

"I suppose she has a cleaner or something?"

Vivi trailed a finger over a shelf in the wardrobe; there was no dust. "Has to be, right? Grey is *not* this tidy."

"What do we do now?" I asked.

Vivi shrugged. "I don't know if we need to worry. Maybe she never even made it home from Paris."

I looked back at Grey's wardrobe. The green tulle gown she'd worn to Cuckoo Club in her Instagram post from five days ago was wedged in there, pressed and lifeless now that it didn't have her body to animate it. "If she's in London, I think I know where she might be."

☾

It felt like some holy ritual. Something I had waited my whole life for. To sit where she sat, to paint my face with her makeup, to slip my body into her clothes. To become Grey.

We thumbed through her wardrobe and draped ourselves in her vestments. Even Vivi, who was generally unimpressed by fashion unless it was ripped or studded, was breathless and giddy at

48

the prospect of unlimited access to Grey's wardrobe. We tried on piece after piece. Eventually, I settled on a gold minidress and a green silk coat that drifted over my skin like cobwebs. Vivi chose a cardinal-red power suit with cigarette trousers and lipstick to match, her peach fuzz slicked flat to her skull with shimmery gel.

I called Grey again and again during the cab ride to Cuckoo Club, certain that we were overreacting, certain that she would answer my next message and Vivi and I would spend the rest of the week cringing at our silliness, but Grey never answered, never read any of my messages.

We got out of the cab on Regent Street and walked beneath a huge shadowed archway to the backstreet that Cuckoo called home. Fairy lights were cast over the street like a net, and restaurants still hummed with late-night drinkers and diners huddled beneath outdoor heaters. There was no line outside the club. The door was unmarked, unassuming. A couple walking in front of us buzzed, and it opened an inch to seep out neon-purple light and electro house music. They had a hushed conversation with whoever answered and were turned away.

Vivi and I stepped up next. I buzzed. The door was opened by a short blond woman with eyes like a cat. "Sur la liste?" she asked, and then she looked at us closely and her mouth fell open a little. We were the ghosts of Grey; of course she would recognize us. "She's not here," she said in English; her accent was so heavy, her tongue sounded swollen.

"Do you know where she is?" Vivi asked.

"I told your friend yesterday—I haven't seen her."

"Someone else was looking for her?" I asked. "Who?"

The woman's expression darkened. "A man. A man who smelled like . . . death and burning."

My heartbeat shifted into a higher gear. I thought of the woman who'd slipped through my bedroom window when I was a child and cut off a lock of my hair, of the man who'd tried to pull Vivi into his car because he'd read about her on the internet. "Did he say why he was looking for her?" I pressed. "What he wanted?"

The woman shook her head. "I didn't let him in. He was . . . His eyes. They were black, like ink. I was afraid of him."

Vivi and I shared a look, and a thought: *We need to find her.*

"We want to talk to this guy." I showed the hostess a picture of Grey's boyfriend. "Tyler Yang. Is he here?"

"Yes, but it's a private event tonight," she said hesitantly. "If you're not on the guest list, I can't let—"

"I won't tell if you don't," Vivi said, practically purring. She put a finger against the woman's lips—and that was all it took. The woman closed her eyes at Vivi's touch, dazed and drunk on the heady smell of my sister's skin. With her eyes still shut, she opened her mouth and sucked on Vivi's finger.

I had seen my sisters do this thing before. I had done this thing before too, a couple of times, though the power of it terrified me. The things I could make people do when they were high on me.

When the woman opened her eyes, her pupils were huge and her breath smelled like honey and rotten wood. Vivi stroked her cheek, then leaned in to whisper, "You want to let us in." The hostess opened the door, giddy, a dumb smile on her face. Her gaze was fixed on Vivi. In the purple light of the vestibule, I saw what she saw: how frighteningly beautiful my sister was, sharper and skinnier than Grey, like a rapier where Grey was a broadsword.

"You shouldn't do that to people," I said as we headed down a hall toward the source of the music. A thick bass jumped in my chest.

"Do what?" Vivi asked.

"Whatever the hell that is."

The club—Grey's favourite, if her Instagram was to be believed—was lit from all angles by screaming pink neon. For the private event, the ceiling had been laced with a forest of cherry blossoms that dripped down over the dance floor. Over-size buckets of Dom Pérignon with glow-in-the-dark labels gave every table a soft green phosphorescence. The bar was gold and glass and framed by a set of sumptuous purple velvet curtains. Drinks were served in tall, impossibly elegant glasses that looked remarkably similar to the tall, impossibly elegant women who drank from them. The crowd was made up mostly of people in the fashion industry—models, designers, photographers—but I also spotted a famous rapper, an actor couple from an American cult teen TV show, the socialite daughter of an old British rock legend. Many did a double take when they saw us, then leaned together to speak in hushed tones.

"Keep your eyes peeled for him," I told Vivi.

"How did you know he'd be here?"

"Grey's here all the time. Tyler is always in her pictures."

Tyler Yang was a heavily tattooed Korean British model who'd gained a reputation in the fashion world for the ease with which his style blurred gender boundaries. Rarely was he seen in something that wasn't daring: Gucci floral suits, bespoke lace blouses, strings of antique pearls, pussybow shirts, heeled loaf-ers. His eyes were always lined, his lids and lips slicked with a candy shop of bright pop colors.

Grey's sexuality was a much discussed but ultimately unconfirmed topic of gossip. Was she dating this Victoria's Secret Angel or that new Hollywood leading man? Vivi and I both knew that Grey was straight. It had always been men for her, the same way it had always been women for Vivi.

For me, it had always been both. My very first kiss had been with Justine Khan in the game of spin the bottle at Jennifer Weir's sleepover. Her mouth had been soft and her perfume had smelled like lip gloss and vanilla frosting. It was supposed to be a bit of giggling fun, but it lit something inside me. A disco ball in my chest, an insistent hunger somewhere within me that made me want to thread my fingers through her then-short hair and press my hips against hers. It confirmed something about myself that I had suspected for a while. The kiss did something to Justine too—something strange and ugly. She kissed me again and again, hungry and insistent, until I tried to push her away and she forced me down, until she bit my lip so hard it burst and bled, until her fingernails raked claw marks into my arms and I had to start fighting her off, until all the girls who were watching us realized it wasn't a game anymore and had to wrestle her, keening and frothing at the mouth, off me. The story had twisted over time, so now girls at school said I was the one who bit *her*; I was the one who wouldn't let *her* go; I was the mad witch who'd tried to bite *her* face off.

It remained the less terrifying of the two kisses I had endured.

"There," Vivi said, nodding toward the back wall.

Tyler was in a pink velvet booth wedged between a pop star and a supermodel. An ex–Disney teen star hovered nearby, trying to find her way into the conversation.

I could see why Grey liked Tyler: the bouffant of black hair tied in a knot at the crown of his skull, the strong line of his jaw, the muscles that moved beneath his tattoo sleeves. Tonight his brown eyes were rimmed with kohl, his lips shellacked with green lipstick. He wore a sheer lilac blouse and high waisted trousers, the kind men favoured in the 1920s. The glowing Dom Pérignon label gave his skin an absinthine quality. The women were beautiful, but Tyler Yang was—like Grey—utterly striking. I licked my lips.

"Damn, is that who I think it is?" Vivi said, eyeing the super-model. "The Victoria's Secret Angel, right? I think she just broke up with her girlfriend."

"Keep it in your pants," I said. "We're investigating our sister's mysterious disappearance. This is no time for fraternizing."

"Says the girl salivating over Tyler Yang. Said missing sister's *boyfriend*."

"I'm *not* salivating."

"At least not with your mouth."

"Gross."

"Yet true."

Tyler spotted us then. We made and held eye contact across the room.

"Uh . . . He does not look super pleased to see us," Vivi said.

Tyler's expression had fermented into vinegar. He was staring now, his eyes dark and jaw set. He raised a thin finger, curled it toward himself. *Come.*

"It appears we are being beckoned," I said.

"Well, that's all the invitation I need." Vivi pushed past me and made a beeline for the model. Shameless. As we approached the table, however, Tyler had a quiet word with the women, and they rose and made their way toward the bar, two goddesses draped in starlight.

"No, why are they going away?" Vivi said, staring after the women as they glided through the crowd. My phone pinged in my hand. I glanced at the screen, but the message was from my mother, not Grey. *Shit*. In all the panic of trying to find Grey, I'd forgotten about my curfew.

Heading home soon, I messaged Cate, then I turned on airplane mode so she wouldn't show up at the club to escort me home.

"Little Hollows," Tyler said, looking from Vivi to me. "You have to be."

"We're Grey's sisters," I said as we sat.

"If she sent you to apologize, I'm not interested in hearing it."

"Apologize for what?" Vivi asked.

"Oh, you know, for being a lying, cheating *witch*."

Vivi raised her eyebrows. I pressed my teeth together. We both hated that word. "We're here because we can't find Grey," she said. "We're worried she might be missing."

Tyler laughed, though not kindly. "No, she's not."

"When did you last see her?" I asked.

"I don't know. A few days ago, when we broke up. I suppose I haven't seen her since then."

"You broke up?" Vivi asked.

"Yes."

"Why? Did you fight?"

"That's usually what happens when people break up."

Vivi's jaw tilted down. There was still the ghost of a smile on

54

her lips, but her eyes were sharp. Going in for the kill. "Did you get angry?" The way she asked it, it was almost like she was flirting. "Did you hurt her?"

Tyler stirred his drink. "I don't like where this is going."

He tried to stand then, but Vivi grabbed him by the collar and pulled him down. She sidled up close to him and hooked her leg over his thigh; to anyone watching, it would look flirtatious, not threatening.

"You're the first person the police are going to come to after we call them," said Vivi, her lips close to Tyler's ear. I sat up straighter at the word *police*. Vivi was bluffing, surely. It wasn't that serious yet—was it? "The ex-boyfriend. You know it's true. So tell us what happened." She stroked his cheek, but whatever cloying spell she'd used on the hostess, it wasn't working on him.

He's quite special, Grey had told me. *You'll know what I mean when you meet him*. Is this what she'd meant?

Tyler looked the way I felt: afraid. "Whoa, whoa, whoa. Police? Why are you getting them involved?"

"Because we can't find her, you idiot," Vivi said. "Grey is uncontactable. The hostess here tonight said a weird dude was looking for her. Something might have *happened* to her."

"Grey is always disappearing. That's nothing new."

"What do you mean?" I asked.

"For days at a time, she disappears off the face of the earth, okay? Won't answer calls, misses work, dates, fittings. Everyone else got used to it. It was part of her mystery. Would she show up or wouldn't she? All very exciting. But it sucks when you're dating her. Your sister was a lousy girlfriend."

Vivi prickled. "Be very careful what you say about her."

"Why? Would I bad-mouth her if I'd done anything to her?

No. I mean it, Grey was a bad girlfriend. There was someone else, I assume. That's why we broke up. That's probably who she's with right now."

"Grey cheated on you?" I asked. It didn't sound like her. Grey was wild, sure, but not flippant—especially not with other people's hearts.

"Well, she didn't admit it to my face, but what else am I supposed to assume? Where does she go when she disappears? All I know is when she was here, she was only ever here halfway—if I was lucky. We were together for a year and I feel like I barely scratched the surface of who she was. She kept so many secrets, so much of herself compartmentalized. Especially the occult stuff."

Vivi and I exchanged glances. Tyler had our attention, and he knew it.

"Oh, I suppose you don't know much about that, do you?" he said. "I don't either, really. All I know is the one time she let me come to her apartment, it was the creepiest place I've ever been. Full of weird shit. Dead things, dark magic. Grey thinks she's some kind of witch."

"We were at her apartment tonight," I said. "There was nothing like that there."

"Everybody keeps secrets, Little Hollow. Perhaps your big sister has been keeping more secrets from you than you realize."

It was no surprise to me that Grey was still interested in the occult. It had been that way all her teenage years. Grey liked things that were obscure and dangerous: older men; drugs; séances in graveyards; heavy leather-bound books that smelled of chocolate and promised spells to commune with demons.

"What did you fight about when you broke up?" Vivi asked Tyler.

"I saw a man leaving her apartment," he replied. Vivi and I shared another look. "That was the final straw."

"Did he . . . ," Vivi began. "Uh, how does one phrase this? Was he, perchance, some kind of Minotaur with all the flesh stripped off the bones of his face?"

Tyler stared at her for a few moments, then smiled. "I think we're done here, Little Hollows," he said as he finished his drink and shrugged on his velvet jacket. "When you find Grey, tell her I hate her."

With that, he stood and was gone.

6

I HAD SEVEN missed calls and a dozen messages from my mother when we left the club, all of them dinging into my phone at once when I turned airplane mode off.

"Damn," I whispered as I tapped Cate's name to call her, my heart fast and swollen with guilt. "Our mother is going to kill me."

"Iris?" Cate said instantly. I could taste the panic on her tongue, a sour scent that made my stomach crumple.

"I'm so sorry." Vivi and I were walking to the Tube, the cold stripping the skin off my legs, turning me inside out. "I'm okay. We're heading home now."

"How could you do that to me?" my mother demanded. "How could you do that to me?"

"I'm sorry. I'm sorry. I'm okay."

"I'm at work. I almost called the police."

"I'm okay, Mama." I hadn't meant to say it. Sometimes it just slipped out.

I could hear Cate breathing on the other end of the line.

"Please don't call me that," she said quietly. "You know I don't like that."

"I'm sorry."

"Go home *immediately*."

"We're on our way already. We'll be there in about half an hour. I'll message you when we're there."

I hung up. The cold had sent my fingers numb and I struggled to bend them enough to slip my phone into my coat pocket. I could feel Vivi staring at me disapprovingly.

"Iris," she said.

"Don't say anything," I snapped.

"What is Cate going to do next year when you go to university, huh? Move to Oxford or Cambridge with you?"

"We've been looking at places and she's been putting some feelers out for jobs."

"Are you *kidding* me?"

"It's not like we'll live *together*. Just close by. Just so I can see her from time to time and so she doesn't feel—"

"*Iris.*"

"Look, it's easy for you to lecture me. You're never *here*. I'm all she has left, okay? I have to be everything for her, every day." Cate Hollow had suffered more grief in her lifetime than most people. Her parents had died suddenly, a terrible thing had happened to her children, her husband had lost his mind and then his will to live, and then her elder daughters had left home so young and all but cut off contact with her. I couldn't understand the way my sisters treated her sometimes, like she was a stranger. All Cate wanted was to be needed. "I'm all she has left," I said again, softer this time. It seemed like the least I could do, to let her track me on an app and braid my hair like she had when I was little.

"That's a pretty heavy burden to bear," Vivi said. "Being everything for someone."

"Yeah, well. Aren't you lucky you don't have to carry it."

Vivi placed her hand in the middle of my back, between my shoulder blades. I felt the warmth of her skin through the silken fabric, felt the cord of power that connected us. Blood to blood, soul to soul. The knot of panic that had been tangling somewhere between my ribs and throat started to come undone.

"Come on, kid," Vivi said. "Let's get you home."

We caught the Northern Line back to Golders Green, the late-night commuters drinking in my bare legs and collarbones with big, hungry eyes. I felt like a thing to be devoured, sucked down to the marrow. I shrank in my seat and tried to stretch my short dress a little farther over my thighs. The Tube rattled and squealed. The woman sitting next to me smelled of sweet alcohol, her breath a cloud of fruit and sugar. The curved windows on the other side of the train carriage reflected a strange beast back at me. There were two Irises: one my regular reflection, one upside down, both joined together at the skull. A creature with two mouths, two noses, and a shared pair of eyes, empty black ovals distorted and made huge by the curve in the glass.

Vivi and I walked home together along our well-trod path, past the red double-decker buses at the station exit, along a long, straight street lined with low houses with darkened leadlight windows. We had always come this way even though the route to our house was faster through the backstreets, because the main road was brightly-lit and busy. We knew all too well what could happen to girls on poorly lit streets at night, because it had happened to us.

Then again, all girls knew that.

Tonight, that old danger felt close. We checked behind us every few paces to make sure no one was following. An old woman in a nightdress and coat stood smoking on the balcony of an apartment block, watching us with sunken eyes as we passed. Would she remember us if we ran into the horned man between here and our house and never made it home? What would she tell the police if they came knocking, looking for witnesses? *They seemed agitated. They were underdressed for the weather. They were in a hurry. They kept looking behind them, as though they were being pursued. What did they expect, dressed like that?*

We turned left, then looped back onto our street. It was darker than the main road and lined with skeletal trees that looked monstrous in the low light.

The man, whoever he was, knew the route I ran through Hampstead Heath in the mornings.

He knew where I went to school.

He knew where Vivi's show was.

He knew, I was certain, where we lived.

After we locked the door behind us, I messaged Cate to let her know I was safe while Vivi checked all the windows and doors were secure. We changed out of Grey's gossamer clothes and into pyjamas—harsh against our skin after designer silk and wool—then sat cross-legged on the kitchen island, eating pasta from a bowl Cate had left in the fridge. Sasha meowed from the floor, begging for more food even though she'd already been fed.

We still hadn't heard from Grey. I called again—nothing— and sent another message that went undelivered. We decided to give her the night before we called the police. There were no signs of a struggle at her apartment, and besides, she was a jet-setter; she could be on a yacht in the Caribbean for all we knew, her phone out of service.

Just because a creep was stalking us and just because a man with black eyes who smelled like death had been asking after her didn't mean something bad had happened to Grey.

I am the thing in the dark, she had said once, and in that moment, I had believed her.

"Why do you think we're so strange?" I asked Vivi as we ate. "Why do you think we can do the things we can do?"

"Like what?" Vivi said around a mouthful of pasta.

"Make people do what we want them to. Other things."

"That doesn't feel strange to me. It feels right."

"Other people can't do what we do."

"Sure they can. Other people can do weird stuff too, you know; they just don't talk about it. There have always been people like us, Iris. Look in any history book, any folklore: witches, mediums, Wiccans. Whatever you want to call it. We're connected to the world and to each other in a different way. We might be peculiar, but we're not *new*."

I shook my head. "There's something wrong with us. I feel it sometimes. Something rotten on the inside." It was why I buried myself in books on coding and robotics and titration, so the wrongness had less room to seep in. I was certain that others—people like Justine Khan and Jennifer Weir—could feel it too. Maybe they were right to be cruel to me. Maybe I let them get away with it because some part of me believed I deserved it. "Do you think that thing—the guy in the skull—do you think he has anything to do with what happened to us? Do you think he's back to finish what he started?" I reached out to trail my fingers over the scar at my sister's throat, hidden now beneath a twisted vine of ink. "Who cuts little girls' throats?"

Vivi chewed her mouthful slowly, her eyes boring into me. "I think it's time we went to bed." She slid off the kitchen bench and left without another word.

I brushed my teeth, tried to catch up on some of the classwork I'd missed that day, then went to find her in her old bedroom, curled up in her childhood single bed. I crawled in next to her. The stink of the perfume had faded, and Vivi's natural scent—sylvan, milky—passed through now. I wiped some smudged eyeliner from her cheek and watched her while she slept. None of us were attractive sleepers. All of the sharp angles that made us striking when we were awake gave way to slack jaws and puddles of drool the moment our heads hit pillows. We'd once spent an entire month seeing who could take the most hideous sleeping pictures of the others.

I stroked Vivi's cheek and felt a pang of longing for her, and for Grey, for the years we'd been inseparable. Not yet split apart by countries and time zones and careers and lives.

I pressed my fingertips lightly to her throat, right at the point where her heartbeat sprang beneath her skin. It was how we'd slept as children, our finger resting on one another's pulse points, a cross-hatched thicket of wrists and necks and hands. For a long time, years, I couldn't sleep deeply unless I felt the heartbeat of both my sisters thrumming beneath my fingers. But they had grown up and left home, and I'd realized there were scarier things in the world than the monsters that lived in my nightmares.

Grey, I thought in silent prayer, knowing somehow that, wherever she was, she'd hear me. *I hope you're okay.*

I woke before dawn, as I always did, and messaged my mother, and checked my Find Friends app, and ran through Hampstead Heath, cursing the Romans for settling in such a damp, miserable place. It was raining again, because it was London. The weirdness of yesterday felt washed away, but I still stuck to the busier paths and avoided the wooded area where I'd seen the man yesterday. I ran until it hurt to breathe and my body begged me to stop, and then I ran some more. I held my phone in my palm the whole time, willing it to vibrate with a message from Grey, but every time I looked, there were no new notifications.

When I got home, Cate was cooking breakfast in her scrubs. Vivi was sitting on the kitchen island again, her long tattooed legs dangling as she plopped cherry tomatoes into her mouth.

"Look who I found," Cate said when she saw me.

"The prodigal daughter returns," Vivi said, opening her arms wide and staring off into the distance like a Renaissance painting of Jesus.

"You know the definition of *prodigal* is 'wastefully extravagant'?" I said as I went to the fridge in search of milk.

Vivi put her arms down. "I thought it meant 'favourite,' and I'm going to stick with that. Pour me one too," she said as I set out a glass.

"Please," Cate said out of habit.

"*Please,*" Vivi said. I handed her a glass of milk and sat at the breakfast bar while Cate scrambled some eggs.

Vivi had an easier relationship with our mother than Grey did. Cate had always been overprotective—how could she be expected to be any other way, after what she'd been through?—which Grey had taken as a personal threat to her freedom. Vivi, on the other hand, was never bothered by our mother's rules, because she never followed them. If Vivi was busted, which wasn't often because she was so good at sneaking around, she would apologize with handwritten cards and breakfast in bed.

They were very different women who had lived very different lives and were interested in very different things, but somehow—despite each considering the other an anomaly—they usually managed to find some middle ground. They spoke on the phone at least once a month. They teased each other constantly: Cate sent Vivi links to tattoo removal clinics, Vivi sent Cate links to pictures of body modders with split tongues and their teeth filed to points, captioned *Do you think this would suit me?* When Vivi sent recordings of her new music, Cate responded with comments like *I think you sent the wrong track? This is a recording of cats being murdered.* They were silly with each other. Sweet with each other.

"Have you heard from Grey?" I asked Vivi.

Vivi shook her head. "Cate doesn't seem to think we should worry."

"Grey can look after herself," Cate said. The way she said it without even looking up from what she was doing made me purse my lips.

My thoughts went to the night Grey left home. They had been at odds with each other for months, Cate and Grey, squabbling over curfews and boyfriends and parties and alcohol. Grey was pushing the boundaries, seeing what she could get away with. One night, she stumbled home rotten drunk and vomited on the kitchen floor.

Cate was furious and grounded her on the spot. Grey was a seventeen-year-old girl, filled with the rage and power of a thunderstorm curling beneath her skin. When she snapped, she put her hands around our mother's throat, forced her against the wall, and whispered something in her ear. A needle. A pinprick. Something that was so small, so quiet, I didn't hear it. Cate was still. Then whatever Grey had said splintered through her, electrifying her. She was a tree split by lightning. One moment a woman, the next something wild and ruptured. She slapped my sister so hard across the face that Grey's lip split; there were still three brown specks on the wall where her blood had soaked into the plaster.

"Get the fuck out of my house," Cate had ordered in a low, steady voice, "and don't ever, *ever* come back."

The sudden violence of it had made me hyperventilate. For years, as my father's delusions had swollen inside his mind, I'd become more and more afraid that he would hurt us, put a pillow over our faces while we slept. It wasn't unusual to wake in the middle of the night to his shadowy form hovering at the end of my bed, whispering softly. *"Who are you? What are you?"* Yet even as the spools of himself unraveled, he never laid a finger on us.

Then here was Cate Hollow, a small, gentle woman who had done something so brutal, so indefensible. I still wasn't sure what terrible thing Grey had said to her to make her snap like that, to pull her so far out of herself.

Grey hadn't cried. She'd set her jaw and packed her bags and done what our mother asked: left the house and never come back, except once, to clear out her room. They hadn't spoken since that night, four years ago now.

"Should we call the police?" I asked. "Should I not go to school?" It was a tempting thought. I wondered what fresh punishment JJ had in store for me for embarrassing them last night.

"You are *going* to school," Cate said as she pointed from me to Vivi. "One day of cutting class with your miscreant sister is tolerable, but no more."

"I think you meant to say 'genius rock-goddess sister,' but okay," Vivi said.

"I would like a doctor in the family," Cate said, her fingers crossed on both hands. "Or at least one daughter to finish high school. So go and get ready."

"What if we don't hear from her?" I asked.

I looked to Vivi, who shrugged. I was immediately frustrated by the sense that if Grey were here and Vivi were missing, Grey would know exactly what to do. There would be forward motion. There would be a plan. Grey was like that: There was no problem so large that it couldn't be solved. The universe seemed to bend to her will. Vivi and I, in comparison, were too used to being foot soldiers under our eldest sister's rule. Without our unifying central command unit, we were lost.

"I was supposed to fly back to Budapest this afternoon, but I guess I can push my flight until tomorrow," Vivi said. "I'll call her agent and manager after nine. I'm sure they'll know where she is."

7

I CALLED GREY on my walk to school and again between each of my classes, already knowing it would go to voicemail. I checked Find Friends—Vivi and Cate were both at home—but Grey's location came back as unavailable. I was distracted in class, refreshing Instagram and Facebook to see if she'd posted anything new.

By lunchtime, I wondered if JJ might just let me get away with the sin of having Vivi for a sister. Justine had ignored me in English, and I hadn't yet seen Jennifer—and then, when I sat down to eat, I found the picture. A piece of printer paper had been folded twice and slipped into my backpack. On it was a medieval image of three women burning at stakes, their hands clasped behind them in irons as flames licked at their toes. Their faces had been digitally altered to look like my sisters and me. There was no accompanying note, though the message was loud and clear.

You will burn.

I sighed. My first instinct was to throw it away or take it to a teacher. Instead, I folded it up and put it back in my bag. Grey would like it, would probably find it funny, would appreciate the artistry that had gone into making the burning women look like us. It was the kind of thing she would have framed and hung on her bedroom wall when she was my age.

I picked up my phone to call her, forgetting, for a moment, that she was unlikely to answer. Instead, I called Vivi for an update, but her phone rang and rang and rang. When her avatar disappeared from Find Friends a few minutes later, I was left with a panicky feeling in my stomach that whatever had happened to Grey had happened to Vivi too.

I cut class for the second day in a row and jogged home through the spitting rain. When I got there, Cate's car was gone and the house was shut up, dark.

"Vivi?" I called when I unlocked the front door.

No answer.

"Vivi?!"

"Up here!" she answered. "In Grey's room!"

I ran up the stairs, my heart thrashing. Vivi was in Grey's old empty bedroom, sitting on the floor with Sasha in her lap and the *Vogue* magazine open in front of her.

"How did you get in here?" I asked, breathless. "The door has been locked for years."

"Grey's gone, Iris," she said without looking up at me.

Lightning flashed outside. Thunder followed a moment later, stuttering through the house and making the window glass jitter. My hair was wet and my teeth were chattering from the cold. Cate told me that the three of us were all born in the middle of storms. Grey was lightning, Vivi was thunder, and I was the sea in a tempest. Grey had always hated storms, but Vivi loved them. When a second curl of thunder crawled in through the open window, I wondered if she'd somehow summoned it.

"What do you mean, Grey's gone?" I asked.

"I talked to her agent, her manager, her publicist, the photographer she was supposed to shoot with yesterday. I talked to her friends in Paris and London. I talked to her doorman. No one has seen or heard from her in days." Vivi held up the latest *Vogue*, the one I'd hidden under my pillow to save it from my mother. "Have you read this?"

"A couple of paragraphs, but—"

"Read some more."

"There are more important—"

"Seriously, *read it*."

"What am I looking for?"

"Oh, you'll know it when you see it."

I opened the magazine and picked up where I left off.

New Year's Day marked the ten-year anniversary of one of the world's most enduring modern mysteries: the disappearance of the Hollow sisters. On a quiet street in Edinburgh, three little girls vanished right out from under their parents' watchful gaze. Then, exactly one month later, they came back, to the very same street they were taken from. They were naked and carried nothing with them but an antique folding hunting knife. They had no serious injuries nor signs of sexual assault. They weren't dehydrated or malnourished. All three of them bore a fine half-moon incision at the base of their throats, nestled in the crook of their collarbones, that had been stitched closed with silk thread. The wounds were healing nicely.

No one has been able to say where they went or what happened to them—not even Grey Hollow, the eldest of the three. She was eleven at the time, certainly old enough to remember snippets of her experience, though she refused to give a statement to Scottish police and has never spoken publicly about her suspected kidnapping.

Conspiracy theories abound, the most popular of which are alien abduction, parental hoax, and (perhaps because of the Celtic setting) fairy changelings.

There were several large out-of-court settlements from news organizations that had falsely accused the girls' parents of being involved in their disappearance. The funds went toward enrolling the three sisters in Highgate School for Girls, a lavishly expensive day school that counts famous actors, poets, and journalists among its alumni. One of the Old Girls recently married into an extended branch of the royal family. The grounds are green and expansive, the main building a timber-framed Tudor mansion with wisteria growing thick on the facade. Grey Hollow struggled to thrive there.

A series of family tragedies followed in the ensuing years, the most devastating of which was a Capgras delusion—Hollow's father, Gabe, reportedly believed his children had all been replaced by identical impostors. After two years in and out of psychiatric institutions, he killed himself when Grey was thirteen.

Little more is known about her teenage years, but at seventeen, she had a falling-out with her mother and found herself homeless. She dropped out of high school, moved into a one-bedroom apartment in Hackney with three other girls, and tried her hand at modeling. Within six months of leaving home, she'd walked for Elie Saab, Balmain, Rodarte, and

Valentino. Within two years, she was the highest-earning supermodel in the world. Now, at the age of twenty-one, Hollow is the owner of and head designer at House of Hollow, whose creations have become some of the most sought-after in the industry after the label's launch at Paris Fashion Week just under eighteen months ago.

One of the first things I tell her is that stitching bits of paper into her creations reminds me of another infamous unsolved crime: the mystery of the Somerton man. In 1948, an unidentified man was found dead on a beach in Australia. All the labels had been cut from his clothing, and police later found a tiny scroll of rolled-up paper sewn into his trouser pocket. It read "Tamám Shud," which means "finished" in Persian. The words had been torn from the final page of the *Rubáiyát of Omar Khayyám*.

"That's where I got the initial inspiration from," Hollow says eagerly as she wraps her long fingers—preternaturally dexterous, like she's a seamstress who's been working for a hundred years—around a cup of unsweetened Ceylon tea. Her voice is surprisingly deep, and she rarely blinks. With white-blond hair, black eyes, and a smattering of freckles across her nose year-round, she is the definition of ethereal. I have interviewed many beautiful women, but none so truly otherworldly. "As a child I was obsessed with mysteries—probably because I was one."

I'm under strict instructions from her publicist not to ask her about the missing month, but since she was the one who brought it up, I press my luck.

Does she really not remember anything?

"Of course I remember," she says, her ink-drop gaze

holding mine. Her smile is slight, sly; the same mischievous pixie grin that has made her famous. "I remember everything. You just wouldn't believe me if I told you."

The article continued, but I came to a snap stop at that line, the line that Vivi had no doubt been talking about: *Of course I remember. I remember everything.*

You just wouldn't believe me if I told you.

The words sank into me like acid, dissolving my flesh. I snapped the *Vogue* shut and sat on Grey's bare bed, my hand pressed over my mouth.

"Yeah," Vivi said heavily.

"That cannot be true."

When I was seven years old, I vanished without a trace for a whole month.

On the very rare occasion she drank enough wine to talk about it, my mother emphasized the impossibility of it. How we were walking through the warren of lanes of Edinburgh's Old Town, back to our father's parents' house. How we were there one moment, then gone the next. How she took her eyes off us for a second or two, long enough to peck our father on the cheek when the New Year's fireworks began. How she heard nothing, saw no one—simply looked up to find the street before her empty. A lace-fine snow was falling through the air, the kind that melts when it hits the sidewalk. The alleyway was lit by oily slicks of light and pops of effervescence from the overhead starbursts.

Where there should have been three children, there were none.

Cate smiled at first; she thought we were playing with her.

"Iris, Vivi, Grey, come out, come out, wherever you are," she sang. We were bad at hide-and-seek, but she always pretended to take forever to find us. No giggles answered her this time. No whispers. Immediately, she knew something was wrong. In her first statement to the police, Cate would say that the air tasted burnt and smelled of wild, wet animal. That the only thing out of place on the street was a handful of fall leaves and white flowers on the stoop of a house that had burned down the month before. That was the first place she looked for us. All that had survived the flames of the fire was a freestanding doorframe, held up by nothing. My mother stepped through it and called our names and wandered from room to room in the shell of burnt-out bricks and rubble, her panic rising.

We weren't there. We weren't anywhere. It was like the cobblestones had opened up and swallowed us.

My father, Gabe, when he was alive, filled in the rest of the story. How he called the police less than five minutes after we disappeared. How he banged on the doors of every house on the street, but no one had seen us. How you could hear people calling our names—*Iris! Vivi! Grey!*—from one end of Old Town to the other, until the sun rose and the searchers went home to rest their throats and hug their sleeping children.

I remembered none of this. Like a language I'd once been fluent in but had long stopped speaking, the memories of what truly happened had faded to threadbare fragments over time and then to nothing at all.

I was grateful for this. I knew what usually happened to kidnapped children. It was better not to know what had been done to us.

My memories began a month later, when a woman found

74

us huddled together at midnight, shivering on the sidewalk of the same street we had disappeared from. Our coats were gone and we were naked in the cold, but apart from that, we were unharmed. Our skin was clean. There were leaves and white flowers in our hair. We smelled of mildew and woodsmoke and milk and death. The police came and took the knife from Grey's shaking hand and wrapped us in foil blankets and offered us hot chocolate and cake made from dark treacle and spices. I was starving. We all were. We gorged ourselves.

After our medical examinations, we were released to our parents. Cate swept me into her arms and collapsed to the hospital floor in a sobbing heap. Her face was wet with tears and her hair was a greasy nest twisted into a bun at the nape of her neck. She couldn't speak, could only rock back and forth on the floor, keening into my ear.

It is the first true memory I have of my mother.

Of course I remember.

I remember everything.

You just wouldn't believe me if I told you.

It *had* to be a lie. Grey didn't remember. None of us did. It was a central tenet of our story. We were taken. We came back. None of us knew what happened, and none of us ever would. We were the miracle that parents of all missing children dreamed of. Spat back from the abyss, unharmed and whole.

"I can't feel her, Iris," Vivi said. "I can't *feel* her."

"What does that mean?"

"Last night, you talked about the strange things we can do. That's one of them. I'd forgotten—I haven't tried to do it for years—but when I woke up this morning and you weren't there . . . I could still *feel* you. I followed your footsteps down the stairs to the front door. We're . . . tethered, or something. We've always been able to find each other. In the dark, across town, even over oceans. My feet bring me to you if I want them to."

I knew what she was talking about. I always knew if Grey or Vivi was calling me without looking at the caller ID. I always knew where I'd find my sisters if I went looking for them—but I assumed the memories of being able to *feel* them, to find them if I needed to, were things I'd half dreamed as a kid, like breathing underwater or being able to fly.

"But I can't feel her," Vivi continued. "Grey is gone—what if whatever happened to us before is happening again? We might be the only ones who can help her."

"Don't say that. Don't even think that, okay? Nothing has *happened* to her." I could hear in the pitch of my voice how desperately I wanted that to be true. "We're not kids anymore. Besides, you heard Tyler last night. She disappears all the time."

"We have to look for her, Iris."

"No, I have to go back to school. I have classes, I have tutoring. There's a titration competition coming up in a month that I haven't practiced for even once and my Python skills need some—"

"Tell me you think she's okay, and I'll drop you at school myself."

"Vivi . . . this is crazy."

"Say she's okay, then. Listen to your gut and tell me you think Grey is okay. Do the thing we can do. Find her."

"I haven't tried that for a long time."

"Do it."

I let out a long breath and did what Vivi asked me to do. I reached out and tried to find Grey, to feel her, the way I'd been

76

able to as a child, but all that came back was an empty sense of nothingness.

I bit my lip. Was that proof of anything?

"That's what I thought," Vivi said. She tapped the *Vogue* cover. "Grey's always kept secrets. When we were kids, she used to hide stuff from us. Her diary, money, booze. She'd squirrel everything away under loose floorboards or behind bookshelves. So where would she keep her secrets now?"

I looked around the room. "How *did* you get in here? Did you pick the lock?"

Vivi shrugged. "The door was open."

"The only person who has a key to this room is Grey." I knew that because I'd tried to get in many times since she left, without success. I thought of the open front door yesterday, of the wet footprints that tracked inside, of Sasha outside on the mat.

"What if . . . ," I started. It was a crazy theory, but we were already talking about crazy things. "What if Grey unlocked the door? What if she was here yesterday? What if she left something for us, something only we would know how to find?"

Vivi snapped her fingers at me. "Now you're thinking like a Hollow."

☾

We spent the afternoon combing Grey's bedroom, excavating for signs of our sister. Vivi found the first: a collection of runes hand-embroidered in emerald thread on the underside of her mattress. I found the second—an annotated page torn from a book of Emily Dickinson poetry rolled up tight inside a curtain rod—and the third.

I was on my hands and knees under Grey's bed, trailing my

fingertips over the baseboard, when my skin caught on a splinter in the wood. A prick of blood welled on my fingertip. I wiped it away on my uniform skirt, then crouched to inspect the offending panel.

"There's something here," I told Vivi. A crack in the skirting board. I slipped my fingernails under the wood and lifted. It gave, but not enough. "Get me a knife from the kitchen."

Vivi was standing over me now. "Why don't you get it yourself?" she said.

I sighed and turned to give her a *seriously?* look.

"Sorry. Old sibling habits die hard."

When Vivi returned with a butter knife, I slipped it into the crack, eased it open.

"You're going to break it," Vivi said as she tried to shoulder me out of the way. "Let me do it."

I stopped and glared at her. "Would you quit it?"

"Fine. Whatever. Just be more gentle."

"I *am* being gentle."

Finally, the wood came away from the wall with a bright pop and clattered to the floorboards. Behind it was a hole in the plasterboard, its edges raw. The exact kind of place Grey liked to keep secrets. "Give me your phone," I said to Vivi, and she did, the flashlight already turned on. I notched it into the darkness, eager to uncover more of Grey's mysteries, the same way I had been as a child. My heart was clucking in my throat. The hole was laced with cobwebs. There were no diaries or cash or condoms or little bottles of elderflower gin, which is what we used to find in Grey's hidey-holes before she left home. There was only a dried white flower, an antique hunting knife, and a brass key with a note attached.

"Now, *this* is more like Grey," Vivi said as I handed her the strange treasures. I could sense Grey in them, feel her energy; she had touched them, not so long ago.

On the scroll attached to the key, there was an address in Shoreditch, followed by a message with yesterday's date:

Vivi, Iris,

First of all, stop going through my private shit. I don't know how many times I have to tell you. (Okay, fine, this time I was counting on you to go snooping—but still. Not cool.)

I hate to say this, but if you're reading this, I might already be dead. There is so much I wish I'd told you. Come to the address above. Bring the key. Find the door. Save me.

And if he comes for you—run.

I love you both more than anything.

Grey

P.S. Regarding the knife, as Jon and Arya said: Stick 'em with the pointy end.

8

I MIGHT ALREADY be dead.

We were in an Uber on our way to the address Grey had given us. The words from her letter were stinging through my nerves, pricking tears at the corners of my eyes. Vivi was silent, her forehead pressed against the window, her jaw set so tight I worried her teeth might crack.

I turned the knife over in my hands. Opened it, closed it again. The staghorn handle had a patina and the blade was pocked with age, but it looked slip-through-your-skin-like-butter sharp. It was the same knife we'd been found with as children, the one police had taken from Grey the night we came back. For a while they'd thought it was an important piece of evidence, but the only fingerprints they ever lifted off it belonged to my sister. I wondered how she'd retrieved it from evidence, considering our case was still open, then dropped back into the pool of my terrible imagination.

A world without Grey was impossible. Both of my sisters were the great loves of my life. I couldn't live without them. I didn't want to.

The Uber pulled up outside a pub in a narrow graffiti-lined street. It was late afternoon and there were a handful of Londoners huddled in the honey glow of the bar, drinking pints. The address Grey had given us was for the flat the next floor up. Vivi and I guessed the passcode to the building—162911, the same as all our phone passcodes—then walked up the winding staircase to the first floor. Grey's door was beetle green, the handle brass to match the key.

Vivi put her hand on the paint and shook her head. "She isn't here either." I knew it too, I realized. I knew what Grey felt like, the way her energy settled in a room. Old memories were coming back to me. How I could follow the trails of her through our house when we were children, retrace the footsteps of where she'd been five, six, seven hours before. What books she'd read, which pieces of fruit she had picked up, inspected, put back. It wasn't like I could see threads trailing behind her, or smell the scent of her skin. It was a sense of general rightness. Yes, she had been here. Yes, she had done this. I could do it with Vivi too, though that held less fascination for me. Grey was my obsession. Grey was who I wanted to be.

One long, lazy summer in France, the first one without our father, I spent two months living an hour behind Grey. She was fourteen and just coming to understand the exhilarating power of her beauty. I was ten. Too skinny, too tall, still shy and awkward. To me, back then, Grey was a goddess. She wore white flowing dresses and wreaths of wild lavender woven into her hair. I copied everything she did, living in the liminal world she left in her wake. I didn't have to see her all day to know where she'd been, what she'd done. Sunbathing on the roof. A midday swim in the river. Nectarines and hard cheese for lunch. A kiss with a local boy in the pews of the medieval church (I improvised and used my hand—still, the priest was not pleased when he found me).

Wait.

A strange memory tugged at the side of my thoughts. Something lost and then found. Another church, this one ruined and half-devoured by the woods. We came across it on our first day there, down by the river. Cate warned us not to go near it. It was derelict. But . . . Grey went. Yes. Went somewhere I couldn't follow. Not because I was afraid, but because her trail just . . . stopped. Because she stepped through a door and wasn't there on the other side. I'd wandered around the old church for hours, trying to figure out where she went. Eventually, Grey was there again, whole and solid. She smelled of burning and had flowers caught in the tangles of her hair.

Find the door, Grey's note had said.

Vivi put the key in the lock and turned. We stepped inside.

The smell hit us first. The wet, heavy stench of fermented shit undercut with a cloying sweetness. We both gagged at the same time and scrambled back into the hall, dry heaving. Vivi looked at me, wide-eyed and knowing. We had smelled a dead body once before. A few years ago, in the week after Grey left but before Vivi packed her own bags, the man in the house next to ours had slipped in his bathtub. It had been eight days before anyone found him. By then, his body had begun to liquefy, and the smell of it had seeped through walls and ceilings and floors. When the paramedics came for him and opened the front door, the stench exploded out onto the street, soaking the air. It hung from the branches of trees like necklaces and took weeks to fade.

The words from Grey's note nipped at my lungs. *If you're reading this, I might already be dead.*

"A dead animal," Vivi said, determined. "Not Grey." Then she pressed inside, breathing through her mouth. I did the same, though I could still taste the dead thing on my tongue, fat and lingering.

We moved through Grey's clandestine apartment together, half looking for the source of the stench, half consumed by the magnificent size of this treasure trove. All our young lives, we had subsisted on morsels of Grey Hollow's secrets. Diary pages read by flashlight after she had snuck out, thimblefuls of sweet wine stolen from the bottle she kept hidden under her bed. And now here was her soul laid bare for the taking. A feast for the starving.

All the curtains were drawn, and the space felt woody and cool. The darkness was tight, damp, the undergrowth of a forest. Vivi turned on a lamp. It was nothing like the first apartment. Here, the walls were painted dark canker green. The floors were bleached herringbone parquet. There were terrariums filled with carnivorous plants and trays full of assorted crystals and delicate animal bones. Vases of feathers and jars of little creatures suspended in formaldehyde. Stacked boxes of balsam fir and red cedar incense. Bottles of gin and absinthe. Books on botany and taxidermy and how to commune with the dead. Pencil sketches were pinned to almost every available surface; Grey's couture creations, but other images too, of strange creatures and ruined houses. Dried bouquets of flowers and fall leaves hung from the ceiling. And perhaps strangest of all was the taxidermy: a snake bursting from the mouth of a rat, a fox emerging from the skin of a rabbit.

The space was thick with Grey's energy, trails of her crisscrossing the hall and rooms in tight webs. She'd been here more recently than she'd been to her other apartment.

The first room off the hall was the kitchen. I paused when I saw it, something hard settling into my stomach. The floor was black and white marble squares, and the opposite wall was entirely covered in shelves bursting with books.

My chessboard floor. Vivi's library. The exact details we'd wanted when we'd dreamed of running away together. Why hadn't Grey shared it with us already?

"Come on," Vivi said. "Keep moving. Let's find what she wants us to find and get the hell out of here."

There were two more doors at the end of the hall. We took one each. I opened the handle and peered into Grey's bedroom. The smell was strongest here, so acrid it stung my eyes and almost physically pushed me back. Some ancient part of my brain begged me not to get any closer, the part that knew the smell of death was a warning. *Stay away.*

"Vivi," I said quietly. "There's blood in here."

I felt my older sister at my shoulder. We surveyed the damage together from the doorway, unwilling to take a step into the room. It was trashed. It was the nightmare scene I'd been afraid of finding at Grey's first flat: Hitchcockian blood splatter on the walls, furniture knocked over, a lamp in shards, a gruesome patchwork of dried brown pools on the rumpled bedsheets. There were boot prints on the wall and holes kicked into the plasterboard and slippery bare footprints in the blood on the floor.

Someone had been attacked in this room. Someone had fought back in this room. Judging by the amount of blood that had been spilled, someone had died in this room.

84

I might already be dead.

I was crying as Vivi pushed past me into the stinking mess and found Grey's iPhone, the screen shattered, on her bedside table, along with her passport. They were both sitting atop a copy of *A Practical Guide to the Runes: Their Uses in Divination and Magick* by Lisa Peschel. I couldn't see Vivi's face, but I could see her chest heaving.

"I will kill anyone who's touched her," she said, her voice harsh and low. I believed her. I would join her.

"What's that sound?" There was a low background hum. An angry buzzing, coming from the wardrobe. I went into the room, careful to avoid stepping in any blood. Vivi opened the wardrobe door and switched on the light.

There was a ceiling access panel in the walk-in wardrobe. A dozen flies whirred beneath it. Black liquid dripped from one corner. It pooled on the parquet floor, where it had turned the wood into a soft fen of decay. Vivi grabbed the pull cord.

"Don't," I said. "I don't want to see this. I can't see this." Not if it was Grey. Seeing her rotting corpse would destroy me.

Vivi ignored me. "It's not her," she said—a wish, more than anything. "It won't be her." Then she pulled the cord. The hatch gagged open and heaved out a body. We both screamed and clutched at each other as it tumbled to the floor and landed with a wet squelch at our feet. It was definitely a human, not an animal.

"Fuck, fuck, fuck, fuck, fuck," Vivi yelped. And then: "It's not her." Not a wish this time: a statement of fact.

I had somehow scrambled from the wardrobe to the other side of the room and was now crouched next to the bloody bed, though I couldn't recall how I'd gotten there so quickly.

"Um . . . Iris, you should see this," Vivi said as she squatted to inspect the body.

I couldn't look. I didn't want to look. I didn't think my stomach could handle it.

I opened a window and took a breath of winter air before I went over to where the body had fallen. It was bruised and bloated but clearly not Grey. It belonged to a man. Young, muscular, naked save for three runes written down his chest in dried blood. The cause of his death was clear: His throat had been slashed.

Yet the fact that he was dead and covered in runes and hidden in our sister's ceiling was not the strangest thing about him.

"What is *happening* to him?" Vivi said. There were waxy white flowers sprouting from his mouth, his nose, the softening remains of his eyeballs. Flowers growing rabid from the gash in his skin, their roots red-black with dead blood. Something moved at the back of his throat, behind his broken teeth. Something alive in the greenery.

"Do we call the cops now?" I asked.

"As soon as we call the police, this will be a crime scene, and we won't be able to find what Grey wants us to find. Look around. Look through everything. There's something here that only we would be able to find."

It was a breeze that saved us. It trilled through the bedroom window and down the hall, where it slammed the front door closed. The door that I'd shut behind me only minutes before.

A fresh sprig of fear twisted up my spine. Not for Grey this time, but for Vivi and myself. Whoever Grey was afraid of, they knew where she lived. They had been here. Maybe they had killed someone. Maybe they were back.

There were heavy footsteps. In the hall, just outside Grey's bedroom.

Hide, Vivi mouthed to me, already taking off her backpack and crouching to slip under Grey's bed. Then there was a hand on the bedroom door, pushing it open. I had no choice but to go back into the wardrobe, over the body of the dead man. Years of following my sister like a spy had given me sure, quiet feet. I side-stepped the pool of decay and pushed myself deep into Grey's clothing, hoping it would be enough to hide me.

A man came to stand in front of the wardrobe door. A bare-chested man who was wearing a bull's skull stripped of flesh to hide his face. The man who'd been following me. He stank of rot and earth, powerful enough to momentarily mask the scent of the body.

The smell of the darkest part of the forest.

The smell of Grey's perfume.

The smell of the missing month.

A memory hummed through me, sharp as a plucked string. A house in the woods. Grey taking me by the hand and leading me through the trees. A strip of tartan fabric tied to a low branch. Grey saying, "It's not far now." Where were we?

I backed farther into the wardrobe, unbreathing, unblinking, as the man discovered the corpse—and was entirely unsurprised by it. The man—in the half-light, his skin looked sallow and seeded with lichen—nudged the body with his bare foot. I thought of the hostess last night, how she'd said a frightening man had been asking after Grey.

The man grunted, hot breath coming from the nostrils of the skull.

Wordlessly, he knelt to scoop the dead guy up and hoisted

him over his shoulder. A runnel of black liquid slipped down his back from the dead man's open throat. I covered my mouth to stop myself from gagging. He dumped the body onto Grey's bed, then worked quickly, moving from room to room, bringing back armfuls of Grey's possessions to stack on top of the corpse. Sprigs of dried flowers, leather-bound notebooks, animal bones. Tapestries, sketches of dress designs, jewelry. Photographs. Many, many photographs, of Grey and Vivi and me, of the three of us together. He piled it into a pyre over the dead man and kindled the flames with scrunched paper, then stood and watched it as it burned.

From where I was hidden, I could make eye contact with Vivi. She had a hand pressed to her nose and mouth to stop herself from coughing in the smoke. Her eyes were wide with panic. If the man stayed much longer, she'd have to scramble out from underneath the bed before the flames ate too far through the mattress or the smoke became suffocating.

Slowly, I moved to cup my hands over my mouth and nose. The man turned to stare into the shadow of the wardrobe, directly at me. I stopped breathing, didn't blink. The firelight danced in his eyes, his irises black inside the skull he wore to hide his face. There were bloody runes written down his torso as well, the same markings as the dead man's. Had this creature snatched me from the street when I was seven? Had he kept me and my sisters locked away for a month?

I waited for a gruesome memory to climb forward, but none came.

The man turned and left.

The smoke was black and choking when the front door finally closed and I burst out of the wardrobe, the air thick with the stink of singed hair and burning fat.

Vivi was fighting for breath as I dragged her out from underneath the bed. "Save it," she gasped through her coughs. "Save it." Grey's things. I yanked a quilt off an overturned armchair and cast it over the pyre like a fishing net, hoping it would work like a fire blanket.

Vivi and I both paused at the sight of it. On the quilt was the hand-stitched image of a ruined stone doorway teeming with white flowers. An odd look crossed Vivi's face, a brief moment of recognition and understanding that gave way to confusion. "I don't . . . ," she said through a coughing fit. "What the hell is going on?"

"What is it?"

"A memory." Vivi traced her fingers over the map's stitching. "Or maybe déjà vu."

I felt it too, a word on the tip of my tongue that I couldn't quite call up.

Vivi smiled. "The Halfway. Grey's made-up place. Oh my God, she used to tell us stories about it when we were little."

I shook my head. "I don't remember."

"It was this weird place somewhere between life and death. Somewhere people ended up if they couldn't let go of something— or if someone couldn't let go of them. Some people get stuck there after they die. The ones who can't move on."

"Like . . . limbo?"

"I don't know. Grey never made it sound religious. It was more like a version of the afterlife that you'd find in a dark fairy tale: Everything was kind of stuck halfway. Like, it was always dusk and always dawn at the same time. All the trees were rotting but they never died. Food only ever left you half-full." Vivi laughed. "I haven't thought about this in years."

"What does the door have to do with it?"

"That's how you get there, I think. You fall through a broken door."

Bring the key. Find the door.

Vivi and I waited to see if the flames would prick through the fabric, but the fire had been starved. I peeled the quilt back slowly, like removing dressing from a wound, and let it fall, still smoldering, in a heap. Smoke curled across the bed but the flames didn't reignite.

"The body burned so quickly," I said as I picked through the journals and drawings and jewelry that had survived. It took hours for muscle and teeth and bone to burn, but more of Grey's possessions had survived than the dead man.

"What answers does she want us to find?" Vivi said as she continued to comb through the charred debris, more frantic by the second. "What door are we looking for?"

My gaze drifted back to the decay the man's body had left. Who was he? Had he attacked her? Had she killed him trying to defend herself, then gone into hiding? Who was the man who came back for his corpse?

Where did she want us to follow her to?

"I need water," I said. The air was still stained with the smell of death, and the smoke from the fire hung over us, snaring in our throats. "Want some?"

Vivi nodded absentmindedly. I wandered out into the hall, rubbing my eyes, and took two or three steps before I looked up and stopped.

"Oh," I said. "Shit."

9

THE MAN IN the skull was standing at the end of the hall, staring at me. He'd come back for something—maybe to make sure the fire had taken, or to retrieve something he'd forgotten. He hadn't been expecting to see me, and I hadn't been expecting to see him, so both of us stood in shock, unmoving. For a sharp, strange second, it appeared that the creature was afraid of me. Then he was fumbling with something at the back of his waistband. I caught a glint of metal.

"Shit, he's got a gun," I said, diving into the room as the first shot rang out. The bullet shattered the mirror behind me and sent a shower of glass into my hair. Vivi slammed the door closed behind me and locked it, but that only bought us a second or two. Bullets ripped through the wood, splintering it into toothpicks.

Vivi yelped and doubled over. My world contracted to the size of a pinhead.

No.

No.

Not Vivi too. I couldn't lose both of them.

But she sat up when the shots stopped, her right hand pressed to her left arm. A red stain was spreading beneath her fingers. "Jesus, he shot me. You shot me, you psycho!" she screamed at the door. There was silence for a moment, then the door began to groan as the man leaned his weight against it. The wood swelled inward, fabric stretched across a fat gut.

"Get it, get it," I said as I collected a handful of singed treasures from Grey's bed and threw them out the window onto the wet street one floor below. Vivi followed suit, using her free hand to pick up a journal, some photographs, her backpack. We both scrabbled out of the window backward as the doorframe popped with a relieved sigh and the man tumbled toward us. I lowered myself down until I was hanging. Vivi, unable to grip with an injured arm and a hand wet with blood, fell and landed in a sprawl below me. Grey's flat was only on the first floor, but the ground still felt far away. I let go and landed hard on my feet, an impact wave rolling up my spine, forcing the air from my lungs and making all my bones feel crumpled. We gathered up what we could of Grey's things and ran. The man in the skull watched us from the window, our arms full of a few of the sodden, bloody trophies he'd tried to burn.

We ran for half a mile, leaflets of paper and drops of blood trailing behind us as we weaved through the backstreets of Shoreditch, past murals and trendy restaurants, sure he was right behind us. Two fire engines screamed past us in the direction we'd come from. We slowed to watch them. A thin column of smoke was rising in the distance now. We stood, breathing hard, and found each other's free hand, knowing that the man had set our sister's life on fire and all that was left of it now was what we held in our arms.

Wherever Grey was, whatever had happened to her . . . we'd have to figure it out using only what we'd managed to salvage.

"Are you okay?" I asked Vivi breathlessly. My fingers were tacky with her drying blood. The left sleeve of her jacket was soaked through. She eased out of it, using the other sleeve to wipe away the slop of red. The bullet had only grazed her arm. There was a lot of blood, and it would leave a scar through her wisteria tattoo as wide and long as a finger, but it wasn't deep. Vivi dug in her backpack for a scarf and started tying it over the wound to stymie the bleeding.

A passerby, an older woman in fur coat, slowed and stared at us. "My cat is *vicious*," Vivi said with a shrug, totally deadpan. The woman hurried away.

"I got shot," Vivi said to me. "Can you believe that? Shot. With a bullet!"

"I know," I said as I helped her tie the makeshift bandage.

"What the fuck?" said Vivi.

"I know."

"I mean, what the fuck?"

"I know."

"Iris, you're not listening to me. What *the fuck*?"

"We need to get off the street," I said as another woman did a double take at the sight of us. Someone might call the police, and I wasn't sure how we'd explain our story. The missing sister, the dead body, the burned apartment, the gunshot wound, the armful of stolen artifacts. Even harder: the man in the skull, the flowers growing rampant in all the soft parts of a corpse. "Follow me." I doubled back the way we'd come, partly to throw our pursuer off our track if he followed Vivi's bloody trail, partly because I'd seen a café a hundred yards back that we could hide in.

It was small and dim inside, the floral wallpaper lit by apricot light bulbs that hung in jars from the ceiling. We slid into a booth at the back. My adrenaline was waning and my body had begun to ache all over. I'd landed badly on one ankle and a bright twist of pain bit at me whenever I put weight on it. The thatch of cuts I'd collected on my palms felt gritty and stung in the warmth of the café. There was glass in my hair, and blood on my hands, and the smell of death still pasted thick inside my nose.

Vivi and I put our salvaged items on the table between us. A leather-bound journal, the edges of its pages wet and flecked with blood. Scrunched, loose-leaf pages that had been torn from a notebook. A handful of drawings, each mostly destroyed now from blood and wet sidewalk and being clutched so tightly during our escape. We laid the drawings out first.

The first four were sketches for House of Hollow designs: Distorted, faceless figures sheathed in layers of dark fabric and feathers, the pencil strokes that made them frenzied. The last was something totally different: A depiction of a tumbledown house with broken windows and withered stone walls and a strip of tattered tartan fluttering from the front gate.

"I feel like I've seen this place before," I said as I leaned over the table to study the picture more closely. The memory was grainy and coated in dust. Had I been there or had I seen it in a movie when I was little? "The fabric looks like it's from the coat I was wearing the day we disappeared."

"It is *vaguely* familiar," Vivi agreed. "I guess."

"Hang on," I said as I snagged the notebook pages off the table. "This is Gabe's handwriting." I knew the tight coils of his writing instantly because I kept the card he'd made me for my fifth birthday in my bedside table. On the front was a hand-drawn iris flower, purple petals mid-bloom, and inside a short message about why I'd been called Iris: They had been his mother's favourite flower.

"What does it say?" Vivi asked.

I scanned through the pages. They seemed like undated journal entries.

My children are home. One week ago, this felt like an impossible fantasy. Now here we are.

"Oh my God," I said. "It's about us." I kept reading.

They don't speak, except to whisper to each other. When we got back to London, they wandered around our house for an hour, as though they'd forgotten it. They won't sleep in their rooms alone. They burrow under Grey's bed and sleep together in a pile. I still have so many questions. What happened to them? Where were they? Did someone hurt them? For now, I am just happy they're home.

I handed the first page to Vivi, then eagerly began reading the next, and the next, and the next.

My daughters have been home for three weeks. I should be happy. I __am__ happy . . . but I still can't shake the feeling that something is wrong with them. Cate thinks I'm being paranoid. She's probably right. What other explanation could there be?

—

Six weeks home today. They eat everything in sight. They're like locusts. Last night, we ran out of food. We found them in the kitchen around 2:00 a.m., naked and shoveling handfuls of cat food into their mouths. They wailed and clawed at us when we tried to take it away from them. Cate cried and left them to it. I couldn't handle it. I couldn't be in the house anymore. I walked around Hampstead Heath until sunrise.

—

When they were gone, all I wanted was for them to be home. For them to be safe. Now they're here, and all I have is bad thoughts. What's wrong with me?

—

It has been three months. When they came back, they looked almost like my daughters, except for the teeth and the eyes. Now their hair is turning white. Why can't Cate see what I see?

—

We used to be happy. Life wasn't perfect or even easy. We weren't rich and we had to work hard every day to support our children, but we were happy. I loved my wife. Cate was . . . effervescent. She had this high laugh like a tropical bird. We went to the movies on our first date and she laughed so hard and so loud that the rest of the theater laughed at her, and then with her. It was

magical. I haven't heard her laugh in months.
She is so thin. She gives all her food to the
children and barely eats anything herself. They
are draining us of life.

—

Maybe I am going crazy. I feel like it. Cate
thinks I am. My therapist thinks I am. He keeps
telling me my theory is wrong and impossible,
that it's a manifestation of my PTSD. That my
children are acting strangely because they also
have PTSD.

—

There is something wrong with all of them, but
especially with the one that looks like Grey. I am
afraid of them. I am afraid of <u>her.</u> Where are my
children? If these things are not my children,
then what happened to my girls?

—

I have come to a terrible conclusion:
My daughters are dead.

"Jesus," Vivi said. "Talk about a descent into insanity."

It happened quickly, the unraveling of Gabe Hollow. When we first returned after our kidnapping, he'd been exuberant. He'd swept us into his arms, a grown man turned to wet pulp by the miraculous return of his three daughters.

He was the one who noticed something wrong with my teeth and eyes, before we even left Scotland. He took me back to the police station without telling my mother and explained the strange problem to the detectives who handled our case: "One month ago, on the night before she disappeared, Iris lost her two front wiggly baby teeth on a hard candy cane. She had been so excited," he told them. Seven was old to lose your first tooth and I had been enthusiastic to finally meet the tooth fairy.

"So what's the problem, then?" the detectives asked.

"Look at her teeth now," my father said, pulling my top lip up as he pushed me in front of them. "Look at them." My mouth was full. I had no gaps. The teeth I had lost had grown back, but they'd grown back as baby teeth, teeth I would lose again only a few months later. "Look at her eyes, too," Gabe insisted. "My daughters all have blue eyes; this child's eyes are black."

I blinked a few times at the detective, who smiled at me sadly.

"You have your daughters back, Gabe," she said as she closed the file in front of her. "You got the one-in-a-million, impossible happy ending. Go home."

And so we did go home, and for a little while, everything was fine. Gabe was a tall man and his skin was always warm, and in the weeks that followed our return, I grew extra attached to him, grew fond of curling up on his lap and falling asleep in his arms. I liked to push his hair back off his forehead and study the soft features of his face, and when he got up to go anywhere, I liked to go with him, my arms wrapped tight around his neck. For a time, Gabe liked the attention. "My little leech," he called me.

I can't say for sure when exactly his mind began to slip, though I suspect it was our hair changing color that first triggered him. All three of us had dark hair as children, like our parents, but in the weeks after we came back, it lightened to white-blond. It wasn't unheard-of for those who'd suffered a severe trauma to spontane- ously develop white hair over a short period of time. It even had a name: Marie Antoinette syndrome, named for the queen whose hair supposedly turned stark white the night before her appointment with the guillotine. It was unusual and extremely rare, doctors said, but nothing to be concerned about.

Life continued on. We went back to school. Gabe seemed wary around us. He didn't like to have me on his lap anymore, didn't like my little arms clasped around his throat. Something sour and treacherous began to sink into him. I don't know how he came to the idea that we were impostors, whether it was a fairy tale from his childhood that made sudden sense or he read it on a conspiracy-theory forum, but it settled into his head and collected there like dust, until it coated everything.

Even when doctors told him our change in eye color had a name too—aniridia, the absence of an iris, a disorder caused by blunt trauma—Gabe had already made up his mind.

"What if Papa was right?" I said.

"Right about *what*?" Vivi picked up the sheets of paper and shook them in my face. "These are the deranged ramblings of a madman."

"Well, what happened to us, then, Vivi? What happened to us? Yes, okay, maybe Gabe went crazy, but something triggered that. Who took us? Where did we go?"

"I don't know!" Vivi snapped. She threw the papers on the table. "I need a drink."

"Maybe if you dealt with what happened to you as a kid," I said, unable to look at her, "you wouldn't need to numb yourself with drugs and booze." We all had different ways of coping, but Vivi's were the most destructive, filled with powders and poisons designed to lessen the pain of a tragedy we didn't understand.

My sister was silent. I chanced a glance at her. Vivi stared at me with cool slate eyes, her bottom jaw set forwards so her lips gathered into a scowl. "Maybe if you dealt with what happened to you as a kid," she said, "your mother wouldn't be your only friend."

I let out a long breath, all the fight suddenly gone from me. "Let's not do this."

"Well, don't come in with a big swinging dick accusing me of being an alcoholic."

"You *are* an alcoholic."

"Oh, screw you, Miss Perfect."

"Please, Vivi. Christ. Let's not fight about this right now."

"Whatever. Fine. You started it."

We flicked through the journal together. It was filled with newspaper clippings and printouts of news stories. At the beginning, they were all about us, all written during our disappearance. I'd avoided reading much about our case. I thought we all had. Apparently, I was wrong.

"Wow, she was obsessed," Vivi said as she turned the pages. "She never talked about it. She never wanted us to talk about it either. And the whole time she was scrapbooking like a bored housewife?"

The rest of the articles and Wikipedia printouts were about other missing people, all of whom, like us, had disappeared under strange circumstances. Grey had highlighted and underlined and made notes in the margins. Things like:

Same? Unlikely. Probably murdered.

Just one door, or many?

Hard to replicate. Fluke? Maybe my memories aren't real?

I want to go back!

Nothing in common.

How many come home? V. few. Maybe none?

Night? Three sisters? Scotland?

Liminality! NYE. Dusk, dawn, etc. Time when veil is thin.

If my memories are true—what does that make me?

Broken doors!

Go back to Scotland? (What if I can't get back?)

<u>WHAT DID I DO?</u>

The writing was bubbly and cute, the *i*'s dotted with pink hearts. Grey had written this when she was a kid, maybe only twelve or thirteen, before she'd switched to the acid-green pens and thin script she'd favoured in high school. *WHAT DID I DO?* was the last annotation. It was in the margin of a Wiki printout about the disappearance of Mary Byrne, a British teenager who'd gone missing from Bromley-by-Bow on New Year's Eve in 1955. Folded into the pages were a handful of Polaroid pictures Grey had taken when we went to Bromley-by-Bow to stay with my mother's cousin the week after our father died. We'd stayed near the station, across the water from where Mary Byrne had last been seen decades ago.

What I remembered from that week: The four of us slept on an air mattress, our bodies stuck together in the heat, a fen of salt and sweat and grief; I fell over in the long summer grass of Mile End Park and skinned my knees on hidden rocks; I wore pink shorts and applied chocolate-flavored lip gloss at an alarming rate; my mother cried every night; I stroked her hair until she fell asleep; Grey slept rigid against the wall, her back to the rest of us; I missed my father.

Grey had been obsessed with Mary Byrne, another inexplicableNew Year's Eve disappearance, and had spent much of her time in Bromley-by-Bow wandering the streets from dawn to dusk. Vivi and I had been too young to go with her, and Cate and the other adults were too distracted with funeral planning to notice or care much what Grey did. It was a rare opportunity, this relaxing of Cate's constant surveillance, and thirteen-year-old Grey took full advantage of this taste of freedom, slipping into the streets of East London by herself every day and returning every night, frustrated.

Then, on our last night there, the night before our father's funeral, Grey had come back giddy with excitement and grinning from ear to ear. It was the happiest I'd seen her in a long time. She smelled of something wild and green.

The photos in the journal were all dated from that day, the day before we buried our father. The first four were of areas around Bromley-by-Bow: the Greenway, a footpath and bike freeway that stretched for miles through London, bordered in Grey's picture by tall white apartment blocks set against a darkening sky; the boxed-in metal footbridge that stretched over West Ham Station, the last place Mary Byrne had been seen; an exterior and interior shot of the House Mill, a huge old tidal mill on Three Mills Island that had burned down and been rebuilt in the nineteenth century.

The final picture showed a ruined doorway: a freestanding stone wall with an archway at its center. It was inside, perhaps in the basement of the mill, persevered by the new buildings that had been constructed above it. White flowers grew rabid across its surface. It looked much the same as the doorway that had been embroidered on Grey's quilt.

A chill settled across my skin.

"Did she think she'd figured out the Mary Byrne mystery or something?" I said.

The rest of the journal was filled with nothing but sketches of ruined doors, their location and a date recorded beneath them. Doors in Paris, doors in Berlin, doors in Krakow. Doors in Anuradhapura, doors in Angkor Wat, doors in Israel. Had Grey been to all of these places?

The barista leaned over the counter then. "You guys . . . uh . . . you guys okay?" she asked.

"We're fine, thank you," I said. "Sorry, we'll order something in a second."

"No, I meant . . . um . . . you're bleeding on the floor just a tad."

"Oh. Yeah. We, uh . . . fell off our bikes. Do you have a first aid kit?"

The barista brought us the supplies and a free cappuccino each to boot. Vivi and I sat together at the back of the now-empty café, drinking coffee, the green-and-white box splayed open on the table between us.

Vivi sat with her hands resting on her knees, palms up, as I swabbed her cuts with iodine.

"Grey's dead, isn't she?" she said flatly. Her eyes were deep wells. She didn't even wince at what must have been stinging pain. "There's a crucial time frame of forty-eight hours, and after that, they're dead."

"Don't say that," I warned. "That isn't what happened to us."

"What do you remember about being gone?" Vivi asked.

"I don't remember anything."

"I know that's what we tell each other. I know that's what we tell the world. But I remember white petals drifting through the air like autumn leaves. And smoke. And dusk. And . . ."

A fireplace. A girl with a knife in her hand.

"Don't," I said. "You were nine. I was seven. We can't trust those memories. Let me see your arm."

"There was a girl."

"Stop it."

"I think she did something to us. I think she hurt us."

"Vivi."

"You asked, 'Who cuts little girls' throats?' Don't you want to know what happened to you?"

"No."

"Why not?"

"Because . . . I'm afraid."

"You shouldn't be afraid of the truth. It'll set you free, right?"

"Unless it's so terrible it screws you up entirely. No, thank you. Maybe I'm totally fine with my repressed memories. Now show me your arm."

Vivi shrugged out of her jacket and rolled up her bloody sweater, her skin prickled with goose bumps. I unwrapped the scarf we'd used to stanch the bleeding. The fabric was sodden with gelatinous blood and smelled heady and wrong.

I faltered when I saw the wound. "Hold still," I ordered as I swabbed it with an alcohol wipe to get a better look. "There's something here."

Vivi wasn't paying attention. "We are going to get her back, Iris," she said as she stared at the ceiling, still unconcerned by the pain. "I will not live in a world without her."

"I agree," I said, but it was my turn to be absentminded. There was something translucent curled up inside her flesh. I used the fine point of Grey's knife to lift it out. It wasn't hard to dislodge: a single, anemic flower. I gave it a gentle tug and plucked it from her wound, tiny root system and all. The same kind of flower that had taken over the dead man's body. The same kind of flower that had been growing from Grey's eyes in the photograph.

It had been budding inside Vivi, feeding off her blood, blooming in her scored-open flesh.

What the hell was going on?

I twirled the bloody flower in my fingers and felt suddenly, desperately sick. My throat swelled. I swallowed a sob. Grey was gone, and the weirdness I'd been trying so desperately to escape had found me again.

"At least I'll have a gnarly scar. Chicks dig scars, right? Does it look infected?" Vivi asked. I crushed the bloom between my fingers before she could see it. Acknowledging it made it real— and I was not ready for whatever was happening to be real.

"It's fine," I said as I dressed her arm with more iodine and wrapped it in gauze, hoping that would be enough to prevent any more gardens from sprouting out of her. "I think it's time to call the police."

10

TWO DAYS LATER

ANOTHER FLASH WENT off, leaving a new cluster of sticky white spots in my vision. I looked down at my dress and tried to blink them away. A thread was coming loose at the hem. I picked at it, watching the stitching come undone as I pulled. It was a House of Hollow piece taken from Grey's wardrobe. We'd all dressed in House of Hollow clothing to show solidarity. A blazer for Vivi. An emerald-green velvet dress for me. A brooch for our mother, despite her protests. A dash of Grey's gag-worthy perfume at our wrists and throats, so we all stank of smoke and the dangerous part of the woods.

The dress was high-necked and rubbed against the scar at my throat, making it raw and itchy. I pulled the seam away from the scar, but it still felt like sandpaper working away at my skin.

The lead detective was standing, giving his opening remarks. "Miss Hollow does not have her cell phone with her," he said. "We have not been able to track her through any social media. We are concerned for her safety. We are asking the public to be on the lookout for her, and for anyone who has any information regarding her whereabouts to come forward."

The journalists were immediately feverish. "Do you think this disappearance is in any way linked to her disappearance as a child?" one of them asked.

"We don't know," the detective said. "We're liaising with Scottish authorities to determine if there are similarities, though at this stage there doesn't appear to be any correlation."

"Where was her last confirmed location? Who was the last person she spoke to?"

"We can't release that information yet. I'll answer more questions in a moment. At this time, Miss Hollow's family would like to make a brief statement."

In another universe, I was in my Friday English class discussing *Frankenstein* with Mrs. Thistle. Instead, Vivi, Cate, and I were together at the front of an event room inside the Lanesborough. A crystal chandelier glinted overhead. The walls were richly paneled and gilt frame portraits lined the space; only the leopard print carpets felt modern.

My mother sat to one side of me, woody and brittle. Vivi sat to the other, slouched back with her arms folded. She stank, the oily smell of stale booze and sweat and cigarette smoke. Cate hadn't been able to force her into a shower, so she'd sprayed her with extra perfume to mask two days of hard drinking. It didn't help.

It was Grey's agent who'd made the call to the police two days ago. We'd waited for them in her office, a chic, modern space adorned with framed pictures of our sister. They'd taken hours to arrive. There was no emergency, after all. No crime scene anymore, no body. Just a burned-down apartment and a missing girl—and girls went missing every day.

The police had arrived around sunset to take our statement. We had left out the details we couldn't explain—the flowers growing on the dead man, the bull skull the man wore over his face—and told them only the bare-bones facts. Grey had left a note saying she was in danger. There had been a corpse in her apartment. A man had broken in and set the place on fire. He had shot Vivi.

The cops had been thorough yet workaday in their questioning. They had exchanged disbelieving, exasperated glances approximately every thirty seconds. I got it. Even with the craziest bits left out, it was a wild, implausible story from a wild, implausible family.

When the police left, Vivi called our mother, and the agent called Grey's publicist. An hour later, the world knew that Grey Hollow—beautiful, strange Grey Hollow—was missing. *Again.* If Grey had been a famous supermodel a week ago, she was now something ten times more intoxicating: an unsolved mystery.

It was official. It had begun.

Which brought us to the press conference. The event had been planned for the dingy conference room of a local police station, but Grey's publicist changed it to the Lanesborough.

We'd been instructed to look sad, demure, and helpless, which wasn't hard. We *were* helpless. Grey had counted on us coming to look for her, and we had. Grey had squirreled away secrets that only we would find, and we had. Grey had left bread crumbs and bet on us saving her—and we had failed.

We'd missed something, some vital clue, and now Grey was really gone, and the only two people who might have a hope of finding her had screwed it up completely.

Something twisted in my heart at the thought of Grey alone somewhere, afraid, waiting for Vivi and me to rescue her. Waiting, and hoping, certain that we'd come—and eventually realizing that we wouldn't.

I love you, I thought, gulping back a sob. *Please know I love you. Please know I tried.*

The journalists drank my moment of grief in hungrily. The flash of photographers left me headachy, disoriented. Cate stood and muttered her way through a plea for Grey to come home, her words never quite sounding convincing. Lips pursed, affect flat. I'd seen the footage of the press conference our parents gave the first time we went missing, in which our mother had verged on mania. Then her cheeks had been slick with tears, her eyes wide and red and wild, a wet tissue dabbed to her nose every ten seconds as she begged, begged, *begged* for us to be returned.

This was nothing like that.

It had been the hardest month of my parents' lives. It had twisted and cracked them, both individually and as a couple.

They blamed each other. They blamed themselves. It had been Gabe who'd pushed to go to Scotland to visit his parents over Christmas and New Year's. It had been Cate who'd wanted to take us walking through the streets of Old Town at midnight so we could see the fireworks and the revelry. It had been Gabe who'd decided the route. It had been both of them who'd taken their eyes off us to share a midnight kiss.

His fault.

Her fault.

Their fault.

Our fault.

Hadn't they taught us not to speak to strangers? Hadn't they taught us not to wander off? Hadn't they been hard enough? Soft enough? Enough, enough, enough?

In the days that followed, our grandparents' home was searched for blood, signs of a struggle. Cadaver dogs slunk through the halls and bedrooms, hunting for death. The gardens in the backyard were dug up, destroyed. Their car was seized as possible evidence. Dozens of witnesses were interviewed to try and piece together a picture of what had happened earlier in the day. Nearby bodies of water were dredged for our bodies. My parents took lie-detector tests. They were fingerprinted. They were photographed. They were followed, by police and journalists alike. The press took pictures of them at their worst moments. If they cried too hard, people accused them of faking it. If they tried to keep it together, people accused them of being cold.

God help them if they smiled.

No one believed their story—and why would they? It was impossible. Who could snatch three children without being seen, being heard? Who could do that in a matter of seconds? They couldn't leave Edinburgh without an answer either way. They couldn't work. They couldn't stay at my grandparents' house now that it was the scene of a suspected crime. They spent all their savings on hotels and rental cars and billboards with our faces on them. They barely ate. They barely slept. They knocked on every door in the Old Town. They drifted through the streets desiccated by despair, oily and fetid and thin. They oscillated between comforting each other and hating each other for what had happened.

Their souls—and their marriage—came apart at the seams.

They were perhaps only a couple of days away from being arrested for our murders when they made their pact.

"If they're dead," Cate said to my father, "do we kill ourselves?"

"Yes," Gabe replied. "If they're dead, we do."

A woman found us on the street that night, naked and shaken but unharmed. The papers that had hounded my parents apologized for libeling them and paid big out-of-court settlements for damages—enough to enroll us all in a fancy private school.

Gabe and Cate had never recovered. They had been wounded too deeply, and wounded each other too deeply in turn. The *worse* in *for better or for worse* had been so much heavier than either of them could have imagined.

Now my mother was reliving that same tragedy. I squeezed her hand; she squeezed mine back.

Then our part in the press conference was over. It had been decided that Vivi and I wouldn't speak, that we would take the focus off Grey, so as we all got up to leave the room, the whole press galley was shouting, asking the questions they'd been dying to ask from the moment they saw us.

"Iris, Vivi, is there anything you want to say about what happened to you as children?"

"Will you be assisting in the investigation?"

"What really happened to you in Scotland?"

"Do you think Grey has been taken by the same people who took you the first time?"

"Cate! Cate! What do you say to the people who still think you're guilty of kidnapping your own children ten years ago?"

I kept my head down, eyes on the floor, my gut filled with oil. Police waved us into the next room, a quiet haven away from the vultures. After the doors had closed behind us, my family broke apart without another word. Vivi made a beeline for the hotel bar. I went home with Cate, back to our big, empty house. My mother shut herself up in her dark room, and I was left alone, still wearing my missing sister's clothes.

My phone pinged in my pocket. It had been going off pretty much nonstop since the first press release, with messages from teachers and the parents of girls I tutored and fellow students who'd never actually spoken to me face-to-face but who'd gotten my number off a friend of a friend so they could pass along their thoughts and prayers.

This new message was from an unknown number:

OMG babe, so horrible about Grey! Hope they find her soon!

P.S. Did you manage to pass my modeling portfolio to her agent? I linked it to you on Instagram, remember? I haven't heard anything back yet. They're probably busy with all this missing-persons stuff, but just thought I'd check!

I couldn't stand to have the velvet itching against my skin anymore, cutting a hot path against my scar. I slipped out of it in the hall, then balled it up in my shaking hands and screamed into the fabric. I wanted to destroy something beautiful, so I took the dress and ripped. As I did, a curl of paper, delicate as filament, fluttered from some hidden place inside a seam. I sank to the floor, my back against the wall, and unfurled it. The note was handwritten in Grey's signature green ink.

I'm a girl made of bread crumbs, lost alone in the woods. —GH

Yeah, Grey, I thought to myself. *No shit.*

☽

What do you do when someone you love is missing? When all the looking you can do is done, what do you do in the long hours that linger ahead of you, heavy with absence and worry? Vivi's answer was to get as drunk as possible for as long as possible, to disappear inside herself. My answer was to wander the floors of our house, dusting off memories of Grey in each room, Sasha trailing at my heels as though she could sense my grief and anxiety.

Here, in the cupboard under the stairs, was where Grey had layered the space with blankets and cushions and fairy lights, and read the Chronicles of Narnia to us every night for a year. Where I had pressed the pads of my fingertips into the plasticky bulbs of the lights as she read, and marveled at how the brightness shone through me, made fluorescent red by my blood, revealing capillaries and veins and all sorts of secrets beneath my skin.

Here, in the kitchen, was where she had cooked breakfast every Sunday morning, dancing around to the Smiths or the Pixies as she slammed through cupboards and left chalky storms of flour on the floor.

Here, in my bedroom, was where she had curled up next to

me when I was ill and told me fairy stories about three brave sisters and the monsters they met in the dark.

Here, in her now-empty room, was where she had tacked the "Telltale Hand" palmistry guide poster above her bed and laden her shelves with salves and smudge sticks.

I sat on her bed for a long time, trying to remember what the room had looked like before she left. There had always been clothes scattered on the floor, and the bed was forever unmade. Tendrils of a wisteria vine had crept through her window and always seemed busy overtaking one corner of the room. A pink Himalayan salt lamp had sweated moisture onto her bedside table, curling the pages of her copy of *A Practical Guide to the Runes*, Grey's favourite bedtime read. The dresser had been scattered with pouches of herbs, strings of crystals, and highlighted books on ancient Roman curse tablets.

All of it was gone now, and the girl was gone with them.

My mother was crying. It was not a new sound. It had been the backing track for much of my life. The house moaning in the wind and beneath it, my mother crying. I padded barefoot down the hall to her room, careful to avoid the creaky floorboard that would betray my presence. The door was open a crack; a slice of light jutted out. It was a tableau I recognized: Cate kneeling by her bed, the photograph of me and my sisters and my father in her hand. Her face was buried in her pillow as she sobbed, sobbed so hard I worried she would inhale fabric and feathers and choke.

In the afternoon, I sagged into my bed with my laptop and cycled between Twitter and Reddit and every news story I could find about Grey's disappearance. It had exploded on social media. I followed hashtags and read deep into threads until my head ached with fullness, until my anxiety was a physical weight resting heavy inside my skull, until my body felt gouged out and desiccated. I picked my fingernails until they bled. I couldn't breathe properly but I couldn't stop reading and watching people's reactions. Was it a publicity stunt or a hoax or a cry for attention or a misunderstanding or a murder or a suicide or a government conspiracy or aliens or a pact with the devil? I scrolled and clicked and consumed and filled myself and drained myself until I saw my mother pass my bedroom door around sunset, her scrubs on, her dark hair pulled back in her usual work bun.

I went to the hall and caught her at the bottom of the stairs. "You're *kidding* me."

"The world has to keep turning," she said as she grabbed her car keys and made for the front door. The skin beneath her eyes was distended, her lips bee-stung.

"Why don't you love her anymore?" I demanded, following her. "I mean, what could a seventeen-year-old girl have said to you that was so cruel it made you hate her?"

My mother stopped halfway out the door. I expected her to protest. I expected her to say *I don't hate Grey. I could never hate my own child.* Instead, she said, "It would break my heart to tell you."

I took a few deep breaths and tried to unravel what that meant. "Would you even care if she was dead?"

My mother swallowed. "No."

I shook my head, horrified.

Cate came back to me then, pulled me into a hug, even as I feigned pushing her away. She was shaking, a frenetic energy humming though her. "I'm sorry," she said to me. "I'm sorry. I know she's your sister. I shouldn't have said that." I never felt more alien to Cate than when we were standing right next to

115

each other, the height difference between us extreme. My small, sweet, blue-eyed mother, and then me, towering and angular. We were different species. "Don't go anywhere tonight, okay? Please. Stay here. Stay inside. You know I can't bear to lose you. I'm sorry . . . but I still have to go to work."

And so she did. She left. I sunk onto the stairs, staring after her, a great twist of acid turning inside me. My scar was still itching from the velvet dress, so I dug my fingernails into it. There was a little hard nodule of scar tissue on one end now, inflamed by the rubbing fabric. I scratched it until it bled. The house felt too quiet, too filled with shadow and too many places for an intruder to hide. What if the masked man was already inside? What if he came during the night, while I was here on my own?

I checked Vivi's location on my phone—she was still at the Lanesborough, still probably drinking at the bar. I hadn't spoken to her all day. Vivi was volatile like that. She could be your best friend one moment, your coconspirator in all manner of mischief, then completely withdraw the next.

Another grim thought: Grey was the grounding force in our sisterhood, the sun we both orbited around. What would Vivi and I be without her? Would we drift apart in the cavernous space Grey left behind, rogue planets spun out into the abyss?

Would I lose both of my sisters at once?

When the doorbell rang, I thought it was Cate again, back to explain herself. I took my time getting to the door, opened it slowly.

"I need a drink," Tyler Yang said as he pushed inside, walking straight past me without an invitation.

"Sure, come in, strange man I've only met once before," I said after him, but Tyler had already found his way up the hall and into the kitchen. I heard cupboards banging, pots crashing. I closed the door and followed him inside.

"It's above the fridge," I said, my arms crossed as I watched him. He was more disheveled today, his black hair falling over his forehead, his skinny jeans ripped at the knees, but it worked. Even against the bland background of a suburban London kitchen, there was a swaggering, pirate-like energy to Tyler Yang, intensified by his smudged eyeliner, billowy floral shirt and leopard print House of Hollow trench coat that covered his tattooed arms. He was tall, lean. Inconveniently handsome.

He found the booze stash, picked the gin, and then took a long swig right from the bottle.

"Charming," I said.

"Your sister is *Gone Girl*–ing me, I bloody know it," Tyler said as he paced the kitchen, gin bottle still in hand.

"What are you talking about?"

"She's faking it! I'm gonna go down for this and that's exactly what she wants." He took another long swig, then stopped, eyes darting from side to side in mad thought. "Does England have the death penalty?"

"Wait, you think Grey is faking her disappearance to . . . punish *you*?"

"Would you put it past her?"

I thought of how Justine Khan had shaved her head in front of the whole school. I thought of the male teacher Grey didn't like, the one who kissed her in front of her class and got fired for it. I thought of how he'd insisted that he hadn't wanted to do it, that she had whispered in his ear and made him. Grey Hollow did have a slightly warped sense of crime and punishment, and a way of making bad things happen to people who crossed her.

Tyler was pacing again. "A lot of strange shit happens around that woman. An *unnatural* amount of strange shit!"

I sighed. I knew.

"The police went to my flat while I was out, you know," he continued. "Apparently, they have an arrest warrant." He sniveled. "It's trending on Twitter."

I checked; it was.

"They've got something on you?" I asked.

Another muffled sob. Another swig of gin. "Hell if I know."

"So you came . . . *here*? When the police are about to charge you with . . . what, my sister's *murder*?"

Tyler pointed the gin bottle at me, his fingers dripping with thin silver rings. "You know I didn't have anything to do with her disappearance. I can *see* it in your eyes. You *know* something, Little Hollow. *Tell me.*"

I shook my head. "We thought we knew something. We thought it might somehow be linked to what happened to us as kids, but . . . we've got nothing."

"Fuck!" Tyler ran his hand through his hair, sweeping it back out of his face, then sank onto the kitchen floor, his head bobbed forwards onto his chest and both arms limp at his sides. I went and crouched in front of him. Up close, I caught the stink of gin and weed and vomit, and wondered how drunk and high he already was when he got here.

"You knew her, Tyler," I said.

He shook his droopy head. "I don't know if anyone ever really *knew* her," he said, his words slurred.

"*Think.* Think *hard*. Is there anything you can tell me, anything at all, that might be a good place to start? A name, a location, a story she told you?" I waited for a full minute, then shook his shoulder, but he flopped a hand in my direction with a whimper and then slumped back against the cupboard, unconscious.

"Oh, for God's sake," I said as I stood up.

Tyler was too heavy for me to move, so I found a spare blanket and pillow in the linen cupboard and left him there, sprawled out on my kitchen floor.

☾

I woke on Saturday morning to the taste of blood and the smell of sweat and alcohol. There was a deep, jagged hunger inside me; I'd been chewing on my cheeks and tongue in my sleep. The blood was my own. It had dried on my lips, dripped onto the pillowcase. The smell of sweat and alcohol came from Vivi, still dressed in what she wore to the press conference yesterday, her makeup a cracking fresco on her skin. Her warm body was curled around me, one of her legs draped over my hip bones.

It had been a strange, sleepless night. The hours had clumped together and then fallen away in great chunks. I had only managed to close my eyes as sunrise blanched the winter sky. In the end, I had been grateful for Tyler Yang's uninvited presence. Checking on him throughout the night to make sure he hadn't choked on his own vomit gave me something to do that wasn't worrying about Grey. The news of Tyler's arrest warrant had spread fast and far on the internet, and I fell from one rabbit hole to the next reading about him, about his relationship with my sister and his career and his past. Which inevitably brought me to the tragic story of Rosie Yang.

I had been sitting on the kitchen floor next to Tyler when I came across the headline.

DROWNING HORROR:
WITNESSES TELL OF HAUNTING SCENES AS GIRL, 7,
DIES ON FAMILY TRIP TO BEACH

I picked my fingernails while I read. It had happened years ago, when Tyler was five, at a busy seaside town in midsummer. There had been a heat wave. The beach had been packed with thousands of people escaping the sticky heat. Tyler and his older sister had wandered off from their parents and been found floating facedown in the surf not long after. Tyler was revived on the scene. Rosie could not be resuscitated and was pronounced dead at the hospital.

The article included a picture of her from her birthday party the week before. A little girl in a yellow sundress with the same black hair as Tyler's, the same impish grin, the same dimples.

I had put my palm against Tyler's chest as he slept and felt the steady rise and fall of his rib cage, the strong beat of his heart, and imagined the scene on the beach that day. The hands of a lifesaver against his chest, the compressions so deep they splintered his thin ribs. The bare, wet skin of his back pushed into the hot sand as onlookers crowded around, pressing their fingers to their mouths and holding their own children back so they couldn't see. His parents hovering over him, hovering over his sister, barely able to breathe through the pain and the hope and the wanting. One child sputtering water from his lungs, a sudden intake of breath. The other limp, blue, cold.

Tyler Yang was confident and cocky and cavalier. Tyler Yang did not seem like a man with a tragic past. Yet the worst thing that I could imagine happening, the thing that was maybe happening to me right now—losing a sister—had happened to him already. He was a grim testament to a truth I knew but refused to acknowledge: that it was possible to suffer devastating, incomprehensible loss and continue to live, to breathe, to pump blood around your body and supply oxygen to your brain.

I sat in the kitchen for most of the night after that, checking Tyler's breathing, Grey's knife in my hand in case the horned man came back, until finally, at dawn, I crawled into my bed and collapsed.

I rested my cheek on Vivi's tattooed chest and listened to the beat of her heart, one arm across her stomach. My heart beat in time with hers. The three of us, with the exact same rhythm in our chests. When one was scared, the hearts of the others knocked. If you cut us open and peeled back the skin, I was sure you'd find something strange: one organ shared, somehow, between three girls.

We were puzzle pieces, the three of us. I'd forgotten how good it felt to wake up next to her, curled into her, a whole with three parts. Grey's absence felt raw and aching this morning. I wanted her more desperately than I ever had before. I wanted to find her and collapse into her and let her stroke my hair the way she had when I was little, until I fell asleep cocooned in her arms.

My sister. My refuge.

A tear slipped from the corner of my eye and hit Vivi's warm skin.

She stirred when I started to sob. "Hey," she said groggily, releasing a plume of sour breath. "What's wrong?"

I nuzzled further into her. "I thought I'd lost you too. I thought you might not come home."

"I'm not going anywhere." Vivi shook her head against me. "I . . . I shouldn't have left you here, Iris. After Grey ran away. I should have stayed here and watched out for you, helped you carry the load. I'm not leaving you again."

Tyler burst into the room then, floral shirt crumpled, eyes wide, hair wild atop his head. "YULIA VASYLYK!" he said, pointing at me. "YES!" Then, as quickly as he'd appeared, he was gone again.

Vivi sat up and stared at the empty doorway, as if trying to make sense of what she'd seen. "Am I still wasted or did I actually just see Tyler Yang in your bedroom?"

"I think he's hiding from the police," I said.

"That's . . . kind of genius. It's the last place they'd look."

Tyler appeared again and clapped for us to get up. "Little Hollows. That was a eureka moment. You must *come*."

"I am way too hungover to deal with this," Vivi said as we disentangled ourselves and went downstairs. We found Tyler in the kitchen, his bedding from the night before neatly folded on the bench. He was pacing again. I saw him differently now, this man who carried such tragedy in his heart. Sasha watched him from atop the refrigerator, her tail flicking furiously to show her distaste for this intrusion into her space.

"Yulia Vasylyk," he said. "That's where we start."

"Are you speaking English?" Vivi asked as she sat at the breakfast bar and put her cheek on the kitchen counter, eyes closed.

"It's a name," Tyler said. "A woman. Someone Grey has mentioned before."

I was so hungry, my stomach felt like a black hole expanding up into my rib cage. I pulled out my phone, typed *Yulia Vasylyk* into Google, and hit return.

The disappearance of Yulia Vasylyk three and a half years ago had not been big news. There were only a handful of short articles, and two of them had referred to her as *Julia*.

"I don't get the link," I said. "Another missing woman?"

"Type *Yulia Vasylyk Grey Hollow*," Tyler said.

I was skeptical but did what he said. Google returned only one exact match. I read it out loud.

UKRAINIAN WOMAN FOUND
A WEEK AFTER BEING REPORTED MISSING

Nineteen-year-old Yulia Vasylyk, an aspiring fashion model from Ukraine, has been located one week after her boyfriend reported her missing. Vasylyk was found wandering near her Hackney apartment late Monday night, barefoot and confused. Police took her to a nearby hospital for evaluation. No further details were released.

In a strange twist of fate, Vasylyk shares her small, one-bedroom Hackney apartment with three other girls, among them . . .

I stopped reading and looked up at Tyler.

"Keep going," he urged.

I took a breath and continued.

. . . among them another famous missing-then-returned person: Grey Hollow. Hollow, now eighteen, was abducted from a street in Scotland when she was a child, but found safe one month later.

Neither Vasylyk nor Hollow could be reached for comment.

"Holy shit," Vivi said, lifting her head from the kitchen bench. "It happened again."

Tyler was grinning. "Bingo, baby," he said, snapping his fingers. "Someone else came back."

11

Yulia Vasylyk was easy to track down online. With a hundred thousand Instagram followers, the once aspiring catwalk model had become a makeup artist and hairstylist of some renown. Tyler had even worked with her several times before he started dating Grey. When Yulia found out they were together, she refused to style him anymore, which is when Grey had told Tyler their odd backstory.

Tyler spent the morning calling contacts in the industry to find out where Yulia might be, without much luck: News of his impending arrest had spread quickly, and people were wary of handing over the whereabouts of another young woman, lest he was a budding serial killer hell-bent on murdering her too.

Cate messaged me around the time her shift usually ended to say she was staying late to cover for an ill colleague and did I maybe want to start thinking about going back to school after the weekend?

Routine helps, she wrote. **Normalcy helps. I know you think I'm cold, but I've done this before, remember?**

I didn't message back.

Eventually, after Vivi and I had showered and changed and fed Sasha and eaten three breakfasts apiece, Tyler started pumping his fist in the air while he was on the phone.

"Yulia's on a shoot at a warehouse in Spitalfields," he said when he hung up. "Am I good or am I good?"

"Gee, Sherlock, it only took you two hours," Vivi said, her voice still gravelly with hangover.

Tyler borrowed a big pair of sunglasses for the Uber ride to Spitalfields, though his "disguise" was so clearly an attempt to not look conspicuous that the driver spent most of the journey glancing at him in the rearview mirror. I held Vivi's hand. My right leg jiggled up and down, animated by a new sense of hope. It wasn't much, but it was something. A lead. It wasn't over yet.

We found the shoot in a warehouse, right where Tyler's contact had said it would be. It was an haute couture photo shoot with models wandering around in transparent raincoat ball gowns and jumpsuits made from netted rope, their faces glazed with bloodred eye shadow and neon-pink freckles. The three of us wandered in, our presence unquestioned because we looked like we belonged there.

"Why aren't you in hair and makeup yet?" a woman with a clipboard snapped before looking at us closer and realizing, suddenly, who we looked like, who we were. "Oh," she said. "Oh." Then she hurried away into the next room and left us be.

We found Yulia at the back of the warehouse, painting the face of a man with blue permed hair. Yulia wore no makeup herself. Her dark hair was in a braid, and the clothes she wore beneath her tool belt were functional, sensible: She looked almost out of place in such extravagant surrounds.

"I don't know where she is," Yulia said when she looked up

and saw us. "I haven't talked to her since before I met you," she said to Tyler. Then she turned and went back to her work.

"We're not looking for Grey," I said.

"We're looking for you," Tyler said.

"We know you lived with her," Vivi said.

Yulia looked up at us again. "My parents owned the apartment. They let me live there when I was going to castings, but I needed roommates to help cover the rent. Hence, your sister. I'm not interested in answering any more questions."

"Please," Vivi said as she stepped forwards and reached seductively for Yulia's face.

"Don't," Yulia said, smacking Vivi's hand away with a makeup brush. "Don't you dare do that vile thing to me."

"Ow, ow," Vivi said, her hands up in surrender. "All right. Sorry."

"You're just like your sister," Yulia snapped, stabbing the brush at us. "Manipulative. Now get out of my *workplace* before I call the cops." Her gaze slid again to Tyler. "I'm sure they'd be very interested to know that *you* were here."

"Hag," I heard Tyler say under his breath.

"Please," I said, trying to calm the situation. "*Please.* We promise we won't come near you. We won't touch you, we won't make you do anything you don't want to do. We just want to find our sister."

Yulia exhaled, then nodded and bent to whisper in the ear of the model. When he left, she picked up a pair of scissors and held them at her side. "Don't come any closer," she said. "I will defend myself."

"Is that *really* necessary?" Vivi asked, nodding to the scissors.

"I know your sister. If you're anything like her, then yes," Yulia said. "Ask your questions."

"You have absolutely no idea where she might be?" Tyler asked.

"Last I heard, you killed her. Next question."

We needed a different angle. "What was she like when you knew her?" I asked.

That caught her off guard. Yulia paused before answering. "Beautiful," she said finally. "That's the first thing anyone notices about her, obviously. Also secretive. Quiet. Weird."

"Weird how?" I asked.

"Most girls, when they get into modeling—they're swept up in the scene. It's the first time they've lived away from their parents. They drink, they party."

"You're telling me Grey Hollow *didn't* party?" Tyler said. "Unlikely."

"Not with us," Yulia said. "We would go to clubs and she would stay behind. When we came home, she'd be gone, sometimes for days at a time."

"Gone?" I asked.

"Yes," Yulia replied. "Gone, as in conspicuously absent."

"Where do you think she went?"

"Probably having sordid affairs, as is her custom," Tyler said. Vivi glared at him.

"At first I thought a lover," Yulia said. Tyler threw his hands up. "Then maybe a drug problem."

Vivi scoffed. "Grey dabbled, but she would never have developed a habit."

"What would you know?" Yulia snapped. She grasped the

scissors harder. Her knuckles blanched white. There was an animal flash in her eyes, the look of something ready to fight for its life. What had Grey done to this woman? "Grey kept all sorts of secrets. No doubt she kept many from you. I didn't even know she had sisters until she was famous. She never talked about either of you. She was a nightmare to live with. She had a lot of weird hobbies, but the taxidermy was the weirdest. How many teenage girls do you know who like to skin mice and birds and snakes and make them into weird Frankenstein monsters? That was how she paid her rent, in the first few months, before the modeling money started rolling in. Apparently, her taxidermy was so good that weirdos off the internet would reach out to her for freelance work. Great for her, really shitty for my kitchen table. I never got the stains out."

"And then there was the week you took a little tumble off the face of the earth," Tyler said. "What happened, peach? Where did you go?"

Yulia took a breath. "I was like most people. As soon as I saw Grey, I . . . I loved her. I was obsessed with her. Like a pet following a master. I can't explain why, only that she was beautiful. I followed her around like a shadow. Then it happened. One day when Grey left to go wherever it was she went, I went after her. Trailed her. I wanted to know where she kept disappearing to. Grey came back. I didn't." She licked her lips. "My boyfriend at the time went to the police. Reported me missing and told them he thought Grey had done something to me, but they said girls like me went missing all the time. Nobody cared. Nobody even looked for me."

"So . . . where did you go?" I asked.

"That's the thing. I don't remember," Yulia said.

"Oh, Christ!" Tyler said. "You're all bleeding useless!"

"You were *nineteen*," Vivi said. "You must remember something."

"I know what happened to me. I followed your sister somewhere I wasn't supposed to go, and I paid the price. When I came back, I wasn't . . . right. It ruined me. Now all I dream about is dead people. When I wake up, I can still hear them whispering to me." Yulia glanced at her shaking hands, then looked past us, over our shoulders. The male model with the blue hair had gone to fetch the woman with the clipboard. They were both staring at us. The woman held a phone to her ear and was having a low, urgent conversation. "I have worked very hard to recover from meeting your sister. Now, you should probably go if you want to get out of here before the police arrive."

I looked at Vivi. I could tell she wanted to keep pushing, to shove her fingers into Yulia Vasylyk's mouth and get her drunk enough on the taste of her skin that she'd answer any question we asked. I put my hand on her arm and shook my head once.

"One last question," I said before we left. "Where was the apartment you lived in together?" Grey had been practically MIA those first few months after she'd moved out. We'd never even been to that place, though we knew it was somewhere in Hackney.

"Near London Fields," Yulia said. "Grey won't be there, though, if that's what you're thinking. My parents own the place. No one lives there anymore."

"It's vacant?"

"No one will rent it, and my parents haven't been able to sell it ever since Grey moved out. Whenever prospective buyers or tenants walk through, they say they feel sick. There's something wrong with it. My parents checked for carbon monoxide leaks and black mold, but I think . . ."

"You think what?" Vivi asked.

"I think your sister cursed it somehow."

"Thank you," I said, and I meant it. "Thank you for helping us."

"Hey," Yulia called as we turned to go.

"Yeah?"

"They left something out of the news reports," she said. "When they found me in the street, I was naked except for the bloody runes written on my body. The blood was Grey's."

☾

Vivi, Tyler, and I caught an Uber and had it drop us close to the south end of London Fields, then walked through Broadway Market toward the park. It was packed, as it was every Saturday, with people buying sourdough bread and artisanal doughnuts and bunches of flowers and vintage Barbour waxed jackets. Along the way, we bought fresh coffee and half a dozen croissants, which barely made a dent in the well of hunger still crawling inside me.

"Like a pair of bears preparing for the winter," Tyler said as he watched us eat. He stuck to unsweetened black coffee.

"Why do you think we're hungry all the time?" I asked Vivi as I licked my fingers after my third croissant.

"We are blessed with fast metabolisms," she said.

"Inhumanly fast, some might say," I said.

"Bearlike, some might go so far as to suggest," Tyler said.

My stomach growled. "I need more food."

We stopped again for goat cheese and honey and two sour-dough baguettes, then continued to stuff our faces until, finally, after consuming approximately ten thousand calories before lunch, I was something close to satisfied.

"What do you make of what Yulia said?" I asked as we left the market and entered London Fields. It was my favourite park in the summertime, when the grass grew thick with red and yellow wildflowers and hundreds of Londoners flocked to the shade of trees to drink Aperol spritzes in the afternoon warmth. Now, in late winter, the midday sun felt diluted, far away. The trees were a scraggy mess of naked branches, and the cold was too caustic to allow anyone to linger for too long.

"That this whole situation is way above our pay grade," Vivi said between mouthfuls of bread. "The bloody runes, though. *That* is something else."

"Both of the men in Grey's apartment had runes on them, written in blood," I said. "That is not a coincidence."

"Just so we're all on the same page here," Tyler said, "this is definitely some Satanic cult thing, right? Like some freaky sex cult with blood and human sacrifices. That's where we're all landing at the moment, yeah?"

As soon as we reached the north end of London Fields, we caught Grey's trail. It came to me as a tingle in my finger-tips and a taste on my tongue, an inexplicable certainty that my sister had been here. The area was thick with her energy, though her presence here felt old and faded now. We walked on in silence until we saw a squat row of houses pressed close to the train tracks. Vivi pointed to one and said, "That one." I knew she was right. Grey's energy had nested there, tight

131

and twisted, and it lingered on even years after her departure.

"How could you *possibly* know that?" Tyler asked.

An ominous feeling crawled over me. "It doesn't feel right," I said.

"Yeah, no shit, because you have *no evidence* this is the right place," Tyler said.

"It *is* the right place. Grey was unhappy here," Vivi said. "What she left behind is . . . ugly."

"Ugh, the pair of you are as bad as your sister," Tyler said as he strode ahead of us toward the building. "It's always energy and demons and whatnot. Ridiculous!"

The Vasylyks had struggled to sell this flat. Cate had tried and failed to sell our family home after our father had died too. I thought it was probably because of the suicide, that people either found out about it or could feel the unsettling energy it left behind. But maybe . . . not. Maybe it was because of us. Maybe our strangeness had seeped into the walls and made the space feel haunted.

We buzzed the four flats in the building but all went unanswered. Eventually we slipped inside behind a man with a bag of groceries, then followed Grey's trail to the door on the first floor. Vivi rattled the handle—locked—but the wood was old and thin, the door beginning to curl at the edges like a wet book. She only had to throw her weight against it once for it to pop open with a dry crunch. Then there we were, inside another of Grey's apartments, with more questions than we'd ever have answers for.

There were a few pieces of furniture stacked in one corner of the living room, but apart from that, the space was empty. The carpet was creamy peach, pilled with age, the walls covered with sun-faded wallpaper. The kitchen was all wood, a fashion statement left over from the seventies. Kitchen, bathroom, living room, one bedroom. It was tiny, dark, grim. Grey had lived here with three other girls, all of them packed on top of each other like rats in a nest.

It didn't feel welcoming. It felt watchful and dangerous in a way I couldn't place. Shadows stretched long. A line of ants crawled up the wall in the bedroom, into a tiny pock hole of rot near the ceiling. I could feel why they'd had trouble selling or even renting it. It was haunted by our sister, by the sadness and worry she had left in the walls. She had not been Grey Hollow, supermodel, when she'd lived here; she had been a scared seventeen-year-old girl with no money and nowhere else to go.

"Well, this is grim," Tyler said as he opened a window that looked directly onto a neighboring brick wall.

We performed what had become our usual routine. We ran our fingers over the baseboard, looking for hidden compartments. We opened all the kitchen cupboards and pulled out all the drawers. We searched under the bathroom sink, inside the cistern, in the creepy crawl space beneath the bathtub. We unscrewed the curtain rods to look for rolled-up scraps of paper and held the curtains up to the light to search for hidden embroidery. We turned over the few pieces of furniture and looked for words scratched into the wood.

I caught flashes of her life here, those first few months of freedom away from the burden of high school and two younger sisters. I pictured her coming home from bars, a little tipsy, giddy and grinning because a cute boy had asked for her number. I pictured her in the kitchen in her pyjamas, cooking what she cooked for us every Sunday morning: waffles, scrambled eggs, freshly squeezed orange juice. I pictured the way the bedroom had looked when it had been partly hers, her bunk bed draped with all the trinkets and treasures she'd taken with her when she left home.

"There's nothing left of her here," Vivi said after blowing on all the windows to search for messages written in breath—and yet there was. There was the unsettling energy. Something malevolent, below the surface. I kept coming back to one wall in the bedroom, the wall Grey must have slept against, because I could feel her most strongly here. I trailed my hands over it. There was nothing outwardly strange about it. No bumps or lumps or hidden compartments. Nothing anomalous at all except the line of ants.

"You feel it too," Vivi said as she came to stand next to me. We both stared at the wall. A tangled web of wrongness hummed beneath.

"The wallpaper here is slightly different," I said. It had been bugging me since we arrived, but I'd only just put my finger on it.

"Is it?" Vivi said. She looked from one wall to the next and back again several times. "You're right."

"It's newer." I ran my hand over it again. Yes, it was smoother and less faded than the wallpaper in the rest of the apartment. "They papered over this wall, but only this one."

Tyler was pacing behind us. "You two are supposed to be exonerating me, not critiquing hideous decor choices."

"Well, we already busted down the front door," Vivi said. "What's a peeled wall after that?"

Vivi brought in a chair from the pile of furniture in the living room. I climbed up on it and started in the top right-hand corner where the ants were, fiddling with the paper until an edge came loose enough for me to pull. It was cheap, hastily applied. It came away from the wall in thick sheets, leaving tacky marks on the paint beneath.

"Ugh," Tyler said, gagging as I let a sheet fall to the floor. "The wall is rotting."

"It's not rot," Vivi said. We both leaned in to get a closer look. "It's something else."

Vivi placed her palm against the wall. It was spongy beneath her touch, steeped with moisture. With a little more pressure, her hand sank right through the sodden plaster. The smell exploded out of the dark, a foul, green stench.

"Oh, something's dead," Tyler said, dry heaving.

Vivi pulled away a chunk of wall, and then some more, big clops of it falling to the floor like mud. The plaster was gelatinous, barely even solid anymore. "No. Something's alive," she said as she held a piece of the wall up to me. It reeked—but one side of it was covered in little white flowers.

The same flowers that had been growing in Vivi. The same flowers Grey stitched in lace to her gowns.

"Carrion flowers," Vivi said as she picked a bloom and twirled it in her fingertips. "The punkest thing I learned in high school science. They smell like rotting flesh to attract flies and bugs."

We pulled more of the wall down, excavating a hole big enough to look through. There was about a foot of soft marrow behind it, and every inch of it was carpeted with corpse blooms and the things that liked to live in them: ants, beetles, creepy-crawlies.

"I've seen these flowers before," Vivi said as she leaned her head into the wall, her phone flashlight revealing more of the wet space. "Growing on the dead dude who fell out of the ceiling."

"They're the same flowers they found in our hair when we came back," I said. "The police tried to identify them but they couldn't. I saw it in a file. They're hybrids, pyrophytes."

"Pyro-whats?" Tyler asked.

"Plants that have adapted to tolerate fire. Some of them even need fire to flourish." I thought of the charred shell of the house in Edinburgh, the blaze so hot it left only the frame of the front door standing. The gunpowder heat of the bullet that grazed Vivi's arm. The flames that engulfed Grey's apartment. Heat and flame. Blood and fire. Was there a link?

Vivi pulled her head out of the wall and started rummaging in her backpack. "Here," she said as she held out Grey's journal, the one we'd found in her hidden apartment. We hadn't handed these things over to the police. They felt too sacred, too personal. "The last photo and all of the sketches."

I flicked to the middle of the journal, to the Polaroid photograph of a doorway in a ruined stone wall. It was covered in a carpet of white flowers.

Vivi pointed to the picture. "A door that used to lead somewhere," she said as she turned the pages of the book, revealing page after page after page of sketches, each one of a different doorway, "but now leads somewhere else."

The words felt like poetry, something I'd once known by heart but had long since forgotten. "How do I know that saying?" I asked. "What's it from?"

"In Grey's fairy tale, that was how you got to the . . . in-between place. The Halfway. Limbo. The land of the dead. What-

136

ever. You walked through a door that used to lead somewhere else. A broken door."

My memory reached for something. Yes, a story Grey had told us when we were younger. The place she spoke of was strange, broken. Time and space got snagged there, caught in snarls. "You don't actually think that . . . she's, what, somewhere . . . else?"

"What if the stories she told us when we were little were true?" I laughed and looked at Vivi, but she was serious. "It was a liminal world," she said, her face close to the photograph from Bromley-by-Bow, studying the ruin. "A kind of accidental gutter. Like . . . the gap at the back of the couch that crumbs and coins fall into." Vivi looked at me, her eyes hard as lead. "What if she's there? What if she found a way back?"

"Vivi. Come on."

"Yeah, I'm with . . ." Tyler glanced sideways at me. "The youngest Hollow . . . on this one."

"Oh my God." I narrowed my eyes at him. "You don't even know my name!"

"We were never formally introduced!"

"It's *Iris*. You *dick*."

"Pleasure to make your acquaintance. You *harpy*."

Vivi was ignoring us. "Do you remember what Grey used to say about missing people?" she said. "Some people go missing because they want to; some go missing because they're taken. And then there are the others—those who go missing because they fall through a gap somewhere and can't claw their way back."

"The Halfway was a *story*," I said.

"I know. That doesn't mean it can't be true." Vivi shoved the

137

journal back into her bag, then pulled out the brass key to Grey's burned flat. "Something happened to us when we were kids, Iris. Something no one has been able to explain. I'm starting to think we fell through."

"Fell through what?" I asked, but she was already striding away, towards the front door. "Vivi, fell through what?"

My sister turned and took me by the shoulders, a half-mad smile on her face. "A crack in the world."

12

THE SMELL OF burning still drifted in the air, clinging to the tightly huddled buildings of Shoreditch. There were two piles of blackened furniture and debris stacked high on the sidewalk, covered by blue tarps and warning signs. Only the windows on Grey's floor were boarded up, but there was blue-and-white POLICE LINE DO NOT CROSS tape across the front door. The whole building had been written off. That suited us just fine; it meant we had the place to ourselves.

We broke in through the same window we'd jumped from days before. We propped a charred but still-intact table against the wall and scrabbled up the rest of the way using some pipes as footholds. Vivi dislodged the board covering the window with a hard push. Then the three of us slipped inside like fish, Tyler protesting about the damage to his expensive clothes the whole time. The smell was stronger than I expected, the death stench overpowered now by the reek of burning chemicals, the taste of ash and poison.

It was pitch-dark with the windows boarded up. We used the

flashlights on our phones to navigate what was left of the place. The bedroom, where the fire had started, was a charred shell, the skin of the room eaten away to reveal its wooden bones, now black and warped and blistered. No part of the space was recognizable. The bed frame, mattress, chair, everything had burned in the extreme heat, been reduced to shards. Much of the wall and roof plaster had been torn away by firefighters looking for any hidden snarls of flame still burning in the dark. The floor was spangled with debris.

But that wasn't what we came here to see.

"Holy. *Shit*," Vivi said as she swept her light across the space.

Everywhere, growing on almost every surface, were the death flowers, bursting from the ashes.

"What the ever-loving fuck is going on?" Tyler whispered as I plucked a bloom from where it had taken root in a withered wall beam. They clustered most thickly around the warped frame of Grey's bedroom door, the door to the wardrobe, the door to the en suite.

"Fire destroys, but it also reveals," I said. "They like to grow on doors."

The fire had slammed down the hall and into the kitchen, consuming the walls and everything else as it went. The white herringbone parquet was smeared with soot and ash. All of Grey's treasures were gone. No more crystals, no more terrariums. No more feathers, no more incense. No more dried bouquets or sketches of monsters. No more journals or jewelry or taxidermied creatures.

I couldn't even feel her energy anymore. Grey had been erased from this place, scrubbed clean. The man who'd come here had not only taken her but destroyed proof of her existence as well.

The kitchen was in better shape than the bedroom, though not by much. The wall closest to the bedroom was disintegrated and most of the cabinets had burned quickly, their contents spewed across the floor, but the bookshelves on the far wall were heavy oak and had survived mostly intact. The books they'd once held were scattered on the ground now with the rest of the debris, their pages curled from fire and water.

We picked through what little remained of our sister's life. I felt the grief of losing the contents of her apartment almost as acutely as I felt the grief of losing Grey herself. This place had been a museum devoted to her, a vault filled to bursting with her secrets. Now she and all her secrets were gone. We might never know what had happened to her. If there was anything hidden in the walls, any clues stitched onto blankets or riddles engraved in wood, they were gone now too.

I picked up a charred hardcover copy of *The Lion, the Witch and the Wardrobe*. It was my favourite book as a kid. Grey would read it to me over and over again. I opened its pages. They were filled with annotations in her handwriting; lines highlighted, words circled, notes written in the margins. No doubt she'd written an essay about it when she was supposed to be studying something else. There was a photograph of the three of us as kids being used as a bookmark. I handed it to Tyler. He traced his fingertips over Grey's face.

And then—something. I swept my flashlight over the book-shelves again and noticed the spray of flowers twisting outward from them, across the floor, across the ceiling.

"Do you feel that?" I asked Vivi. Something had begun to tug at the edge of my heart. A sensation that felt familiar and yet alien at once. All of Grey's energy had been burned away from this place—except for a low thrum at the far end of the kitchen. It was a soft, punchy beat.

"What?" Vivi asked as I walked to the end of the room and put my palm against the wood. Yes, there it was again, a fizzle in my fingertips.

"Come here," I said.

Vivi came and put her hand next to mine, then snatched it back quickly. "It's her."

"What do you mean, 'It's her'?" Tyler said as he put his hand on the wood over and over again and felt nothing.

"It's weak but . . . fresh," I said. "Almost like she's right on the other side of the wall."

"Help me move the bookshelf," Vivi ordered Tyler.

They shuffled it forwards together until it toppled down with a crash, its damaged wood splintering into pieces on the floor. The wall behind the shelf had been mostly protected from the flames; its canker-green paint had only buckled close to the ceiling. And there, pressed tightly against the wall, was a hidden wooden doorframe growing thick with carrion flowers. It led to nowhere, but perhaps that didn't matter.

Perhaps all that mattered was that it used to lead somewhere else.

"Where is she?" Vivi whispered.

"In the gap at the back of the couch that crumbs and coins fall into," I said as I ran my hands over the old wood. "Halfway."

Grey had sent us here to find answers—but answers alone weren't enough for me. I wanted my sister back. "Grey, it's Iris," I said to the empty doorframe, to the green wall behind it. "If you can hear me, I want you to follow the sound of my voice.

We're close, but we need you to come to us. We can't find our way to you."

We stood in silence for a full minute, our breaths shallow and hearts racing as we waited. Even Tyler was quiet, watchful.

Finally, he shook his head. "You're both completely bonkers," he said, kicking the fallen bookshelf on his way back towards the hall. "It's been a long, shitty day. I need a nap. And then I need one last line of cocaine before I go to jail."

Vivi exhaled, and then she followed him. I waited a little while longer, my forehead pressed against the doorframe, before my throat grew dry with the taste of smoke and I knew I had to go. Maybe Tyler was right. Maybe we had gone a little nuts.

As I stepped into the hall, something moved in my peripheral vision. I yelped and scrambled back. Someone else was there. A figure had emerged from the warped doorway—from the wall—and was now leaning against it, gasping.

A girl, dressed in white, her fingertips dripping blood.

"Oh my God," I whispered. "Grey?"

My oldest sister looked up at me. Her eyes were black and her white hair hung in filthy clumps around her face.

"Run," she said. She tried to take a step towards me but sank heavily to her knees. "He's coming."

13

My head lolled forwards, searching for sleep, then snapped back at the last moment, the movement dragging a gasp from my lungs and a furious flutter from my eyelids. I shifted in my chair and tried to sit up straighter in the bleach cold of the hospital waiting room.

"Would you *stop* doing that?" Tyler said, his own face smushed into his palm, his elbow balanced precariously on the arm of his plastic chair. "You sound like someone is stabbing you every thirty seconds and it is *very* annoying."

"Sorry," I said, then began the slow slump back into almost unconsciousness. Loll, snap, gasp, flutter. Tyler groaned as I shook my head and sat up straight again. Vivi, who possessed the talent of being able to sleep anywhere, in any position, was fast asleep, her head back and mouth wide open. Cate flicked through a magazine and sipped a cup of tea, her teeth clenched tight.

I caught sight of my reflection in a vending machine. There were dark grooves beneath my eyes, a smudge of dried blood on my cheek. I licked my thumb and wiped the red away.

Outside, three floors below, I could hear the distant click of cameras, the murmur of the growing crowd who'd come to see the missing supermodel, who—for the second time in her life—had been spat back from the abyss. I stood and stretched, then went to the window and parted the blinds to glance out at the swelling mass of fans and well-wishers. They noticed me immediately and turned their phones and cameras my way. A restless field of stars blinking in the dusk.

It had been a confusing, scary afternoon. Getting Grey to the closest hospital had been . . . a challenge. We'd removed the police tape over her apartment door and carried her down the stairwell to the street below. Vivi tried to call an ambulance, but Grey—bleeding, gaunt, and barely able to stand—had pushed us off, thrown Vivi's phone into the road, and screamed at us to listen, *listen*. When we'd hailed a cab to get her to the hospital ourselves, Grey had gone wild. There was still a fizzy sting of pain where she'd scratched my cheek, my neck, my arms as I helped Vivi and Tyler hold her down in the back of the taxi. "We have to run, we have to run, we have to run," she'd chanted, kicking and bucking against us as we struggled to force her into A&E. We were all covered in scratches and bite marks and blood by the time doctors and nurses and security came rushing over to help restrain her.

The police had come, called by someone, and we'd each given short statements as nurses swabbed our wounds and gave us ice packs for our bruises. *Yes*, we'd really found her in her burned-out apartment. *No*, we didn't know how she'd gotten there, or how long she'd been there for.

Then we waited. Waited for news of what the hell had happened to her, waited to hear if she was okay. Waited, along with the rest of the world, to find out the answer to the mystery. Where had she been? For the first time, I understood why people were obsessed with us, why there were Reddit boards with hundreds of comments trying to unravel the answer.

I let the blinds slip closed and went back to the vending machine. I was halfway through my sixth packet of crisps when a doctor finally appeared, a young South Asian woman in glasses and a green checked shirt.

I stood quickly. "Is she okay?" I asked. "Can we see her?"

"Mrs. Hollow," the doctor said to my mother. "My name is Dr. Silva. Perhaps we could speak privately?"

"I don't think so, Doogie Howser," Vivi said. "We want to know what's going on."

Cate nodded. "It's fine."

Dr. Silva looked hesitant but spoke anyway. "Your daughter is stable," she said. I couldn't help but notice the way my mother's lips pursed on the word *daughter*. "We've sedated her to help her rest. Whatever happened to her, it's over now. She's safe."

Safe. Grey was safe. Somewhere, in a room tucked off a corridor around the corner, my sister's heart was beating.

The bones went out of my legs, like some tether inside me had been cut. I sank down into the chair behind me and looked at my hands, at the broken pinkie I shared with Grey. It had taken months to heal, a bruised, fat sausage where a finger had once been. Even now, when I ran my thumb over it, the joints beneath were bulbous, bent out of shape.

Grey was alive. Grey was back.

Relief flooded my body with such force that I gasped and laughed at the same time. With it came a surge of memories. The night my pet guinea pig died, Grey curled up in bed next

to me, teaching me to meditate. Her body next to my body, her lips against my ear, her fingertips trailing down my nose as she taught me to breathe in for seven, hold for seven, breathe out for seven. The day that Vivi bit my arm so hard she broke the skin, so Grey bit her back as punishment. The night Grey pulled me onto the dance floor at a school dance and led me in an exaggerated tango, spinning me so fast I could feel gravity trying to wrest us apart, but our hold on each other was so strong I knew no force in the universe could separate us.

"What happened to her?" I asked as I wiped mist from my eyes.

Dr. Silva glanced at my mother. "As best we can tell, it seems as though your sister is in the grips of a particularly severe psychotic episode. During psychosis, the mind finds it extremely difficult to separate what is real and what is not. Hallucinations and delusions are common. It could explain why she's been off the grid for a week."

Vivi bristled. "You immediately assume she's crazy?" she snapped. "We found her cowering and covered in blood. She could have been taken by someone, she could've—"

"Grey believes she was kidnapped and dragged through a door to another realm by a horned beast, where she was held captive," the young doctor continued gently. "She believes she managed to escape, but that this creature—again, for emphasis, a *fairy-tale creature*—is coming for her. She also believes you—her sisters—are in mortal danger. She told us this herself."

"I want to see her," Vivi said as she pushed past her, but the doctor stopped my sister with a hand on her shoulder.

"You don't. Not right now. We had to restrain her. You don't want to see her like that, I promise you. Your sister is ill. Her mind and body are exhausted. Now, there is a police officer posted at her door for her protection, more police downstairs to keep the press at bay. Even if someone did wish her harm, they wouldn't be able to get to her. Let her rest tonight. Talk to her tomorrow."

"Thank you," Cate said as she pulled Vivi back. "We'll let her sleep."

"Wait," I said. "Whose blood was she covered in?"

Dr. Silva turned back to look at me. "It was her own. There are cuts on her forearms, some so deep they needed stitching. Self-harm."

"You're both coming with me," Cate said as she shrugged on her coat. "I don't want you here tonight."

"What?" I said, unmoving as she pulled my hand. "Your daughter is in the hospital and you're going to *leave*?"

"Grey's here. She's safe. There's nothing you can do for her overnight."

"What if she wakes up all alone?" Vivi asked.

"She's heavily sedated and will be kept that way until morning. You're not going to miss anything by coming home." Cate looked so tired. Her frown lines cut grooves through her forehead and gathered to a pinch above her nose. She was still dressed in the scrubs she'd worn to her last shift. She clasped my hands in her own and pulled me close. "Please. Please come with me. Don't stay here."

I glanced down at her bare neck and ran the pad of my thumb over her collarbone. I remembered the delicate necklace of bruising left on her throat the week after Grey left. I remembered how our next-door neighbor had come by during this time with post that had been incorrectly delivered to his house and how, when Cate answered the door, he had let his eyes linger on the hickey-like thumbprint by my mother's collarbone for too long, the slash of a smirk on his face, like he could judge the type of woman she was from this one small thing.

"Steer clear of him," Cate had said when she closed the door, her skin flush with goose bumps.

It was the first time I had thought of my mother as a sexual creature. I was thirteen at the time and just coming to understand the power and treachery that came with breasts and hips and body hair. Men had begun catcalling me as I walked home from school in the afternoons—but that was my burden to bear. Seeing it done to my mother was something else.

It had made me angry, the look he'd given her. It had filled my stomach with blood and bile. The neighbor slipped in the bathtub that night, split his skull on the tap, and spent the next week liquefying. His was the body I'd smelled, before the dead man in Grey's apartment. I wondered, for a long time after he died, if my hatred of him had cursed him to death.

Part of me was horrified at the thought. Part of me hoped it was true.

"I'm not leaving her," I said. "I can't."

Cate shook her head and left without saying another word, too exhausted to fight.

"That is some *bullshit*, right?" Vivi said. "There is some weird crap going on, but Grey is *not* crazy. We saw those dudes in her apartment. We saw a dead guy fall out of her ceiling. We saw her *step through a doorway from somewhere else* and end up in her burned-out kitchen."

"Did we, though, Middle Hollow?" Tyler said. "I certainly

didn't. For all I know, she could have been curled up in a cupboard the whole time."

"Oh, for fuck's sake," Vivi said. "I'm going out for a pack of cigarettes."

"Do you think she's ever coming back?" Tyler asked as Vivi stalked off. "Or is she skipping town to go and start a new family somewhere else?"

"I didn't pin you for the daddy-issues type."

A quick grin slipped across his lips. "No one who has a good relationship with their parents ever becomes a model. Even if they're as ridiculously good-looking as me."

"Did Grey ever talk to you about our parents?"

"Oh, dribs and drabs. Enough for me to know that she was afraid of your father and that she didn't get along with your mother. *Shocker.*"

"It's not that they don't get along. It's that Cate hates her."

☾

"You are not to speak to her," my mother warned me the morning after she threw Grey out. "You are not to speak to her ever again." I hated Cate a little bit for that. It seemed wholly unfair. The day before, we had been a (relatively) normal and happy family, and then all it took was a drunken whisper from Grey to tear it all apart. Now one of my sisters was gone and the other— though I didn't know it yet—was already planning to go.

Vivi left in the middle of the night two weeks after Grey, without warning or fanfare. That was Vivi's way. Grey was dramatic. Grey liked people to know when she entered and exited the room. Vivi was the opposite. She left with nothing but a backpack and her bass guitar, and left nothing behind to mark her departure except a note on the end of my bed. *Sorry, kid,* it read, *but it's just not the same if it's not all three of us together.* She caught a midnight Megabus to Paris, then spent the next three years making her way east, through the jazz clubs of France and the grungy nightclubs of Berlin and the absintheries of Prague and finally to the ruin bars of Budapest, collecting tattoos and piercings and languages and lovers along the way. It was rarely an easy, carefree life. We never talked about it, but I knew from Grey that Vivi had done things to get by. Pickpocketing tourists. Selling drugs. Working the odd shift at a strip club. At eighteen, when she moved into a converted warehouse overlooking the Danube with seven other musicians and artists, she had already lived and hurt more than most people do in a lifetime.

The first six months after Grey and Vivi left were the worst of my life. They were both mostly MIA, busy transforming themselves into the women they wanted to become. I heard from them only occasionally. A message here, a phone call there. It was like a piece of me had been cut away, two-thirds of my soul suddenly sloughed off.

It was also during those months that something changed in my mother. It was then that she started collecting newspaper clippings and police files from our case, started hiring private detectives to follow leads the cops couldn't or wouldn't or hadn't. Before, it had been enough for her that we had come back. It didn't matter where we'd gone or what had happened to us, so long as we were safe and whole and home. Then suddenly, overnight, she developed this burning desire to *know*. To know *exactly*. I would wake sometimes to find her standing in the doorway of my bedroom, watching me with quizzical eyes as I slept, as though searching for the answer to a question she was too afraid to ask out loud.

Please, I messaged Grey around the six-month mark. **I need to see you.**

Grey came that very night like Romeo and threw little stones at my window until I opened it. It was past midnight. She beckoned me into the dark. I put a coat over my pyjamas and climbed down the tree that grew close to the house. It was the first and only time I have snuck out. We went to a pub in Golders Green and ate salt-and-vinegar crisps in a haze of other people's smoke. It was like meeting in secret with a lover, except I was thirteen and my clandestine liaison was with my estranged older sister.

In the six months since I'd seen her, Grey had cut her white hair into a long bob that skimmed her shoulders. She wore a black turtleneck and cat eyeliner. She looked like an assassin from a spy movie. We talked about what she'd been doing, where she'd been living, the boys she'd been dating. She showed me pictures of herself on her phone, beautiful images that would soon run in magazines and appear on billboards. She was on the precipice of intense and immediate international fame, though neither of us knew it yet.

"Come and live with me," she said at one point. "You don't have to stay there anymore. You don't owe her anything."

It was a tempting offer. I wanted to go—and I wanted to stay. I was split between the two halves of my heart. "She's my mother," I said finally. Grey frowned like she wanted to dispute that but couldn't. "I can't leave her all alone. I'm all she has left."

So I stayed, on the condition that I could see and talk to Grey whenever I wanted. Cate allowed it, begrudgingly.

The first and only time Grey reentered our house since leaving was to pack up her bedroom. We spent the next afternoon dumping all her bric-a-brac into boxes bound for storage until she had enough money for her own apartment. I wanted to linger over each piece of treasure, to slip lipsticks and candle stubs into my pockets to marvel at later, but she watched me with eagle eyes, and it all went where I had chosen not to follow.

"If Justine or her little Barbie sidekick give you any more trouble, let me know," Grey said as she carried the last box out the front door. "I'll take care of them."

Before she left, Grey went upstairs to speak to Cate. I followed behind her quietly and listened at the door, hoping to hear them reconcile, but that was not what I heard. "If you hurt her," Grey said to our mother softly, "if you so much as harm a single hair on her head, I will come back here and I will kill you."

If Cate answered, I didn't hear it. I went to the bathroom and vomited. I thought of Justine Khan and how I could never unleash my sister on her, no matter how mean she became, because Justine was just a girl and my sister was something more, something crueler, the thing in the dark. Grey left without saying goodbye. Somehow, whatever she had said to my mother the night she threw her out was even worse than the death threat.

Here is a terrible truth I had known for as long as I could remember: I was my mother's favourite child. I was orderly and docile and quiet, and those traits made it easy for her to like me, to understand me. My sisters were difficult girls: too sexy, too angry, too hard to handle. They wanted too much. They were too willing to put their bodies and lives in the way of the world. In the months and years after Grey and Vivi evaporated from our day-to-day, life was better. I learned to live without my sisters as my constant companions. I became myself. The strangeness that haunted them decreased to a low simmer when they weren't around.

Cate and I fell into an easy routine. We watched *Doctor Who* and drank herbal tea curled up on the couch. We donned Wellingtons and took long strolls in London's marshes, foraging for knotweed to make jam and elderflower and nettle to make summer cordial. We took flowers to my father's grave every other week. Without my sisters there to cause trouble, I settled into what was left of my little family with ease.

☾

Tyler rolled his eyes. "Ugh, your mother does not *hate* Grey, Iris. So dramatic."

I stared at the door through which she had left. "No, she does." I knew it profoundly. I had known it since the night Grey left home. I knew it on the nights I curled up next to Cate on the couch. I knew it in the mornings when we ate our homemade jam. As surely as many children know they are loved, I knew that Cate despised my sister. "She manages to mask it most of the time, but there's something . . . ugly underneath. I see it sometimes. Cate is afraid of her. I don't know why."

"You sound like you belong in the psych ward with your sister."

"And I thought you were going home."

"Yes, well. I look like utter garbage. I can't let the paparazzi shoot me in this state." A lie to mask the truth: He was worried about Grey too. "I always knew Grey was a bit . . . off. I liked it. It seemed, I don't know, dangerous in a sexy way. I never thought she was completely nuts, though."

"I don't think she is."

"Oh, please. You *heard* what the doctor said."

154

"I've also seen things over the past week that I can't explain. If it's all in Grey's head, why can Vivi and I see it too?"

"Folie à deux, Little Hollow. Or in this case, folie à trois." Tyler tapped my temple. "Sometimes madness is catching."

Vivi came back an hour later, once darkness had settled over the city, the knuckles of her right hand raw and bleeding from punching a photographer as he tried to manhandle her for a picture. The three of us went down to the hospital cafeteria together and ate prepackaged sandwiches and old oranges for dinner, then trudged back upstairs to wait and wait and wait. Vivi went to sleep again, her hand bandaged and iced by a nurse. Tyler stared dead-eyed at his phone screen, scrolling through tweets and Instagram posts about Grey's disappearance and subsequent miraculous return. The story was blowing up on social media. There was already a fan-art meme trending online of Grey as a venerated saint rendered in watercolor, a banner behind her reading "In Hollow we trust." Dozens of celebrities had reposted it, rejoicing at our sister's return. I watched over Tyler's shoulder for a while, and then, even with the plastic chair beneath me biting into my bones, I eventually slipped into a fraught and fitful sleep.

14

I WOKE JUST after midnight with my head on Tyler's shoulder. My neck was pinched at an angle, my bladder urgently swollen. I stretched off some of the sleep, then made my way to the toilets. The hospital was darker and quieter than it had been earlier in the evening. No lights came on in the room, so I peed in the dark, my eyes still drooping shut as I rested my elbows on my knees and cradled my chin in my hands. The scar at my throat was crawling again, begging to be scratched. I pressed my fingertip to the familiar ridge of scar tissue—and felt something *move* beneath my skin.

"Jesus, fuck," I spat, lurching off the toilet seat, sending droplets of piss down my thighs, over the floor.

You imagined it, you imagined it.

I sat back down and finished peeing and cleaned myself up, my heart whipping an angry beat inside my chest. My whole body was fizzing.

You imagined it, you imagined it. Don't touch it again.

I flushed and went to wash my hands with my head down,

too afraid to look up at the mirror. What would I see at the base of my neck? The pale-fleshed bud of a carrion flower about to burst through my skin? Or something worse?

I looked up. The room was too dark to make out anything but the vague outline of my body, so I turned my phone flashlight on and rested it on a soap dispenser, the beam of light pointed in my direction. The light wasn't kind to my features. It scrubbed the color from my complexion, carved any softness from my bones. I was a demon in this light. A monster. I couldn't look myself in the eyes without feeling a snap of fear.

Don't look. Don't look. Don't look at her.

I leaned in. I looked. There was a small pustule erupting at one end of my scar, its head hard and shiny black. As I watched it, it moved again, the flicker of something beetle-dark and spindly beneath my skin.

A tear slipped down my cheek. What the fuck was happening to me?

I pressed the sharp edge of my fingernail into the lump, enough to break the skin and tear the head away, then waited and watched to see what was beneath.

Something unfurled. Tiny legs. A black body.

An ant.

It crawled out of the wound and made its way across my collarbone, tickling my skin. A second followed it, popping from the tiny bore hole in my flesh, and then a third, until the pustule was empty. Thoughts of Grey's abandoned apartment filled my head. The line of ants and something dead and gruesome hidden beneath the wallpaper. I leaned in closer to the mirror, closer to the light, and gritted my teeth as I took out Grey's knife and used the tip to open the wound wider. The hot pain made more tears skim down my cheeks. A bead of blood slipped between my breasts. I blotted it away with a paper towel.

There was something there, beneath my skin. Something smooth and pale.

"What the *hell*?" I whispered.

It was *skin*, I realized as I leaned in for a better look. *More* skin. A second layer of it beneath my own, just as there had been a second layer of wallpaper beneath the one we'd peeled away.

My phone slipped from the soap dispenser then and clattered to the floor, sending the room strobing. The phone landed at my feet with a glassy clack and shot a beam of light at my face from below. For a second, it was not myself I saw in my reflection, but someone else. Something else.

I grabbed my phone and clambered back into the waiting room, madly swatting the ants from my body as I went. I thought I might vomit. I wanted to find one of the nurses, get them to rinse out my wound with alcohol and tell me I was imagining things, but there was no one around. Vivi was sprawled out on the floor, her head resting on her rolled-up jacket, her backpack tucked under one arm. Tyler slept sitting up. Apart from that, we were alone.

I hurried to the nurses' station, where the medics who'd cared for us all afternoon and evening were nowhere to be found.

"Hello?" I said. A sandwich sat unwrapped and half-eaten on a stack of paperwork. A can of Coke had been knocked over and left to drip into a puddle on the floor.

I went from the waiting room to the corridor where Grey's room was. The lights above me flickered. A clot of darkness swelled at the end of the hall where the ceiling lights had already been choked out. To my right, a doctor and a nurse squatted in an alcove, their bodies pressed together like soft fruit. Each took quiet, shallow breaths. They were holding hands, shaking, their eyes wide and wet. I looked down the corridor towards my sister's room, then back at them. The nurse shook his head. *Don't go.*

I went. I pushed into the stuttering dark, down the long corridor. Grey's room was easy to identify. It was the one with a chair out in front. Except the chair was toppled on its side, and the police officer who was supposed to be guarding my sister was sprawled facedown on the ground. There was blood. Not a pool of it, but slashes.

Grey's door was locked. I jiggled the handle, then pressed my face against the glass to see inside. It was soaked in shadow. The curtain was drawn around her bed. There was no movement.

Just as I was about to bang on the door, to try and wake her, a bloody hand closed hard over my mouth and yanked me back. I tried to scream, tried to thrash against my captor as they dragged me into the room opposite Grey's, but they were stronger than me.

"Stop," ordered a low voice as they pushed me roughly against a wall. "Stop. It's me."

Grey lifted her hand from my lips and pressed a blood-slick finger to her own.

My sister was a caricature of a madwoman in a red-spattered hospital gown. Her eyes and hair were wild, her lower jaw shaking. In her bloody hands she held a scalpel. What remained of her restraints hung loose and tattered at her wrists. A spark of déjà vu: Grey with a blade in her hand, and then gone, the familiar image there and then already fading from my mind like white spots left after a flash.

"What's going on?" I whispered, horrified.

"He's coming here," she said. "To take me."

"Grey," I whispered. I spat onto my sleeve and scrubbed the blood from my lips, then took my sister's face in my hands and tried to get her to look at me. She was skinnier now than when I'd last seen her, her collarbones pushing through her skin, and her hair had been lopped off above her shoulders. "Grey, look at me."

She did, eventually. She was calmer now than this afternoon, no longer rabid. I let the joy of her being alive, alive, *alive* flood me again. I wrapped my arms around her wasp waist and squeezed her close, my head on her shoulder. Grey was rigid for a moment, and then she melted into the hug.

"I'm sorry I hurt you," she said as she pulled back and trailed her fingertips over a soft bruise along my jaw. "I was scared."

"It's okay. It's okay. It doesn't matter. I'm just glad you're okay. Where were you? What happened?"

Grey's eyes welled and she pressed her lips together. "He took me. That bastard. I thought I'd never see you again."

"Who . . . who do you think is coming for you?"

"Wait," she said. "Watch."

I glanced at the floor, where arterial blood dripped from the tip of the scalpel, the tips of Grey's fingers. Another smack of déjà vu. Why did this scene feel familiar? "Did you . . . did you hurt the policeman, Grey?"

Grey's eyes went to his body, then back to her ward door. "He was not what he seemed."

I swallowed my horror and took Grey's free, bloody hand in my own. What would this mean for her? A lifetime in prison for his murder? Or would they go easy on her because of her mental state? Not guilty by reason of insanity, the rest of her twenties

160

spent in a mental institution? Both options were grim, life-destroying, but she had done something gruesome to an innocent man whose only crime was trying to protect her.

We waited together. We watched together.

In the minutes that passed, my sister stood unmoving and unblinking by the glass panel, her eyes bolted to the door of her hospital room across the corridor. I thought about what the doctor had said earlier in the evening, that Grey was in the grip of psychosis. It ran in our family, this predisposition to derangement. It had happened to our father, after all.

The day he killed himself, Gabe Hollow woke us in the early hours of the morning and bundled us into the family car. Cate was still asleep. We went quietly, without complaint. We could sense the danger in him—he handled us roughly, slammed the car doors, screeched out of the driveway—but what could we do? How could we fight? We were only little girls.

Gabe drove erratically. He was muttering to himself, crying, screaming that he was going to drive the car off a cliff and kill us all if we didn't tell him the truth.

Where were his children?

What had we done to them?

Who were we?

What were we?

Vivi and I bawled our eyes out in the back seat, but it was Grey, sitting in the passenger seat up front, who talked him down.

"Please, Papa," she whispered.

"Don't call me that!" he said with a sob, knuckles stone-white on the steering wheel.

Grey put her tiny hand on his arm. "Take us home." Her

morning breath smelled strange, both syrupy and sour at once. It wasn't until a year later, when I saw her kiss the woman who broke in, that I began to suspect Grey had compelled our father—and probably saved our lives in doing so.

Gabe took us home and killed himself later that day, while we were at school. We found him when we returned, hanging from the banister in the entranceway. Vivi and I screamed, but Grey didn't. She dragged a chair over to his body, patted him down, took the note he'd folded in his pocket, read it, and then tore it up into small pieces and threw it out the window. I spent the afternoon in the garden, collecting all the scattered scraps in my pocket, while Cate called relatives and made arrangements for his funeral. It was late spring, an unusually hot day in London, the afternoon temperature climbing past thirty degrees Celsius. I sat in my room and taped all the pieces of his note back together with sweaty hands.

I didn't want this, it had said. Four words to sum up a whole life.

I wondered if the same thing was happening to Grey right now. I wondered, for a few brief moments, if Tyler was right, if Grey's hysteria was catching. How much of what we had seen was real? Had there really been a dead body in Grey's ceiling? It had happened quickly and I had no physical proof of the strangeness, only scent and blood and memory. No one but Vivi and I had seen it. We had not been sleeping well, had been fueled by caffeine and adrenaline. The edge of our reality had begun to twist and burr as it brushed up against something else.

There was a hitch in Grey's breathing. She closed her fingers around the door handle, still holding the scalpel, still staring at her room across the hall. "Take off your shoes," she said.

"What?" I looked down at Grey's own bare feet. The nail beds were blackened, her ankles rubbed raw from restraints. "Why?"

"Do it. He's here," she said. The flickering lights went out, and darkness dropped over the hallway like a stone. I scuffed out of my shoes and held them in one hand.

Then he was there, just as she said he would be. I knew him from his silhouette, even if I couldn't see his face: the man from Grey's burned-out apartment. Tall and thin, the skull of a dead bull worn over his face. The stench of him palmed my face, driving splinters of rot and damp and smoke into my nose. A flicker of broken memories skipped across the surface of my thoughts: a decomposing forest, a hand with a knife, three children warming themselves by a fireplace. Three little girls with dark hair and blue eyes. Us. Whose house were we at?

I was crying, though I didn't understand why. We were not safe here. Whoever he was, he had found us, again. Found Grey. Come to take her away from me. I wanted to run, I wanted my feet to move as fast as my heart was beating, but my sister tightened her grip on my hand. *Not yet.*

The man knelt by the body of the police officer and turned him over—except he was not wearing a police uniform. A thicket of white flowers was bursting from the dead man's eyes, his nostrils, his mouth, their petals waxy in the low light. Something was happening to him, something I'd seen before. Hair-thin vines grew from the roots of the flowers in his mouth, twisting their way across the skin of his face. There was the smell of blood, yes, but also something green and sour. I covered my mouth to keep from gagging.

He was not what he seemed, Grey had said. Not the police officer who'd been tasked with guarding her door. Someone else.

The man tried the handle to Grey's hospital door. When he

found it locked, he used his elbow to break the glass, then put his arm through and unlocked it from the other side. He slipped into Grey's room and shut the door behind him.

"We have to go now," Grey whispered. "Follow me." She opened the door and padded quietly into the hall, her feet bare, tiny drops of blood slipping from her hand as she moved. My own blood was thundering rapids, but my footfalls were silent as I followed her, also barefoot, crouching low as we moved past her room, careful not to step on any glass as we moved under the broken window.

"You have to hide," Grey whispered to the doctor as we crept back past her. The nurse had already disappeared, but the doctor was now an empty shell, gone from her body. There was a crash from Grey's room, an animal growl: He'd found her bed empty. The doctor looked that way and swallowed but didn't move. Grey knelt by the woman's side, tucked a strand of her hair behind her ear, and then leaned in to press her lips against hers. It had been a long time since I'd seen Grey do this thing, and for a moment I wondered if it would still work, but then whatever sweet potion we carried on our breath, our lips, every inch of our skin worked its way into the doctor's bloodstream, and I saw her melt beneath my sister's touch. When Grey pulled back from the kiss, the woman's pupils were saucers, and she looked at Grey like a bride walking down the aisle on her wedding day. Awed. Overwhelmed. The most in love she'd ever been. "Hide now," Grey said. The doctor smiled, punch-drunk and dazed, and slipped into the room behind her.

My pulse was a flurry. "Come," I whispered urgently. We ran then, hard but silent, towards where Vivi and Tyler slept, rounding the corner as Grey's door slammed open, sending more broken glass jittering across the floor. The noise made Tyler jump awake. Grey pressed her palm over his mouth and shook her head. Tyler swallowed. I woke Vivi with a finger against her lips. Her eyelids lurched open, but she was quiet as I pulled her to her feet and motioned for her to take her shoes off, carry them in her hand. Grey removed her hand from Tyler's face and knelt to help him pull his shoes off.

All was silent. Then came the crunch of heavy boots on glass. The footfalls were headed in our direction, following the line of blood drops Grey had left on the floor. Vivi put her backpack on. Grey pulled Tyler out of his seat and wiped her hands on her dress, and then the four of us moved softly, swiftly towards the next hallway, making it around the corner a moment after the man stepped into the waiting room, the shadow concealing our retreat. I watched his diluted reflection in a panel of glass. There were three fresh runes written down his chest in blood. He crouched and placed his palm where I had been sitting. He picked up Vivi's rolled-up jacket from the floor and pressed it to the stripped-bare bones of his mask, inhaling deeply. He nudged Tyler's shoes with his toe.

From the back of his waistband, he pulled his gun and started in our direction. We peeled away from the wall we'd been pressed against and ran soft-footed down the corridor, as quickly and quietly as we could manage.

As we rounded the next corner, Grey slammed into a body. A green aura of stink exploded in my head.

"He—" breathed the figure (a woman, I could see now, in the half-light), but Grey drove the scalpel up under her chin and cut off her cry when it was still no more than a breath. Grey yanked the scalpel out of her head and held the woman tightly against her as she lowered her, gushing blood, to the floor. The blood was full of clots and smelled of decay.

We kept running in the dark then, turning corners, back-tracking when figures appeared at the end of a hall or when a wall of smoke and rot stench hit us. Grey was doused in blood—but was it blood? In the half-light, the stain down her front seemed to twitch across her like shadow.

"We need to get off this floor," Grey whispered. "Out of this hospital."

"There," I said, pointing to a door at the end of the corridor. EMERGENCY EXIT ONLY, it read. ALARM WILL SOUND WHEN DOOR IS OPENED.

"Do it," Grey said. "Run, and don't stop running."

We ran. Vivi reached the door first, slammed into it at the same moment the alarm split my teeth open. I followed her, and Grey came up behind me. Tyler hurled himself through the door last. When I looked back, the man was coming straight for us, the bone of his mask catching shards of light as he charged in our direction.

"Go, go, go, fucking go!" Grey screamed as Tyler pulled the door closed, the man hitting it three seconds behind us, popping it from its hinges like a craft Popsicle stick. We flew down the stairs, taking them three at a time, our feet slapping the concrete, our lungs sucking hard. The man was fast and agile. As we tore down the stairwell, gripping the handrails to swing around corners faster, we heard him gaining on us. Then we smelled him gaining on us. Then we *felt* him gaining on us, the wet hotness of his breath, flecks of sweat from his arms and chest flicking the back of my neck. Tyler screamed. I turned. The man held him by the collar and had him pressed up against a wall. Grey was already there. She plunged the scalpel into the creature's chest and fell back. The gun went clattering down the stairwell, lost somewhere below us. The surgical implement looked comically small lodged in his flesh, a toothpick stabbed into a watermelon. He dropped Tyler, who scrambled towards us, choking. We backed away, down the stairs, as he plucked the scalpel from his chest like a splinter and flicked it to the ground, where it made a pretty twinkling sound.

"Run," Grey said. We turned and hurled ourselves downward again, out the door at the bottom of the stairs and into the cool night. After the shrill alarm of the stairwell and the thick stink of the horned man, the night felt crisp and quiet. We'd been spat out at the back of the hospital.

The man burst out of the stairwell behind us, clipping the horns of his mask on the doorway.

Grey was the fastest out in the open and she ran hard through the gap between hospital buildings until she reached the street, where she flung herself in front of a passing car. It screamed to a stop, curls of rubber smoke rising from the asphalt beneath it. The driver wound down his window and started yelling obscenities. Grey pitched herself through the window and planted a desperate kiss on his lips. The man went quiet as she spoke in his ear, quickly, urgently, as we all piled into the car. Then Grey folded into the back seat, and the man shoved the car into first and smoked the tires again before we'd all even closed our doors—and not a moment too soon.

The man landed a fist on the back bumper, making the car fishtail as we sped away. Then he ran alongside us, almost keeping pace for a second or two, before we finally pulled ahead and left him in the middle of the road, doused in the faded red of our lights.

15

"IT'S TIME FOR some *bloody* answers," Tyler demanded as I put my shoes back on. I couldn't disagree with him. "My love," he said, holding my now-unconscious sister's face in his hands. "You must wake up. You've got some explaining to do."

"Would you let her rest?" Vivi said.

"No! I just saw my girlfriend *murder a woman* with a *scalpel*. And that man—that *thing*—its skin was scabby and rotting. No more excuses."

"I don't think being unconscious is an *excuse*, you twat."

"Nor do I! So wake up!"

I turned around from where I sat in the front seat. "Let's just calm down and debrief for a minute."

"Oh, you want to debrief? You want to debrief? A murderous bull just crushed my esophagus, Little Hollow. I am not okay— and I am still not convinced this isn't all an elaborate ploy to ruin my life," Tyler said to a still-unconscious Grey. "Do you hear that, darling? I know what you're up to."

I sighed and turned back around. "Where are you taking

us?" I asked the driver as he pulled onto the highway, heading north. He stared, dead-eyed, out the windshield, but he was under Grey's spell, not mine, and had no interest in me. The inside of the car smelled like honey wine on the verge of turning to vinegar. The air was close, thick with blood and some invisible magic. I cracked a window to let in some fresh air and clear my heavy head.

How long would it be before someone realized our driver was missing? The Uber app was open on his phone. In the glove compartment was an assortment of things no doubt shoved in there before his shift started: three colored pencils, a pair of women's sunglasses, a charging cable, and one pink and one purple hair bobble, each with fine blond hairs caught in the elastic.

"What if one of us has to pee?" Vivi asked. "Is he going to just . . . keep driving?"

"Now might be a bad time to mention that the hospital cafeteria sandwiches seem to be disagreeing with me," Tyler said.

I thought about messaging my mother—but what would I say to her?

We're driving north but I don't know to where.

I don't know how long we'll be gone for.

A masked man is trying to kill us all.

Don't stress.

In the end, my phone died in my hand before I could send anything. Maybe it was better that way. Cate would be sleeping in her lonely room in London, dreaming of a time before her children disappeared.

Peeing didn't end up being a problem. We ran out of fuel less than two hours after our escape, not far past Northampton. The car rolled to a sputtering stop on a quiet street next to a field hemmed by a low fence. It was the early hours of the morning. No one else was around. The driver, still under Grey's spell, got out of the car, left the lights on and his door open, and started walking along the side of the road.

"Hey!" I shouted as I ran after him. "Hey, where are you going? Are you just going to leave us here?" Even when I grabbed his arm and tried to stop him, the man kept his pace. Mouth slightly open, eyes unfocused. I let him go, let him sink into the waiting dark.

"Excuse me, I'm going to go and shit in the woods like an animal," Tyler said as he hopped over the fence and wandered into the field.

"Charming," Vivi said. "You can really see why Grey dated him."

"I heard that!" Tyler called.

"You were supposed to!" Vivi shouted back.

We waited. One minute stretched to five stretched to ten. I kept wandering around the car, waiting for another vehicle to pass us by. Vivi kept holding her phone high like they do in horror movies when they're looking for a signal. Like that ever worked.

I wondered if the driver would continue on foot all the way to the destination Grey had given him. I wondered how far that might be and if the man would stop at all along the way. Would he walk until his feet bled, until his stomach growled and his joints ached? Would he break for food and water, or would he walk until he died? Did we have the terrible power to do that to people?

"Iris, come here," Vivi said as I paced. I went to where she had trained the beam of her phone flashlight, by the open door of the car. Vivi stepped aside to reveal Grey's waxy face, her eyes rolled back in her head, her skin tight and slippery with fever sweat.

"Oh my God. She looks terrible." I crouched and put my palm on her forehead. "She's burning up. What do we do?"

"Take her to the hospital again?" Vivi suggested.

"Because that worked out so well the first time."

"Well, shit, I don't know. What if she's dying? We can't do nothing."

"We could call Cate," I suggested, wondering if our mother would be willing to provide urgent medical care to the daughter she had thrown out of her house.

"Even if I had a damn signal, I'm sure Cate would be *super* enthusiastic about helping."

We found a half-empty bottle of water and a gym towel in the trunk, then soaked it through and mopped Grey's forehead, trying to bring her fever down. Tyler came back, holding his stomach. "Now that that's out of the way . . . what's going on?" he asked.

"You didn't notice that she was as hot as an oven, you incompetent dunce?" Vivi snapped.

A noise then, from the darkness: footfalls on gravel and a sloshing sound.

"Who's there?" I asked, but it was only the spelled driver, now carrying a large red jerry can. "Oh, thank goodness."

"Well, look who it is," Tyler said. As the man passed, Tyler put his foot in front of the man's legs to try and trip him. The man stumbled, then kept on walking as if nothing had happened. "What's wrong with him?"

"Don't torment him," I said as the driver went by me, in a world entirely his own. "He's not himself."

"*What* does that even mean?" Tyler asked.

Vivi took Tyler's face in her hands, looked at him for a moment, and then leaned in to kiss him. It was a deep kiss, rich with whatever elixir lived on my sister's lips. My lips. Even I felt the power of it and, underneath that, something else—a pinch of envy.

Vivi pulled back and watched Tyler carefully.

"Well, I feel violated," he said as he wiped his wet mouth. "Yuck. Not interested, FYI. Been there, done that. You're all as bonkers as each other."

"Interesting," Vivi said to me. "He's entirely unaffected. Maybe because he has no brain."

"How *old* are you?" Tyler said.

Vivi could tease him all she wanted, but I knew why Grey dated Tyler.

The second time someone kissed me was backstage after Grey's very first House of Hollow catwalk at Paris Fashion Week. The show had been a resounding success, but I didn't feel like celebrating. A hard stone sat in my stomach because a man had been watching me for two days. I never learned his name. All I knew was that he was an up-and-coming photographer who wore a brown leather jacket and tied his light hair in a bun. He was tall and young and handsome and spoke with a purring accent. Women should have been all over him, but he lingered for too long around the models, and he liked to look at me too much. I suppose he figured that a teenage girl would be thrilled by the attention from a grown man. I suppose he figured that I liked the way he brushed his fingers across the back of my jeans when he asked me for a selfie together.

I suppose he figured a lot of wrong things.

What I figured was this: It was vitally important that I was never alone in a room with him. I had spent two days making sure he never got the opportunity, not because I was certain something bad would happen, but because I couldn't be certain that nothing bad *wouldn't* happen. Now that the show was over, I could let my guard down. I was flying home to London the next morning, Grey had organized an Uber back to my hotel room, and the creepy man wouldn't be there.

All I needed was to dash backstage to get my coat.

Backstage had been chaotic for hours before the show started, busy with filament-limbed models and makeup artists and producers darting across the space, yelling into headsets—but it was quiet now. The chemical smell of hair spray lingered, as did the burned-hair tang of curls left in irons for slightly too long. The Hollywood lights bordering each of the mirrors were dark, and the dresses that each of the models had worn on the catwalk had been packed into garment bags and hung on rails along one side of the room. I couldn't help smiling as I passed them in the lowlight, these small miracles of thread and fabric born from my sister's wild brain. I'd seen rough sketches of her creations in the months leading up to fashion week, but nothing had prepared me for seeing them in real life, the beauty and grotesquery of them.

I found my coat draped across the back of a folding chair and shrugged it on.

"Hello, Iris," a male voice said. I turned. It was the photographer.

Here, with me. In the dark. Alone.

"Oh. Hello. I didn't know anyone was still here."

"They're not. Everyone's gone to the after-party."

"Where's Grey?"

"I just saw her get in an Uber." That didn't sound right. Grey was supposed to take me back to my hotel before she went partying. Cate had made her promise. "I can give you a lift home, if you want."

I tried to slip past him, to see if he was telling the truth, but he caught my wrist and sent my heart cartwheeling in panic.

"You're beautiful, you know," he said with his lips, but with his fingers gripped tight enough around my arm to leave bruises, he said something different. And then it happened. He leaned in to kiss me. He got too close. He breathed in the untamed power of me, fizzing with sweat and fear, and it sent him wild, the same way it had sent Justine Khan wild. His eyes turned to saucers, and the next thing I knew, I was on the ground, under him, under his weight and his hardness as his fingers scratched at my waistband, trying to force their way into my jeans. I screamed and I fought beneath him. I thrashed and scratched his face with my nails, but the sudden scent of his own blood only made him more rabid. The hot stink of his breath in my face. The warm trail of saliva he left on my skin as he kissed me, bit me, licked the wounds he left on me.

I'm not sure if Grey heard my scream or felt my distress instinctually, but suddenly she was there—not gone, like the photographer had said—standing over us, wearing the face of a vengeful god. She took the man by the throat and wrenched him off me with one hand, then slammed him against a mirror, shattering the glass and light bulbs behind him. Her slim fingers were so tight on his neck, he could barely breathe, but—though his face was red and his throat made clucking sounds as it struggled to pull air into his lungs—the photographer did not seem to mind. He was already violently high on her, giddy and lovesick.

Why was it a useful, easy power on Grey, but on me, it made me a victim?

Grey was breathing hard, spitting venom with every exhale. She squeezed the man even harder, until I could see the capillaries bursting beneath her grip. "You are going to go home," Grey ordered, "and when you get there, you are going to kill yourself. Make it slow. Make it painful. Do you understand?"

The man bit his lip and smiled, then nodded coyly, like he was flirting with her.

"Grey," I said through my sobs. "Don't. Don't make him do that. It's . . . It wasn't entirely his fault. It was . . . more of an accident. I got too close and he went too far. I don't know how to . . . Please. Please take it back. Just let him go."

Grey let go of the man's throat and slapped him hard across the face. A tinkling rain of glass shards fell from his hair. "You're lucky my sister is more merciful than I am. Don't you ever, *ever* fucking touch someone without their consent again. Get out of my sight. Get out of Paris and don't come back."

When he was gone, Grey rounded on me. "And you. You have to be more—"

"What?" I snapped as I pulled myself off the ground. "Careful?" I was shaking, bleeding. I wanted Grey to fold herself around me like a blanket and make the hurt go away, but she didn't. She stood there and watched me, unmoving, as I did up the top button of my jeans and pressed cotton makeup rounds to the bleeding bites on my neck, my shoulder.

"You have to be *stronger*, Iris."

"Are you *kidding* me? It's not like I asked for it! He followed me back here. Why are you angry with *me*?"

"Because you're weak. Because you let lesser people push you around. Because you are afraid of how powerful you are and you shrink away from it. Because I won't always be around to protect you and I know, *I know* you are capable of protecting yourself, because you're more like me than you realize."

"Who the *fuck* are you?" I asked, because this person was not my sister. Her words were so vile, so wrong—how could they have come from Grey? How could this person who claimed to love me more than anything hurt me so deeply after what she'd seen happen to me? I thought, then, of the broken pinkie finger on my sister's left hand. On my left hand.

"Does it hurt?" I'd asked her when it happened.

"Yes," she'd whispered, cradling the swollen bones to her chest. "It hurts so much."

"How can I make it better?"

She'd looked up at me, her eyes black, her breath coming in sad little drags. "Break your finger too."

On my way out, Grey snatched up my bruised wrists in her hands. I winced at the layered pain, hurt on hurt. "Use the gifts you have been given," she said to me. "No one should be able to lay a finger on you. You can bring them to their knees, if that's what you want. You can make them pay."

"That isn't what I want," I said as I twisted out of her grip, the way Vivi had shown me after one of her Krav Maga classes. "That's never been what I want. Why can't you get that? What I want is to be *normal*."

Later that night, in my hotel room, I spent two hours in the

176

shower trying to scrub the smell of him off me, and then, when it was gone, trying to scrub out whatever rotten thing lived under my flesh and made me so weak. I scrubbed my scar so raw, it bled for days.

So yes. I thought I knew why Grey dated Tyler. Because to be near a person who wasn't prey to your intoxicating power, to kiss someone who would never become crazed at the scent of you—someone you couldn't *make* want you, someone you couldn't *make* love you, someone who desired you of their own free will—was something I had daydreamed about but thought was impossible for me.

We watched as the driver used a funnel to refuel the car, then got back in the front seat and turned on the engine.

"Hey, hey, hey!" I yelled as he put the car into first and began to roll away without us, all of the doors still open. We all piled in—Vivi in the front this time, Tyler and me in the back—and slammed our doors shut.

"I must say, I am *not* a fan of this Uber," Tyler said. "One star. Two at most."

I sat with Grey's clammy head in my lap, her bare legs draped over Tyler's knees. Her hair was sodden with sweat, and her skin smelled sharp and wrong, meat and vinegar undercut with something sweet and floral, like gardenia. I pushed her hair off her forehead. Even like this, even ill and sallow and shaking, Grey was beautiful.

I'd never seen her really unwell before. It had always been Grey taking care of Vivi and me when we were little girls, not the other way around. Grey had always been the one in charge. Grey had always been the strongest.

"I'm going to keep you safe," I whispered to her, just as she had whispered to me every night when she tucked me in. "Forever. I promise."

☾

We stopped for more fuel not long after, at a twenty-four-hour service station along the highway with acid-white lighting. I dashed inside while the driver filled the tank. I bought a liquid painkiller meant for kids and water to try and lower Grey's fever. I was back in the car, my arms full of medicine and snacks from by the register, before the guy had even finished refueling. Tyler was walking around, stretching his legs. Vivi twirled an unlit clove cigarette in her fingers, maintaining eye contact with the glaring station clerk the whole time.

"Grey," I said as I slipped back inside the car and rested her head in my lap. The man docked the nozzle at the pump. "Grey, you need to take this." I thought the man would head into the station and pay, but he opened his door and started the ignition. "Shit, Tyler!" I called as the car jerked forwards. "Get in!"

Tyler legged it after us and made it inside as the driver pulled out of the station, the clerk already outside yelling after us.

"Dude is gonna get us arrested," Vivi said.

"Help me with this," I instructed Tyler once we were back on the highway. I hiked Grey's limp shoulders farther up on my knees and held her head so Tyler could open her mouth and pour some of the painkiller in.

Tyler leaned over and stroked the side of her cheek. A tender moment. He ran his thumb over Grey's bottom lip, then opened her mouth.

"There's something . . . something in there," he said.

"In her mouth?" I leaned over and looked. There was something green and rank lodged at the back of Grey's throat. I put my fingers in past her teeth and tried to scoop it out: a slop of rotten leaves covered in a fur of powdery mildew. The tinny stink of it made my eyes water. Tyler and Vivi both gagged as the close air of the car ripened. I turned on the car's overhead light and looked in Grey's mouth, then immediately wished I hadn't. I gagged too. A nest of rotten leaves and carrion flowers and ants, all growing in her. Swollen with her blood. Bursting from the flesh of her throat.

"What is it?" Tyler asked.

"An infection," I lied. "Drive faster," I instructed the driver, though I knew he likely wouldn't listen to me, "or she might not make it to wherever we're going."

We drove for four or five more hours, until dawn began to leech the dark from the edges of the sky, and all of us sat with our legs crossed, our bladders pressed tight and low. Grey's fever waxed and waned, but her skin remained slick with sweat, her lips sapped of color, her breath stained rotten green.

I sank in and out of sleep. I wished I'd had the opportunity to tell Cate I was okay. Soon, she would wake to the news that we had disappeared from the hospital overnight, that we were gone without a trace. What would that do to her?

In the shadow light of the early morning, I saw ants slip from the corner of Grey's mouth and walk a tight trail over her cheek, towards her eye.

Vivi yawned and stretched. "Where are we?" she asked as we pulled past the outskirts of a city.

"Edinburgh," I answered. I'd suspected as soon as we'd crossed the border into Scotland that this was our final destination. Where it all began, a lifetime ago, on a quiet street in the

Old Town, in a slip of moments between one year and the next.

When I thought about that night, when I tried to remember it, nothing came back to me. It was only through the retellings of others that I could get a sense of what it had been like.

The way Cate told it, there was no magic hanging in the air, no sense of foreboding, no tall stranger in dark clothing following unnoticed behind us. It was a normal night on a normal street. We were a normal family and then, just like that, we weren't. Something terrible and impossible happened to us here, and I couldn't remember what—but maybe Grey did. Grey, with her secrets and her perfumed lips and her unnatural beauty that had brought the world to its knees before her.

Grey, who said she remembered everything. *Everything.* All the answers, wrapped up on the other side of a fever. All we had to do was break it.

A few minutes later, the car rolled to a stop on a tight, cobbled street. The city was still soaked in darkness. The light here was old, borrowed from another century. Even the modern streetlights seemed unable to fully shift the weight of the Scottish night.

Tyler stretched and went to open his door.

"Stop," Vivi said, looking up out the windshield at something I couldn't see. "There's a kid pointing a gun at us out her window."

"A kid?" I asked.

"Yeah, a creepy-looking little girl with a shotgun," Vivi said.

The driver got out of the car slowly and stood there, staring up at her with his hands raised. I heard a gun pump.

"You owe her," the man said, and then he turned and—without closing his car door—began walking back the way we came. How ruined would his life be from his night of driving three strange girls and a male supermodel across the country?

"What's she doing?" I asked Vivi, who was sitting very still in the front seat.

"I think she's contemplating shooting me in the face," Vivi answered. "The odds are not looking in my favor."

I opened my door then, slowly, the way the man had, and slipped out from beneath Grey with my hands held over my head. The barrel of the shotgun moved to me. Vivi was right—the person holding it was only a child, a little girl of no more than ten or eleven.

I didn't say anything. I didn't have to.

The girl broke her stance, glancing over the gun to get a better look at me: my white-blond hair, my black eyes. If the girl knew Grey, she would see her in me. She drew the gun inside and closed the window.

"I think it's clear," I said.

Tyler and Vivi opened their car doors and got out. I thought for a minute that that would be it, that the child would shut up the windows and lock the doors on us—but no, the front door opened, and the girl stepped out onto the porch with the gun slung over one shoulder. She was tangle-haired and squalid, her hands and bare feet thick with grime. She wore a cotton nightgown that might once have been white, but was now soiled with earth and muck. It looked like she'd been buried alive in it and then dug herself out of her own shallow grave.

Her eyes traveled from Vivi, to me, back to Vivi's tattooed throat, and then to my throat, to the shiny hook of scar tissue that glittered in the early morning sun. Her eyes were wide and her lungs drew the rapid, shallow breaths of a hare watching a wolf across a field—as if deciding whether she should run or remain stock-still.

Tyler looked over her shoulder and into the house. "Are your parents home, sweetheart?"

"Shut it, Tyler," Vivi said.

I took a step towards the girl, my hands raised. "We need you to help her," I said. "Grey sent us here because she knew you'd know what to do."

The child looked at me, questioning. I nodded towards the back seat, where my sister lay shaking.

The girl stepped barefoot onto the cold cobbles and came to look at Grey. "Bring . . . ," she said, her voice a dry and strangled thing. I wondered how often she spoke to anyone. "Bring her inside," she rasped—and so we did.

Vivi, the strongest of us, held Grey under the arms while Tyler carried her feet. They set her down on a dust- and crumb-covered rug in the living room just off the hall. I ducked back outside to close the car doors and the front door. There was a stack of two dozen or so unopened envelopes piled up in the hall, all addressed to Adelaide Fairlight. Our grandmother's name. It was also the name Grey used to check in to hotels to hide her identity. So this was another of our sister's hidden nests. How extensive was her web of mysteries?

I knelt by Grey's side with the others and looked around the space for more signs of our sister. Green things had begun to grow through the windows and floorboards. Tendrils of vine snuck in through the window frames. Yellow pops of lichen burst from the walls. The wood stacked by the fireplace was cocooned in a fuzz of mold. The rug under Grey's back was spongy with some kind of fungus that grew in coral-like polyps that swayed softly when the air shifted.

It felt like a place Grey belonged, yet the furniture was sparse and there were none of the trinkets she liked to pack her hidey-holes with: no incense or crystals or candles. I could only guess the apartment was a safe house of some sort—or that Grey had rented or bought it in our grandmother's name *for* the little girl. For a moment I wondered if the child was Grey's secret daughter, born after she ran away. I searched her features for similarities, but there were none. The girl had chestnut hair and green eyes, and besides, she must've been ten or eleven, and Grey left only four years ago.

The girl left us then and went into the adjoining kitchen. There was banging, the sound of glass bottles clinking together and a spoon stirring. When she came back a few minutes later, she was holding a bowl. I caught the smack of vinegar and salt, mixed with the licorice of anise and the bitter, medicinal tang of wormwood. A witch's brew.

The little girl motioned for me to open Grey's mouth and pinch her nose shut. When I had done what she asked, she poured some of the liquid down Grey's throat. Grey gagged and swallowed, then immediately vomited, a placental sac of rot and roots and greenery slopping out of her and onto the rug.

"Oh God, I *cannot* handle this," Tyler said as he stood and went outside. I heard him retching a moment later, the few snacks we ate in the car splattering onto the sidewalk as he made his retreat.

The girl motioned for me to hold Grey's nose again while she poured more of the draft into her mouth. Again, Grey gagged, swallowed, vomited, this time bringing up sticky strings of bile laced with flowers and thin worms.

The girl noticed the bandages on Grey's arms and laid her blackened palms over them. Then she went to the kitchen and returned again with a pair of meat shears and slipped them under the coils of cotton, slicing the bandages off. Beneath, the skin of Grey's arms was covered in three cuts, two of them closed with sutures that looked like barbed wire. White death flowers grew from each wound, a carpet of them, their roots vein-blue from drinking deeply of Grey's blood.

"Jesus," Vivi whispered. "What's happening to her?"

The girl took the scissors she'd used to cut Grey's bandages and drew one of the blades across her own palm. I cringed at the thought of the pain, but when she opened her hand there was no blood, only a runnel of brown liquid that smelled at once of iron and sap.

"It gets . . . ," the girl rasped, but her throat closed. She swallowed, tried again. "It gets inside you." She used two fingers from her opposite hand to hold her wound open. Inside were no capillaries or tendons or raw red flesh, but what you might expect to find on a decomposing tree on the forest floor: a fen of rot and moss and mold.

A tear slipped down Vivi's cheek. "What are you?" she asked.

"It is in me," the girl said, placing her hand over her heart. "In her." She put her palm on the scar at Grey's throat. Finally, she pointed at Vivi. "In you."

Vivi shook her head, slowly at first and then more angrily. She smacked the tears from her eyes and stood. "*Fuck* this," she said. She kicked the bowl of witch's brew, which went clattering across the room, and did what Vivi does: stormed out, probably to find an off-license that would sell her booze before ten a.m.

The girl tore a strip from the bottom of her dress and soaked it in the puddle of leftover tincture. "For you," she said as she handed the material to me. I was confused, but then the girl tapped the soft basin of flesh between her collarbones, and my fingers instinctively went to my own, went to my scar, where the knot beneath my skin had re-formed. I pressed the wad of wet fabric to my skin. Something beneath the surface squirmed in protest.

The girl soaked Grey's cut bandages with what remained of the remedy, then laid them over the cuts.

"Why . . . ," the girl began. She swallowed. "Why did she do this?" she asked as she ran her fingers over the wet strips of cotton.

I held my sister's hand. "I don't think she did. Grey's been missing for a week. We found her like this. I think someone did this to her. A man. A man who wears a bull's skull to hide his face."

"He . . . cut her?" the girl rasped.

"I don't know. I don't know why anyone would do that."

The girl stood and grabbed the shotgun and pointed it squarely at my face.

"You cannot stay here," she growled.

"Whoa, whoa, just wait a—"

"No," she said, slamming the barrel of the gun into my shoulder, toppling me over. *"Go."*

"Please just tell me what's going on!"

"He has her blood." The way she spoke was like a wild animal that had been taught human language. "He will always be able to find her. If she is here, he will come. He is already on his way."

"You owe her," I said quickly, echoing what the driver had said before he left. I didn't know exactly what a child could owe Grey, only that reminding her had gotten us inside, and maybe it would be enough to let us stay a little longer. Grey was weak and dehydrated. I worried that moving her again would do more damage, and besides, the girl seemed to know how to care for her when a hospital couldn't. We needed to be here. We didn't have anywhere else to go. "We need your help and you owe her. Please. Please."

The girl was breathing hard. "When she wakes, you go," she ordered, and then she dropped the gun and followed Vivi and Tyler out onto the street.

16

VIVI CAME BACK not long after, much to my surprise, not with a bottle of tequila but with fresh bread and fruit and coffee. We ate together on the front porch in the cold morning sun. I told her about what the girl had said, that the man looking for Grey would find us here like he'd found us at the hospital, that our time here was limited.

Vivi sucked on a clove cigarette and breathed out a plume of smoke, her thoughts ticking.

"What?" I asked her.

"It's like . . . Well, maybe it's like how the three of us can find each other," she said. "He has her blood, and so now he can find her too."

"How does that make sense?"

"Fuck, Iris. I don't know. I don't know what any of this means. I have no answers for you. I'm just throwing some thoughts out there, trying to get a brainstorming session rolling."

"Okay, okay. God. What do we do now?"

"Keep moving, I guess."

"Forever?"

"Until we can figure this thing out."

"What is there to figure out?"

"How to kill a Minotaur? We're humans, right? We're, like, the dominant species for a reason. We're terrifying. We have guns. We should easily be able to kill an upright cow." Vivi stubbed out her cigarette. "I don't have patience for this anymore," she said as she stood and went inside. I heard her muttering to herself as she knelt by Grey's side and slid a pillow under our sister's head. "I want to go back to Budapest. I want to go back to drinking elderflower beer and making out with beautiful Hungarian women every night. Do you hear me? Wake up and sort out your mess. I like my life."

I took a long inhale, then spotted Tyler at the end of the street, walking towards me with new sneakers on his feet and a Nike shoe box tucked under his arm. In his floral shirt and leopard print coat, he was an anachronism set against the cobbled road and stone houses.

"Nice kicks," I said as he sank to the porch beside me. I offered him a banana and what was left of my coffee.

"Yes, well," he said after taking a sip. "They're not exactly my usual style, but they'd run out of lizard-skin Gucci loafers, so what's a man to do?"

"I thought we might have seen the last of you."

"I went to the train station and bought a ticket. I even got on the train and found my seat."

"So why are you back here?"

"Oh, some kind of fire alarm went off and they evacuated all the passengers. I obviously wasn't going to wait on the platform in the cold."

"And here I was thinking you were suddenly struck by a moment of conscience."

"God, no." Tyler stretched out his long legs in front of him and tapped his new shoes together.

"I read about your sister."

Tyler said nothing.

"If you don't want to talk about her, I—"

"It's fine. I just . . ." He scratched the bridge of his nose. "It happened a long time ago. I'm the youngest of four. The only boy. We were at a beach in the summer. I was five, Rosie was seven. We were good swimmers. We were daring each other to swim farther and farther out." He recounted it like it was a Wikipedia article. It was the same way I talked about my abduction, if I had to. Removing the emotion and stating the bare-bones facts made it easier. "We got caught in a rip. We both went under. When they pulled me out, I had no heartbeat for three minutes. Eventually, they revived me. They couldn't bring her back."

"I know it's not enough to say I'm sorry, but I'm sorry."

Tyler had only 3 percent battery left on his phone, but he unlocked it and navigated to his Favourites folder in his photographs and showed her to me. Rosie. The little girl I'd seen in the news article, with long dark hair and a heavy fringe. There were pictures of her visiting family in Seoul. Pictures of her toothless grin on her first day of school. Pictures of her playing with her siblings: her two teenage sisters and Tyler. "Rosie was the bravest and most mischievous of the four of us. Always getting into trouble."

"Sounds like Vivi."

"Vivi reminds me of her, actually. Both full of attitude and *incredibly* annoying at times but endearing, somehow." Tyler put his phone away. "Grey thinks I went there, you know."

"Went where?"

"The Halfway. For the few minutes my heart stopped, that's where she thinks I went."

"Huh."

"*Huh*, what? That was a very epiphanic *huh*."

"Just that . . . Grey told me once that she thought you were special. I wonder if that's why we can't make you do whatever we want." Tyler had died. Tyler had come back. Tyler was impervious to our compulsion. "I thought you thought this was all in my head?"

"Well, the way Grey talked about it—I mean, I assumed, like a *normal* person, that it was a fairy tale. I don't remember much about that day, after I went into the water, but I do remember the smell of smoke when I came to on the beach. My mother told me—when I coughed up water from my lungs during the CPR, she thought she saw me coughing up flowers. I just never . . . It's real, isn't it? What's happening is real."

"Yeah. I think it is."

"I bought you a gift," he said. Tucked inside the Nike shoe box were three new iPhone chargers. Tyler handed me one. "One for you, one for me, one for your aggressively tattooed sister."

"Thank you. That's weirdly thoughtful."

"People are always *so* surprised when I turn out to not be an absolute dick."

"To be fair, you do seem to go out of your way to *act* like an absolute dick."

"All part of my image, Little Hollow. Bad-boy swagger. I'm actually *very* deep."

"I knew there had to be some reason Grey was dating you."

"Beyond my outrageous good looks, you mean? I didn't really go to the train station, you know." Tyler took another sip of my coffee and then turned to look through the door, to where Grey slept on the squalid rug. "I want her to be okay. I *need* her to be okay."

"Me too," I said as I patted him on the back. It felt so strange and so good to be this close to someone without having to worry about them sinking their teeth into my skin to taste me. "Me too."

☾

I steadied myself with three deep breaths before I plugged my phone in to charge.

For the first time ever, I edited my Find Friends app to remove my mother from the list of people who were allowed to see my location. If she knew where I was, she would be on the first flight here to bring me home. I couldn't let that happen. It wasn't safe for her.

I tapped her name in my Favourites list and called her.

"Iris, Iris, Iris," my mother sobbed a half second later. "Oh my God, talk to me, baby."

"I'm okay," I said. The pain in her voice was corrosive. I felt it in my blood. God, how could I do this to her? "I'm okay."

"Where are you? I knew I shouldn't have let you stay with that *thing*. I'm coming to get you."

That thing? "I can't tell you. I'm safe, but I can't come home yet. I don't know how long I'll be gone for." *I don't know if I'll ever be able to come back.*

I thought about school then, and the carefully constructed

fantasy future I'd allowed myself to dream about for years. The one in which I wore a navy Oxford University sweatshirt as I carried textbooks across the lawns of Magdalen College. The one in which I had classmates who didn't know me as a famous missing person or the younger sister of a supermodel, but as Iris Hollow, medical student. The one in which I had a girlfriend or a boyfriend and kissing them didn't feel scary. The one in which I went punting on the River Cherwell and drank cider at summer picnics with my friends and spent long hours studying in libraries built inside the hallowed halls of old churches.

A future that, at this moment in time, felt like it was slipping away—but I had my sister back, and that was what mattered more than anything.

"That thing has taken everything else from me," Cate said. "I'm not going to let her take you too. *Tell me* where you are. You are mine, not hers. Do you hear me? You are *mine*."

"Are you talking about . . . Grey?"

"Stay away from her, Iris. Please. Wherever you are, just get away from her. You are not safe, you are—"

"Cate. Stop. I'm *not* leaving her. I'm not abandoning my sisters."

"Don't trust her. Run. Listen to me. Please. You have to run. Run. *Run.* She is not—"

I hung up and pressed the heel of my hand against my mouth to keep from sobbing. My phone vibrated with an incoming call. A picture of my mother and me together filled my screen, my opaline hair and pale forehead pressed close to her flushed cheek, her mop of dark curls. We were both smiling. Our features were startling in their dissimilarity. The call ended, and then my mother called again, and again, and again. I blocked her number.

My mother had called my sister a *thing*. My mother had told me to run from her.

I didn't know what to do with that, except swallow my revulsion and lean back against the wall. The house was quiet. The three of us were together. Grey was alive. That was enough.

I savored the calm for a handful of minutes—then I typed *minotaur* into Chrome and tapped *Go*. The search returned images of a hulking demon bull with an axe, cartoonish in its size and evilness. It was frequently depicted with washboard abs, cloven hooves, and glowing red eyes. Nothing like the man who was following us.

The Wikipedia article recounted the Greek myth, of a flesh-eating monster trapped at the center of a labyrinth by the master craftsman Daedalus. I scrolled down. The Minotaur appeared in Dante's *Inferno*, which piqued my interest—it was one of Grey's favourite books—but the mention was brief, and Dante and Virgil passed by it quickly. Picasso included the creature in several of his etchings. There were Minotaurs in *Dungeons & Dragons* and *Assassin's Creed*. Useless.

Under the *See also* section, there was a list of comparable entities: I tapped on *Ox-Head*, "guardian of the Underworld in Chinese mythology," and read about it and Horse-Face, two guardians of the realm of the dead who captured human souls and dragged them to Hell. I navigated back and tapped another name I vaguely recognized: *Moloch*. "A Canaanite god associated with child sacrifice." I pressed my lips together and skimmed the entry: archaeological evidence of children sacrificed in Carthage, Cronus eating his children.

I stopped at the Peter Paul Rubens painting that had been included alongside the text: *Saturn Devouring His Son.* In it, a naked male god with gray hair and a gray beard bent over the small child he held in his hand, his teeth ripping at the flesh of the baby's chest.

"*Jesus,*" I whispered.

I put my phone down and ran my hands through my hair. I needed a shower. I needed to sleep.

I went upstairs. There were two bedrooms, though one was unfurnished and the double bed in the other was stripped of sheets, its bare mattress stained and sagging. The girl slept, I figured, in the nest of fetid blankets in the corner of the room, its layers lined with leaves and bits of paper. I knelt and unfolded a square of newspaper, a clipping that had turned brittle with age. *Missing Child,* the headline read, followed by a black-and-white photograph of a little girl. Underneath, the caption read: *Eleven-year-old Agnes Young, the only daughter of Phillip and Samantha Young, has been missing for five days.* I trailed my fingertips over the girl's face, over the familiar white cotton nightdress she wore. Another clipping was the death notice from last year of one Samantha Young, aged ninety-six. *Reunited with her beloved daughter, Agnes, at long last,* it read. I folded them both and put them back where I found them, my thoughts snagging on the dates.

I sat in the shower for a long time after that, my knees tucked up to my chin, arms wrapped around my shins until I was curled as tight as a river stone beneath the falling water.

I cried. Not a lot and not easily, but a few hard sobs clutched at my ribs and squeezed me. I cried for the days Grey had been missing and I cried in relief that she was here and I cried for myself, for the life I had worked for and the life I wanted, the life that seemed so fragile now. I cried because my mother thought my sister was dangerous and I cried because a part of me knew it was true.

I felt better when I was done. I changed back into my sweaty T-shirt and jeans, my skin protesting at the salt and grime clinging to the fabric.

Tyler took first watch while Vivi and I slept on the living room floor next to Grey. The day was unseasonably bright for winter in Edinburgh. The room was hot from the boiler, and the air felt close and stank of rotting forest, but none of us had really slept the night before, and the nights before that had been riddled with stress and waiting and wanting, so we both fell into heavy, dreamless sleeps. I slept more deeply than I had in weeks, my fingertips pressed to Vivi's wrist on one side of me, Grey's throat on the other. The rhythm of their pulses like a metronome.

I woke through a hazy curtain sometime in the afternoon when the girl—Agnes—came back. I watched her for a little while as she sat in a chair by the front window, the shotgun resting across her lap. When I woke again, it was night. The house was dark, but there was a light on in the kitchen and the hushed voices of Vivi and Tyler—made soft and giddy at the edges, I guessed, by several servings of alcohol—drifted through. I put my palm on Grey's cheek. Her fever had broken sometime during the afternoon and her skin no longer felt sodden. When I peeled back the bandages on her arms, the flowers were wilted, the wounds they grew from almost healed.

"Hey, kid," a gravelly voice whispered.

I looked up. Grey's eyes were cracked only a sliver, but she wore half a smile.

"You're awake!"

"Shhh," Grey said, laughing weakly. "I just want a few more minutes of peace before I have to get up."

"I thought you were dead," I whispered as I buried my face in her neck. "I thought you were dead."

"Hey, hey. No. I'm here. I'm here."

"There was a body in your apartment. There are people following you. A man who wears a bull skull on his head. The little girl—Agnes—says he'll be able to find you here."

"How long have I been out? We should probably get back on the road before he tracks us down."

"Who is he? What does he want from you? Did he kidnap us when we were children?"

Grey ran her fingers through my hair and tucked a strand of it behind my ear. "No, he didn't take us when we were children."

"You said in *Vogue* that you remember. You remember everything that happened to us. So what happened to us?"

There was a noise from the kitchen, a round of Vivi's snorted laughter. "Who else is here?" Grey asked.

"Vivi and Tyler."

"Tyler came?"

"We haven't been able to get rid of him."

Grey smiled. "Can I see him?"

"What are we going to do, Grey?" Where would we go now? How could we run from an enemy who would always be able to find us? Grey tried to speak, but her throat caught and she coughed. "Hang on. I'll get you some water."

I stood and stretched and went into the kitchen, where Vivi had stripped down to a crop top and jeans, her bare feet up on the table, a clove cigarette in her mouth and another tucked behind her ear. She and Tyler were playing cards and drinking whiskey. Vivi's wisteria tattoo had grown since I last saw it. It now twisted under her bra and around her rib cage, across the flat plane of her stomach and around her portrait of Lady Hamilton before it dipped below the waistband of her jeans. Purple water-color blossoms bloomed from the vines. Some of the leaves had begun to curl and blacken with rot. I wondered if she'd purposefully added to it, or if the ink had grown wild across her skin, unable to be stopped.

"Care to join?" Tyler said around one of Vivi's clove cigarettes. He, too, was shirtless in the warm kitchen. I tried not to let my gaze linger on him for too long.

"You two are playing poker and getting pissed on your watch?" I asked as I poured a glass of water from the sink.

"We both have extremely high alcohol tolerances," Vivi said.

"By that, she means we're high-functioning drunks who require at least a few shots of medicinal booze every day to remain operative. Really, getting pissed was the responsible thing to do," Tyler said. "How's Grey?"

"Awake," I said, then nodded at Tyler. "She wants to see you." Tyler stood so quickly that his chair toppled over behind him. I handed him the glass of water. "Take this to her."

"How is she?" Vivi asked.

"Weak. I'm so used to her being strong. It feels wrong to see her like this."

"Well, thank God she's awake now to tell us what to do. If I had to make *one* more decision . . ." Vivi mimed her head exploding.

"Where's Agnes?"

Vivi looked puzzled. "Who?"

"The little girl."

"Oh. The kid climbed up on the roof with the gun. Said if he's going to come, he's probably going to come at night. Thinks she's Clint Eastwood or something."

"I'll take her some tea." There was no kettle, so I put a pot of water on the stove and waited for it to boil. "Grey's fever has broken," I said as I searched the cupboards for cups. "We should get out of here as soon as she's strong enough. Preferably *sober*."

"Yeah, yeah," Vivi said as she leaned over the table to peek at Tyler's cards.

I found two mugs in the sink, crusted with grime. They looked familiar: raw clay on the outside, green glaze on the inside, imperfect handles. *GH* stamped on the bottom, the mark of their creator: Gabe Hollow. Grey must have brought them here from London. I put my hands around one, cupping its form, holding it the way he must have held it as it turned beneath his fingers on the wheel. My hands, exactly where my father's hands had once been.

I stirred dark leaves into them both.

Tyler and Grey were huddled together on the couch when I went back in the living room, her head against his shoulder, his fingers in her hair. I lingered on the stairs and listened to them speak softly to each other, relieved whispers of *I missed you* and *I love you* and *I'm sorry* drifting to where I stood. I continued upstairs to find Agnes. She was in her room, sitting on the roof just outside her window, blackened feet still bare even in the caustic cold that had settled in after sunset. I handed her one of the steaming cups of tea. For a moment she hesitated, but then she took it.

I crawled through the window and sat next to her and looked out over the city. The sleet light of the winter sky had turned the world grayscale. For a while, we sipped in silence.

"You were there," I said finally. It was a guess. "You fell through. To the same place my sisters and I ended up when we were children. Except you didn't get to come home like we did. You got stuck." Agnes sipped her tea and didn't disagree with me, so I continued. "Then Grey found you and brought you back somehow—but wherever you were, you'd already spent too long there. It got inside you. Changed you."

"The Halfway never lets you go," she said. "Not really." The tea had wet her throat, smoothed over the roughness. For the first time, she sounded almost like a child and not like something wild. "It's supposed to be a one-way ticket. Things that end up there are not supposed to be able to find a way back."

"What is it? The Halfway? My sister seems to think it's somewhere between life and death."

"Your sister is right. It's a liminal place on the borders of the living and the dead—though I thought of it more as a kind of hell. Everything that dies passes through there. People, animals, plants. Most things move on quickly, as they're supposed to, but some things get stuck. Humans, usually. The ones who can't let go, or who are mourned too deeply by those they leave behind. There's an old folk song—'The Unquiet Grave.' Perhaps you know it?"

I breathed into my cup. My breath rose off the surface of the tea and sent a warm, moist cloud to linger about my face. I did know the song. In it, a woman died and her lover mourned her so hard, weeping by her graveside for a year, that she couldn't find peace, couldn't move on. Was Agnes saying that the grief of the living could disturb the dead, could trap them in a slip of space between life and death? "How did you end up there if you didn't die?"

"When I was a child, I was playing in Holyrood Park at sunset. There were old chapel ruins there that people said were haunted. My parents had banned me from playing there, but I was curious. I heard a voice on the other side of a ruined doorway. I followed it. I ended up somewhere else and I couldn't find my way back. Sometimes the veil between the living and the dead grows thin. Sometimes the dead speak to the living and lure them through."

"Is that what happened to us too?" I whispered.

Agnes sipped her tea. "You disappeared on New Year's Eve?"

"At the stroke of midnight."

"Between one year and the next. It makes sense. The veil is thinnest at liminal times. Sunset, sunrise, midnight." Agnes looked like a child, but didn't speak like a child. She had been missing for decades. I wondered how old her mind was. "If you were near a ruined door, perhaps you heard the dead calling. Perhaps you followed."

"We were in the Old Town, on a street where a house had burned down a few weeks before. It was all destroyed—except for the front doorframe. That was still there, freestanding."

Agnes nodded. "A door that used to lead somewhere, but now leads somewhere else."

"You came back. You're like us."

"I am not like you. You must understand, by now, that you are different. Why are you so beautiful, do you think? So hungry? So able to bend the wills of those around you? You are like the death flowers that grow rampant in your wake: lovely to look at, intoxicating even, but get too close and you will soon learn that there is something rank beneath. That's what beauty often is, in nature. A warning. A disguise. Do you understand?"

"No." Yet I did understand, on some basic level. The purple, otherworldly petals of the monkshood flower concealed poison that could deliver instant death. Poison dart frogs were pretty as jewels—and one gram of the toxin that coated their skin could kill thousands of humans. Extreme beauty meant danger. Extreme beauty meant death.

"There is something in your blood that lets you slip between the place of the living and the dead—and back again—as you please."

"Well, then, how did you get back?"

"Runes written on my skin in your sister's blood. The rune for death." Agnes took my hand and drew a shape on my palm with her finger: a line with three prongs at the bottom in the shape of an inverted arrow. "The rune for passage." Agnes drew the shape of a capital M. "The rune for life." This time, she drew the inverse of the first rune: a line with three prongs at the top. "Grey figured it out. I don't know how. An incantation in blood and language to allow the dead to slip through to the world of the living."

"You're not dead, though."

"No. The man that hunts you is, though. I can stay here because I belong here—I never died—but he can only cross over temporarily using Grey's blood and the runes."

"What makes us different? Why were we able to come back? Why does our blood let us come and go as we please?"

"Your sister is a wily one. A trickster. A wolf in sheep's clothing." Agnes reached out to trail a gangrenous fingertip over the scar at my throat. "Do you think there is any terrible thing she wouldn't do to save you? Any line she wouldn't cross? Any sacrifice she wouldn't be willing make?"

"Tell me. Tell me the truth."

"Your life would be happier if you didn't know."

"Knowledge is power."

"And ignorance is bliss."

There was a muffled yelp from downstairs then, followed by a thump. Agnes snatched her hand back from my throat. We looked at each other for a moment, each questioning the other: *Did you hear that too?* There was silence for a few heartbeats. Then Vivi's scream bolted us both into action. I scrabbled to get inside, but slipped down the old roof tiles. Agnes was faster than me, smaller and more nimble. She was already on the stairs by the time I hauled myself through the window, my limbs windmilling and adrenaline slamming. I heard glass break; a gasp of pain; Tyler swearing. I took the stairs three at a time and stuttered to a stop on the last one behind Agnes, who was standing with her shotgun aimed across the room.

The man had found us. In one hand he held Grey by the hair, her chin lolling on her chest, her hospital gown a Jackson Pollock painting of blood and vomit. Vivi, still dressed in a crop top and jeans, was hefted over his shoulder, biting and clawing and kicking, trying to break free. Tyler brandished a broken wine bottle and was trying to stab it into the man's chest, but he was too slow, his reflexes softened at the edges by booze. Then he caught one of the horned man's fists full in the face and collapsed, boneless, to the ground.

Agnes screamed. The man looked towards us. Agnes pumped the shotgun and, without hesitation, pulled the trigger. The gun went off and made a stippled mess of the man's shoulder, but he didn't bleed. He grunted and dropped Vivi and let Grey go, then came barreling towards us. Agnes shot again, but the man was furious now, and even a second shot that tore a chunk of dead flesh from his neck and sent shattered particles from his bone mask flying like grains of rice wasn't enough to stop him. He slammed both of us into the wall, the wood and plasterboard tearing like paper beneath our weight. It was suddenly dark and I couldn't breathe, the heft of two bodies on top of me, a pile of rubble digging into my neck, the soft parts of my back. Then the weight of him was gone and I sucked in a breath. The world blurred and rippled around the pain. I coughed up a wad of blood and spat it to the side.

We'd burst through the wall and were sprawled out on the kitchen floor. I pushed Agnes off me and stood, trying to ignore the too-limp feeling of her body, the ugly angle of her neck. None of my limbs were broken, but whenever I inhaled, a bright pop of pain in my ribs made me gasp. I staggered back through the hole in the wall—which, I noted dully, was filled with crawling things and black mold. Tyler was slack on the floor, one side of his face bloody and sunken. The room was trashed and the front door was open.

Both of my sisters—and the man—were gone.

I didn't stop to check if Tyler was alive. I fished Grey's knife out of my coat pocket and lurched down the front steps onto the street. There was a sharp, tugging pain across my collarbone that brought tears to my eyes. Somewhere, not far away, Vivi was still fighting, giving the man hell. I could hear her strangled shrieks, the slap of her fists against his skin, just around the corner. "Vivi!" I tried to scream, but the impact had crushed something in my lungs, in my throat, and I couldn't get out more than a wheeze. I tried to run but kept teetering sideways if I moved too quickly. A concussion, maybe.

Then Vivi's screams abruptly stopped midway, fizzling out

like hot metal plunged into water. I turned the corner, half expecting to find the man standing over her lifeless body, but the street was empty. I caught the scent of smoke and rot. A handful of dry leaves curled across the cobblestones towards me.

There was nothing else.

They were both gone.

They had both been taken.

"No," I rasped, limping down the street. "No, no, no, no, no."

They could not be gone.

I would not allow them to be gone.

Not both of them.

Not again.

I banged on doors and windows, wheezing a broken animal moan. "Vivi! Grey! Vivi! Grey!" I rattled door handles and rang bells. Lights came on in windows. Sleepy residents came to their doors and swore at me. *Didn't I know what fucking time it was?*

Somewhere, not far from where I stood, my sisters had been dragged through a crack in the world. I didn't know how to follow. The one person who did—a little girl with rotten limbs—was, I suspected, already dead. Tyler might be too.

Something tightened in my chest, picking holes in my lungs. I couldn't stand anymore. I sank to my knees in the middle of the street, struggling to suck air past my broken ribs, and cried with my forehead pressed against the cobbles until I heard sirens.

17

I HOBBLED BACK to Agnes's house in a daze, before the police arrived to arrest me. What could I say to explain myself? *Well, you see, Officer, my sisters were kidnapped and taken to a mysterious limbo for unknown reasons. I suspect this is not the first time it's happened.*

I closed the front door behind me, then drew the curtains and turned off all but one light.

Tyler was alive. Agnes was not.

He sat on the kitchen floor next to her small, broken body, crying quietly. There were flowers teeming from her eye sockets, vines growing from her mouth, lichen colonizing her face and neck. I sat down on the other side of her and put my hand on Tyler's bare shoulder. We sat like that for a while, both of us with tears running down our cheeks. Then I crossed Agnes's arms over her chest. Her skin already felt desiccated, her joints creaky and dry. Carrion flowers grew from under her nail beds, cracking and peeling the fingernails to make way for their blooms. Ants and beetles had already made their home in the soft hollows of her face. The pungent stink of her made the warm kitchen air taste green, wild.

Tyler looked at me. One of his eyes was shot with red, a burst blood vessel. The cheekbone beneath it jutted awkwardly, broken and pressed painfully against the skin. His expression was one of searching. Asking.

I shook my head. "He took them," I managed to rasp. "I couldn't follow. I . . . I lost them . . . I lost them both."

Tyler said nothing.

We burned Agnes's body in the fireplace. It seemed wrong to leave her abandoned on the floor of an empty house, her death unnoticed and unmourned. When I lifted her, she was light and hollowed out, like a long-fallen tree. We burned her wrapped in her blankets and used the newspaper clippings she slept with as kindling. It didn't take long. The pyre smelled not of flesh and hair, but of smoking greenery and forest fire.

I hoped that, wherever she ended up now, she was at peace.

"I suppose you have a plan," Tyler said as he buttoned up his floral shirt. "You Hollows always seem to have a plan."

I shook my head. "Grey's the planner. Not me. I'm a follower. I didn't even fight. I just . . . stood there while Agnes shot him. I let a *kid* defend me."

"Well, not fighting it turned out to be a good idea," Tyler said as he touched his fingertips to his broken cheekbone. "Look, you are Grey's sister. You are as strong and smart and, frankly, as terrifying as she is. How do we follow them?"

"I don't know."

"You do know, because you've been there before. *How do we follow them?*"

I let out a frustrated exhale. "How do you get to the land of the dead?" I was certain that that's where we were trying to go: a strange sliver of space between here and nothingness.

"I suppose dying would get you there, though that seems to be a very permanent solution."

I locked eyes with him. "It wasn't for you."

"Yes, well. I'd rather not do *that* again."

"That's fine," I said, already making my way towards the stairs. "I can go by myself. I'll fill the bathtub, you can hold me under until I die, then give it a minute or so and do some CPR. I'll find them." Hadn't I seen that in a movie or read it in a book? It had worked then—why wouldn't it work now? I wanted Tyler to say yes before my adrenaline waned and I chickened out. My heart was beating so fast, I felt like I might vomit it up. I was already imagining the terrible moment my burning lungs sucked in a flood of water while he held me, thrashing, under the surface.

"Iris," Tyler said, pulling me back. "I won't drown you. Don't ask me to do that."

I snatched my hand away from his. "Do you want to save her or not?" I yelled, because I felt my courage breaking. Didn't I always think I was willing to die for my sisters? Here was an opportunity—was I too weak to take it?

"We both have to go," Tyler said. "Together."

I sighed and softened. "Your eye looks terrible."

"Well, I did take a right hook from a demon, bang in the socket. Frankly, it's a miracle I'm not dead. My delicate bone structure was not built for physical combat."

I grabbed an old bag of frozen vegetables from the freezer and threw them to him. We should both go to the hospital, but there was still a tinge of something otherworldly in the air. I thought, if we didn't follow them tonight, we might not ever be able to follow. We would forget that impossible things were possible. It was now or never. It had to be.

I pulled back the curtain an inch and looked into the sloe-black Edinburgh night. Somewhere out there was a door to another place, a crack in the world into which girls and boys slipped, never to be seen again.

Well, almost never.

The three of us had come back, somehow. We had found a way.

"Did Grey ever talk to you about what happened to us when we were children?" I asked Tyler as he pressed the vegetables to his face. The flames of Agnes's body had simmered down to smoke and bone.

"Of course not. I would have immediately sold the story to the *Daily Telegraph* if she'd told me the truth." When I glared at him, Tyler rolled his eyes. "I'm kidding. It was off-limits to even ask."

"Did you ever wonder?"

"Oh, I wondered. I grew up reading the Reddit threads and watching the unsolved-crime specials the same as everyone else. *Of course* I wanted to know the answer. Sometimes when she was drunk, she talked about it in a vague way, like it was a thing that had happened to someone else. It was almost like . . . a dark fairy tale about three sisters who fell through a crack in the world and met a monster who did something terrible to them."

"What did the monster do to them?"

Tyler stared at me, peas still pressed against his face. "I don't know for sure, Little Hollow. But I can imagine. Can't you?"

I went to pick up the shotgun from where Agnes had dropped it. I'd never held a gun before and it felt heavier and more lethal than I expected.

"So where are we going?" Tyler asked.

"Back to the beginning."

"Stop speaking in riddles, for Christ's sake. What does that *mean*?"

"Look, whatever happened to us happened here first, in Edinburgh. It happened in the Old Town, not far from here. There's a door there. Or, at least, there used to be. A door that used to lead somewhere, but now leads somewhere else. We're going back there. We're going to find a way to follow them."

I watched a YouTube video on how to load a shotgun while Tyler stuffed Vivi's backpack full of some meager supplies scavenged from Agnes's kitchen. We put on our coats—his ridiculous, mine functional—I slipped Grey's knife into my pocket, and then we set off.

Outside, Edinburgh was steeped in predawn darkness. We headed towards Saint Giles' Cathedral, in the direction of the narrow street I had disappeared from. We walked, shivering, through the Old Town's warren of narrow lanes, retracing my steps from that night, though I knew them not from memory but from snatches of police reports and the witness statements of my parents.

Grey's energy was here, though it was no stronger than a whisper. She had been here, though not recently. Years ago. I felt Vivi's energy too, and my own. Yes, we had come this way.

And then we were there. *The* street. The stone walls were close on both sides, and I could see all the way to the end. I could understand why the police thought it impossible for three children to disappear from right under their parents' noses: because it *was* impossible.

"I know this place," I said quietly. "We were here visiting our grandparents for Christmas. We were walking down this street right as the fireworks were going off. My parents were just behind us." I ran my hands over the bricks. Being here felt wrong, like we were disturbing the dead. "This one," I whispered, looking up at a stone terrace. It was newer than the others. The brick was milk and bone, not yet covered by centuries of grime. "This is the one."

There was a bronze plaque set into the cobblestones to the right of the front door. *Here, on this spot in January 2011, sisters Grey, Vivi, and Iris Hollow were found alive and well after being missing for 31 days.* Our names had been burnished gold, presumably from all the tourists who came to this place and rubbed the bronze for luck.

The memories I had were slippery; they kept sliding through my mind, slightly different each time. I was no longer sure which ones were mine and which ones had been stitched in from elsewhere to make a more complete picture. Did I remember walking down this street that night? Or did I only remember coming back?

"It had burned down a few weeks before the night we went missing," I said. "It was just a shell back then."

Tyler nodded. "Yes, we've all seen the pictures."

"There are pictures?"

Tyler stared at me. "You *haven't* stalked yourself online?"

"I try to avoid reading anything about the catastrophic disaster that destroyed my family, actually."

Tyler sighed, pulled out his phone, and googled *hollow sisters disappearance*.

The picture he showed me had been posted to r/Unsolved-Mysteries on Reddit and appeared under the title *I was in Edinburgh the day the Hollow sisters vanished and have a bunch of pictures from the street they were on when it (supposedly) happened. Thoughts?* The poster went on to state that there was no way, in his humble opinion, that our parents' story could possibly be true. His charming theory was that our mother had sold us to sex traffickers and then panicked and repurchased us a month later when the heat from the media got to be too much. While the hypothesis was bunk, the pictures of the street from that day seemed real enough. I thumbed through them and then scrolled down to read some of the comments.

I'm sorry, but there is just no way—NO FUCKING WAY—that three kids could disappear from this street if their parents were actually there watching them. I don't know what they stood to gain or how they hid their daughters from police for a month, but Cate and Gabe Hollow were absolutely in on it.

> I'm willing to bet you don't have children of your own. You can be actively watching your kids and then, poof, nothing. They are sneaky little bastards. Case in point: I have a three-year-old son. Yesterday, I was following behind him in the grocery store. (He likes to point at stuff on the bottom shelves and guess what it is. "Is this pasta? Is this pasta? What about this, is this pasta?" Newsflash, kid: Unless you're in the pasta aisle, it's usually not pasta. Hours of fun.) Anyway, he turns a corner into the next aisle, so I follow him—except he's not there when I get there, or in the next aisle, or in the

next aisle. I found him ten minutes later on a bench in the car park, waiting with a nice old lady. His disappearing act immediately made me think of the Hollow sisters and has honestly changed my mind about the case. My theory: The girls walked ahead of their parents, took a wrong turn, got lost, then got found by an opportunistic predator who got cold feet a month later.

> Yeah but there aren't even any corners on this street. It's not like they ran ahead and turned a corner and then they weren't there. Cate Hollow has maintained that they disappeared from this street while she was on it. Two seconds, she says. For two seconds she turned her head to kiss her husband, and in that time, her three daughters vanished without so much as a peep? I'll say it again. NO FUCKING WAY.

"I don't need to read conspiracy theories about my parents," I said as I handed Tyler's phone back to him. "I can tell you right now: They weren't involved."

"Keep reading, would you?" Tyler insisted.

I scrolled down to the next comment thread.

Okay, the freestanding door is creepy af. How have I not seen this before?

> Reminds me of the search-and-rescue guy who posted about random staircases deep in the woods. Cate Hollow said the three girls were playing right near the burned-out house the last time she saw them. I wonder if that has anything to do with it?

> I can't remember where the folklore is from exactly, but I've heard stories of people (mostly children) disappearing after walking through freestanding doors they found in the forest. There were ruins near my grandparents' house growing up that we were banned from going near because three kids had disappeared from there over the years. Kids being kids, we went to investigate once and found nothing but a door just like the one in Edinburgh. We were so creeped out, we ran all the way home and didn't go back.

> Reminder that this is a thread for genuine theories, not fairy tales. Let's not let this devolve into a thread about alien abduction (again).

> Sure, sure. That being said . . . Anyone brave enough to try walking through it?

> Alas, it's not there anymore. It was demolished a few weeks after the girls came back and has since been rebuilt. But yes, obviously, lots and lots of people walked through it in the month that the Hollow sisters were missing: police, volunteers, forensics, etc. Again, it's not a door to Narnia.

> Damn it! My dreams of making sweet, sweet love to Mr. Tumnus are once again dashed!

I scrolled back up to the photograph the original poster had included. It was a low-quality image taken a decade ago on a crappy camera phone, grainy and strangely cropped. It depicted the blackened remains of a stone house, taped off, some bricks gagging onto the sidewalk. The freestanding doorway *was* creepy. It emanated wrongness. I, too, had heard stories about abandoned staircases in the woods and how people had been warned not to go near them for whatever reason. I'd seen pictures of some of them; they felt out of place and otherworldly. The burned-out door had the same effect.

I couldn't remember the night we disappeared very well, but I remembered the night we came back. I remembered standing in this exact spot, naked and shuddering between my sisters. I remembered Grey whispering something to me, whispering something to Vivi, tucking a strand of hair behind each of our ears. I remembered how the cold made my skin tight and numb, made it feel like it belonged to someone else. I remembered how we stood stock-still, not speaking, as we waited. I remembered a young woman turning down the street and screaming and dropping the bottle of wine she held when she saw us in the dark. I remembered her running to us, draping her heavy coat over my shoulders, yelling for the neighbors to call the police as she struggled out of her sweatshirt and gave it to Vivi. I remembered red and blue flashing lights reflecting off the slick cobblestones. I remembered the ambulance ride to the hospital, the three of us sitting pressed together on a stretcher, draped in aluminum blankets and harsh light. I remembered how Grey refused to let the nurses take her blood and how, when they tried to convince her, she'd freaked out and they'd backed off, whispering things like "Haven't they been through enough already?" I remembered the way Gabe held Vivi's little face in his hands after he scooped her up, his expression going from elated to searching and then to confused, like he already believed in that moment that we weren't quite right.

I remembered that Cate carried Grey out of the hospital the next day, her little legs wrapped tightly around our mother's hips.

I remembered Grey looking back at me over our mother's shoulder as we headed into the light, safe in the comfort of her arms.

I remembered the way my sister held eye contact with me for a moment, the spark of a grin at the corner of her lips.

I remembered that she winked.

I could remember so much, but I couldn't remember where we had been only minutes before the woman found us on the street.

That part was gone. Everything before it was a black abyss.

"The door," I said. I zoomed in on the picture. Even though it was slightly out of focus, I could make out white flowers growing at the base of the stone. "It's still the place, even though it's changed," I told Tyler. "I can still feel her. I can feel all of us." I put my hand on the glossy black door of the rebuilt house. "We passed through here. We came this way."

I could feel it. I felt Grey's pulse in the wood, weak as a bird's heart.

I took a deep breath and swallowed my revulsion. I had spent much of the last ten years trying to forget this place. I had poured my studies like cement over the radioactive thing that had happened to me here in my childhood and that continued to poison me. I had ached to be older. To be finished with university, to have a career, to be preoccupied with the small stresses of daily life that adults were always complaining about. Bills. Taxes. Health insurance. The dentist. I wanted the years to fill and stretch and stack, to put as much time between myself and this place as possible.

And now here I was, back again, trying to follow my sisters wherever they had gone, to the place I had sworn to never return to.

"It has to work," I whispered to myself, staring at the door. "It has to work, it has to work, it has to work."

I turned the handle. It was unlocked. I pushed the door open and stepped inside.

"Hollow," Tyler growled. "You can't just go wandering into strange houses! Get back here."

"No," I said. I was too far into the hall for him to drag me out. "I'm not leaving until I find them."

My jaw was quaking. I pressed my lips together.

"They're *obviously* not here," Tyler said. "This is just a house!"

My throat was thick. I knew he was right because I could feel it. Grey and Vivi weren't here and hadn't been here for a very long time. The energy they'd left behind was ten years old, crumbled to dust. The thing that linked me to them felt thin and weak, but it was all I had. I pressed forward into the dark hall.

"I will leave you here," Tyler whispered, but his feet were moving forwards to follow me. The hall smelled sour, of milk with base notes of urine. I knew that smell from the handful of babysitting gigs I'd done. A boiler was on somewhere. It congealed the baby odor into something oily and solid. The warm air cocooned me, felt too heavy after the February cold. Sweat prickled under my arms, on my palms. My cheeks were hot coins.

"There are whispers of us here," I said as I made my way down the hall, fingers trailing the wall. "In the foundations. We were here. This place remembers us."

The hall opened onto a softly lit kitchen and living area. A redheaded woman was sitting on a couch, breastfeeding a baby with her eyes closed.

I still had my palm on the wall, feeling the pulse of the stone. Tyler was tugging at the back of my coat, trying to get me to leave. The woman opened her eyes. Saw us. Tightened her grip around the baby, then stood and started to scream.

I crossed the floor in three strides and hooked a finger into the woman's mouth. The effect was instantaneous; I might as well have plunged heroin into her veins. The woman's muscles relaxed, and she folded into me like she was lovesick, her head nestled on my shoulder, the baby pressed between us.

I was breathing hard. I had not done this thing for a long time. Not since the photographer. I had never done this thing intentionally. It had always been a cursed power, far out of my control. A thing that made me weak, like Grey said.

I wasn't sure what had changed, except that I was furious, a barb of rage twisting at the center of me. My stomach was filled with blood, my mouth slick with venom. The other two times that I had compelled people, I had been vulnerable and unsure, and my attackers had fed on that.

Now, this time, I was the one who would feast.

"What's your name?" I asked the woman.

"Claire," she answered.

"Tell me where my sisters are, Claire."

"I'll tell you anything you want," Claire whispered softly. Lovingly. She kissed my collarbone, but tears were streaming down her face. There was fear in her eyes, but her lips betrayed her. "I'll give you anything you want."

"Tell me where Grey is. Tell me where Vivi is."

"Gray," the woman said. "Gray is . . . the color of stones and the sky during a storm."

"Tell me where she is!"

"Bloody hell, Iris!" Tyler snapped. "She doesn't know!"

Tyler pulled me back from the woman, who reached out to touch my face even though her lip was trembling. I shook Tyler off.

"Three little girls went missing from right outside your house ten years ago. Did you know that?"

"Yes," Claire said. "Of course. Everybody knows that."

"Do you know where they went?"

"No."

"Shit!"

Claire's baby started screaming. "When it happened," Claire said as she slipped her nipple into the baby's mouth, "my grandmother kept me close for weeks. A little girl had gone missing when she was growing up, and my grandmother thought the same thing had happened to those sisters. 'Stay away from Saint Anthony's Chapel,' she said. 'Stay away from the door, or you will end up like Agnes Young. You will end up like the Hollow sisters.' So I did. I stayed away."

A chill rolled over me. "Don't remember this," I ordered her. "Forget that we were here."

"Of course," Claire said as she stroked my cheek, the baby snuffling as it suckled at her chest. "Of course."

Tyler yanked my jacket again, and this time I let him drag me back into the hall.

Out on the street, we saw Claire watching us from her front window, her baby crying again as she juggled it over her shoulder, trying to soothe it. The spell had broken as soon as she could no longer smell me, and she stared at me now in the dark with a look of confusion, as though she was experiencing intense déjà vu. I knew the feeling of that look; it was something I regularly suffered myself. The feeling of knowing you had memories about something but were unable to access them.

I shuffled off Vivi's backpack and flicked through Grey's journal with shaking fingers, looking for something I was sure I'd seen before. And then, there it was—a detailed sketch of a freestanding stone wall, into which was set three windows and a door. Beneath it read *Saint Anthony's Chapel, Edinburgh—July 2019*. The same door Agnes had fallen through.

I typed *Saint Anthony's Chapel* into Google Maps and set off into the dark, Tyler swearing after me that I was reckless, stupid, just like Grey. Yet just like he had followed Grey, he followed me. I felt the power in that. We hurried through the Old Town, along Cowgate and Holyrood Road toward Arthur's Seat. The dawn was coffin-cold, the streets wisely abandoned in favor of warm beds and sleep.

My hands were numb and my breath short by the time we arrived. The ruins of the chapel sat on a squat hill overlooking a small loch in Holyrood Park. Beyond that, the lights of the city dotted the land toward the sea. The ruins were two stories tall; only the corner of the chapel remained now, the walls rendered in rough stone in some century long passed.

Saint Anthony's Chapel was now nothing but a single wall, the north side of a ruined church. There were windows, but most importantly, there was a door. It used to lead somewhere, but now—maybe—it would take us somewhere else.

Tyler and I stood panting, staring through the doorway, both knowing how crazy this was. We were far too old to still believe in fairy tales, and yet here we were.

We'd come this far; no matter how insane it was, we had to know. We had to try.

I checked the weather app on my phone for the exact moment of sunrise: 7:21 a.m. The veil between the realms of the living and the dead was thinnest at dusk and dawn, when the world was on the edge of day and night.

We waited in the winter cold until the sky began to lighten at the edges and then we held hands, both knowing that if this didn't work, we had nothing. There were no more clues to follow.

The air around us was bitter enough to make our teeth chatter, but it in the minutes leading up to sunrise, it smelled strangely burnt. At 7:20 a.m. we stepped closer to the door.

"Wait," I said to Tyler. "Are you sure about this? I don't know how it works. There's no guarantee we'll be able to get back. Even if we do, once it gets inside you, you can't get rid of it. It will change you."

"I'm coming," Tyler said. "I'm sure."

The sky was lightening quickly then. The first sliver of sunlight would fall over us in under a minute, and then it would be too late.

"Please work," I said. I squeezed Tyler's hand, took a deep breath, and stepped over the threshold with him.

18

I WAS SEVEN the first time I slipped from the land of the living to the land of the dead.

The second time, I was seventeen.

I stepped through a broken doorway that once went somewhere, and then went somewhere else.

The first change I sensed was the smell. Somewhere between one inhale and the next, the air became tainted. The clean scent of Edinburgh—grass and sea and stone—was usurped by smoke and wild animal and rot.

We stepped from dawn to dusk.

From cold to humidity.

From ruins in Scotland to ruins . . . elsewhere.

I blinked a few times and tried to get my vision to adjust. My stomach turned, an untethered sac inside me. I tasted fat and metal. My skin fizzed, prickling with the remnants of whatever violent energy had brought us here against the rules of nature, living things transported to a dead place. Tyler was already bent double, elbows on his knees, the contents of his stomach leaking from his mouth and nose in a sour waterfall.

We were in a dying forest. Hazy light filtered through the wiry canopy to the ground below, which was covered with long grass, rotting leaves, and white petals. Tyler groaned and sank to his hands and knees, then vomited some more, flecks of it splashing over his fingers. I stumbled away to keep from puking myself, feeling hungover and shaky. I squatted and cupped my hands over my mouth and tried to take deep breaths to weaken my nausea, but the pain in my chest kept sparking with every inhale.

"God," Tyler said as he crawled away from his vomit and collapsed onto his back in the grass. "Dorothy and Alice and the Pevensie children didn't suffer like this."

I couldn't help myself. "I didn't know you could read," I said through my fingers. My stomach tightened and my vision jittered like I was drunk, but the sick burn was almost worth it.

"You would kick me when I'm down?" Tyler said, almost in a whisper.

I peeled my fingers away from my face and forced myself to take a deep, fetid breath.

"Why do I feel so god-awful?" Tyler dry heaved a few times. "And why does it stink so badly?"

It did stink. It stank of rot and smoke, each breath sticky yellow on my tongue. It stank of my worst memories and worst nightmares come to life. I knew this smell, because I had been here before.

The Halfway.

"It's putrid," I said. "It's a slowly rotting canker somewhere between the realms of life and death." A decaying tooth, lodged deep at the back of the mouth. A gangrenous limb, turned swollen and black from a lack of blood supply. A dying thing, soft and bloated and bleeding, but still attached by thin threads to our living world.

The forest around us was thick but decomposing and misshapen, stuck in a perpetual state of decay. The tree closest to me was soft with rot, its roots arthritic, its trunk split open and oozing what looked very much like pus. A threadbare smattering of leaves still sprouted from its sagging branches, but they grew gray and moldy, and when they fell, they landed in blighted fens on the forest floor.

Above, the sky was flush with gunmetal light. Vivi had said that in Grey's stories, the sun never set in this place, nor did it rise. The sky here was jammed halfway, always on the precipice of dusk. The shadows were always stretched and sunken, full of twilight things.

The wood was sick. The wood was angry. It did not feel welcoming.

There was a low moan of faraway wailing in the air, something that sounded almost human but not quite. For a moment, I thought it was the trees, whispering to each other. The ruins of Saint Anthony's chapel looked almost the same here as they had in Holyrood Park, still a freestanding church wall of harsh hewn stone, except here they were in a forest and were covered in dollops of mold and carrion flowers. Through the door, I could see only more hazy woods.

We had fallen through a crack in the world.

This is where we had come as children and wandered for a month. A place of the dead. What had happened to us here? Why had we stayed so long?

"How can a *place* be dying?" Tyler asked, but I wasn't watching him. I was looking at his vomit. It had started sprouting flowers. How long would it be before this place crawled inside him and started nesting?

"Oh shit," Tyler said, his gaze set on something behind me. He sat up and grappled with Agnes's shotgun as I spun around. There was a pale man standing in the trees not far away. Dead-eyed and sightless, a slick of dark gloss where his irises should be. Runnels of liquid leaked from his orifices: his mouth, his nose, his eyes, his ears. He was naked and his skin was thick with a garden of green and white lichen.

There were clusters of others behind him. At first I thought they were statues, effigies in the shapes of men and women, sitting in tree roots, standing in the long grass. They reminded me of the death casts of the victims of Pompeii, all captured in moments of movement that had, very suddenly, ceased. The Halfway had grown on them, in them, had pulled them apart from the inside out. Some were so fresh they had fabric decaying on their bodies, and a few still smelled like people: of sweat and oil and the sharp tang of urine. Others were much older, and so misshapen it was hard to tell they'd once been human apart from the teeth and nails and clumps of hair erupting from knots of wood.

"What are they all doing?" Tyler asked.

"I think they're drawn here by the door." All of them were facing toward it; some were even reaching out to it. "Agnes said the veil is thinnest at sunset and sunrise and that sometimes the dead whisper to the living. Maybe it goes both ways. Maybe they can hear and smell life, but they can't cross over, so they wait here—forever."

"They're all dead?" Tyler whispered.

I approached the closest man and moved my hand in front of

his face. Something registered beneath the dark veneer of his eyeballs, and his black irises slid in my direction. Though his body had ossified and his skin had the texture of rough-hewn stone, there was still something locked away inside him. "They're whatever is left over after a person dies." I looked around the wood once more, understanding: Agnes had said that everything that dies passed through here.

These people were ghosts, as were the trees. Everything here had lived, once, in our world and gotten stuck here in the Halfway after they died.

I set off into the forest, weaving through the sea of frozen spirits. "Try not to wake them," I said to Tyler.

"Do you think all the dead are here?" he asked quietly as he trailed me. "Do you think Rosie is here?"

"Everything that dies passes through—but only those who can't let go get stuck."

"Part of me hopes she's here. So I can . . . see her. Say sorry. If I could just see her one more time . . ."

I wanted to say: "Don't hope for that fate for her." But I said nothing. If Grey or Vivi died, I would want to see them again.

"Do you hear that?" Tyler asked. "Running water."

We followed the sound over a small rise and found a milky green river bordered on both sides by brushwood and dead weeping willows that drooped like tangled hair into the water. The water moved quickly and was swollen with bodies that drifted along with the current. Men. Women. Children. All of them naked. All of them with wide black eyes.

A river of the dead.

"Oh God," Tyler said as he gagged.

"We should move quickly," I said as I stared at the flowing

water. "We shouldn't stay here. Get in, get my sisters, get out. I can feel them." I'd felt them since the moment we stepped through. Grey and Vivi's presence was stronger here. Not close, but tangible at least, a ropy tug around my heart. My sisters had been here before—and so had I. Not to this exact part of the afterlife, but here. All I had to do was let my feet carry me to them.

"This seemed like such a good and noble idea ten minutes ago," Tyler said. "I forgot that I'm not a good *or* noble person."

My sickness was fading now, replaced piece by piece by the thrill of our plan having *worked*. We were *here*. We had *done* it. And there, seeded beneath the excitement, was something else: the sense of familiarity.

The answers to long-asked questions felt suddenly possible.

"Let's go," I said. When I started walking, I knew it was in the right direction.

Toward my sisters. Toward some answers.

☾

We walked for what felt like an hour through the wood. Or was it two hours? Time moved strangely here. Dusk continued to fall and fall and fall, but night never came. Tyler complained about the smell and the damp and the throbbing pain in his face and the destruction of his expensive clothing until I told him to shut up, please, for the love of God, shut up. The pain in the side of my chest nagged at me, a needle pricking against my lungs anytime I breathed too deeply. The rest of my body was covered with slow aches that crept in and nestled in all the bruised parts of me, making their homes there, throbbing in time with my heartbeat.

For a time, we saw other doors, all freestanding and half-ruined, held up by nothing. Stone archways and burned timber, doorways back to desolated parts of our world. Around each of them we found clusters of spirits turned to wood and stone, things that had once been human but were now only memories. I wondered about the people they had been before their souls had gotten snagged here on the way to death. What did they long for so badly that they had been unable to let go? Love? Power? Money? The chance to say sorry?

It was near one of these doors that I spotted the first swatch of fabric: a torn strip of red-and-black tartan, tied around a low tree branch. I stumbled toward it. Despite a few spots of mold, it looked out of place against the forest: red and man-made where everything else was green and gray.

"I know this pattern," I said as I rubbed it between my fingers. I thought back to the photograph I'd found in Cate's bedside drawer what seemed like a lifetime ago now but was really only a week. "I was wearing this coat when I went missing."

"I can see your terrible taste in clothing hasn't changed in over a decade" was Tyler's contribution to the discovery. "What *are* you doing?" he said as I weaved through the trees and the statues of the dead, moving outward in a circular pattern, looking for another flash of red.

"Testing a theory," I said.

"Well, I'm sitting," he said.

A few minutes later, I spotted what I was looking for and grinned. I went back to Tyler—who was, indeed, sitting cross-legged on the ground—and pointed through the trees. "There," I said. "Do you see it?"

"More decomposing forest? Oh, yay."

I smacked him gently across the back of the head. "Look harder."

"Another one?" Tyler asked. Just visible in the distance through the trees was another strip of red fabric, hanging limply. "So what?"

"Bread crumbs," I said breathlessly, giddy with the thrill of the clue. I moved toward the next strip of fabric as fast as my broken ribs would let me. "Don't you get it? We came this way as children, and we left bread crumbs to find our way—"

My next step did not find ground but air and I suddenly found myself tumbling through mud and forest, down a slope, until I came to lie faceup in an inch of fetid water.

"Are you alive?" Tyler called from somewhere above.

All I could do was let out a low moan. Pain cascaded through my side and wrapped tight around my lungs. I heard him sigh and start to make his way down the bank.

"Can I leave you behind if you die or do you expect me to be heroic and drag your corpse home?" Tyler asked.

It took him a few minutes to reach me, which suited me fine, because I had no desire to move. I lay in the water, drawing shallow breaths as I waited for the pain to ebb. Eventually, the sting in my bones loosened enough that I could prop myself up on one elbow to see where I was.

"Oh," I whispered. The water I'd fallen into was black and smooth as glass. Distended bodies floated on its surface for as far as I could see. They paid me no mind. When Tyler slid down the bank, they blinked open their black eyes and watched him, but they didn't come crawling from the water to attack us.

"Well, we are obviously *not* going in there," Tyler said as he reached me and helped me stand, then turned to scrabble his way back up the bank. Drowned trees grew out of the water, bone pale and stripped bare of leaves. It was a marshland of some sort, a dead place inside a dead place.

"Wait," I said. I pointed to what I wanted Tyler to see: another red-and-black way marker called us deeper into the fen.

"No," he said as I took a step into the water. *"No."*

☾

Eventually, of course, he followed. There was only one thing more frightening than wading into a swamp of the dead, and that was being on your own in this place. Our feet sank into the ankle-deep water and mush as we trudged over spongy ground. Here, the tree branches sagged into the shallows, making the terrain hard to traverse. It seemed darker in this part of the forest. The trees seemed wilder. The going was slow. Things moved around us, unseen. Bodies bobbed by, eyes flicking open like lamps as we passed. We abandoned our coats to the marsh; they were too heavy to carry. I tucked Grey's knife into my bra and folded my jeans up to keep them out of the water.

We came across more ruins sunk into the marshland. Not doorways now, but low stone walls ground down to hip height by age. The bricks that made them were crumbling into the moor, greedily devoured by hungry tree roots. Soon we began to see other structures, tumbledown stone houses that were infected with lichen, their windows smashed and trees bursting from their roofs. Many were surrounded by decaying stone walls. I'd seen a documentary on ghost towns once, about how nature slowly reclaims signs of human habitation and leaves only eerie remnants behind. Roads eaten through by vegetation. Unkempt buildings withered by sun and wind. Concrete dissolved by rain, terra-cotta red roofs caked in grime. That was nothing compared to the utter desolation of these ghost houses. The forest crept in and around them, tearing them apart, but they also rotted from inside, sagging into the water, their walls collapsing into soft masses of putrefaction. And in each one, the spirits of the dead drifted from room to room, window to window, unable to let go or move on.

The hours bled together. There was no sunrise, no sunset, no time. We walked until our legs ached and we began to drift into sleep standing up. I hadn't eaten since Vivi brought me breakfast the morning before and my hunger was a chasm inside me. We steered clear of the empty shells of houses, cautious of what we might find inside. We followed the tartan way markers deep into the marsh, where the water was hip-deep and so dark I couldn't see my fingers in it if I submerged them. Fog curled across its surface, squeezing our visibility to no more than six feet.

Bodies drifted everywhere. The twisted skeletons of dead things floated by. I lifted the skull of a bull from the water and stared into the hollows where its eyes should be.

And then the fog curled back like a curtain to reveal her.

A child sat cross-legged and naked on a low mud island, her dark hair stuck to her back in wet curlicues. Tyler and I both stopped when we saw her through the haze, afraid of catching her attention, but she already seemed to have heard us and half turned her head in our direction. She was sweet-faced and very young, perhaps only six or seven. I could see webs of veins beneath her sodden flesh. Her black eyes reminded me of spider eyes. There was mud and reeds matted into her hair, mud leaking out of her ears, as though she had recently emerged from the water.

"Rosie?" Tyler said quietly.

"Oh my God," I breathed as Tyler thrashed through the shallow water and sank heavily into the mud in front of the girl.

In front of his sister.

19

"No," Tyler said as he cupped Rosie's small face in his hands. The last time he saw her, he would have been younger than her, smaller than her. Now he was a grown man and she was still a child. Her face fit in his palm like a piece of fruit. "No, no, no, no, no. Why are you here? Why are you here, Rose?"

Rosie mirrored Tyler's gesture. She reached out to stroke his cheek, leaving a stripe of mud beneath his swollen eye. There seemed to be a flash of recognition behind her dead eyes, a moment of sadness and longing that crinkled her young brow. That was all it took. Tyler scooped her out of the mud and held her like a baby against his chest.

"What are you doing?" I whispered as he waded back into the water, in the direction of the next way marker.

"I'm bringing her with me."

"You can't bring her home."

"Why not?" he snapped. "*You* came back. *You* got your sisters back. Why shouldn't I get mine?"

"Because . . . she died, Tyler," I said gently. "Rosie is dead. She can't come back."

"You said she wouldn't be here!" he yelled. "You said she had no reason to be caught here! Why is she here, Iris? Why did you lie to me?"

"I thought—because she's so young. What unfinished business does a kid have?"

"I left her once. I'm not leaving her again," Tyler whispered, and then he was striding ahead through the water and mist, his dead sister clinging to him like an insect. "I can see something!" came his voice a few moments later.

Ahead of me, another house appeared from the vapor. It was a roofless stone structure built on a slip of island. Water lapped at the stone wall built around it. Like everything else in the Halfway, it was abandoned and tumbledown, overrun by a fever of flowers. Windows smashed, bits of it sliding into the water. A rudimentary gravestone had been erected on one side of the yard.

And there, fluttering on the twisted metal that passed for the front gate, was a strip of red tartan from my coat.

It was still dusk, the haze rolling across the swamp tinted the color of late evening. If it were not for the stink and the thousands of bodies floating in the marsh, the place might have been beautiful. We stood for a long time, watching and waiting in the stillness, and then we took a silent loop around the place, peering through the windows for signs of habitation. No shapes moved in the half-light. The house appeared empty.

As we stood in the water, I took out the journal and handful of drawings Vivi and I had saved from Grey's apartment, back when I had understood less of our story. I shuffled through the pages. The fifth page was the one I was looking for: a sketch of a tumbledown house with broken windows and withered stone walls and a strip of tartan fluttering from the front gate.

I held it up next to the house Tyler and I stood before. It was a match.

We had been here before. Grey had been more than once, had come back to sketch the place.

Whatever had happened to us as children had happened here.

"I'll go in," I said, "and make sure it's safe."

"Do you want me—" Tyler began, but I stopped him.

"No. I want to do this alone."

We walked up to the house together, out of the marsh onto drier ground. Tyler put Rosie down on a carpet of carrion flowers, where she resumed the cross-legged, dead-eyed position we'd found her in. "Call me if you need backup," he said as he sat next to her.

I tried to steady my breath. My stomach squirmed the way it does when you're watching someone watch someone else in a horror movie.

There wasn't much to the house, if you could call it that: It was a single large room, with rusted pots and cracked stoneware collected around the hearth and broken wooden furniture scattered about the place. I kept waiting for a cascade of memory and understanding. Here, in this pile of fetid blankets—is this where we had curled up together, limb on limb, seeking shelter far from home? Here, by this fireplace—had we warmed our hands, dreaming of a way back to our parents?

I had spent so many years trying not to think about what had or hadn't happened to my sisters and me in this room. Something that had changed us. Something that had sent us home with black irises and scars at our throats.

I knelt by the hearth and reached my hands out as if to warm them. Three dark-haired children by the fire, each wearing a different colored coat. Yes, that felt right. I swept ash and debris away from the pale hearth stone. There was dried blood here. Generous pools of it, like an animal had exsanguinated and its life force had soaked into the floor.

I took Grey's knife out of my bra and unfolded it. Grey, with a knife in her hand, no fingerprints on the handle but her own. Yes, that felt right too. *Do you think there is any terrible thing she wouldn't do to save you?* Agnes had said. *Any line she wouldn't cross? Any sacrifice she wouldn't be willing to make?*

I followed the blood across the floor. It was faded now, hardly more than a shadow—and then I saw something out of place. A tuft of wine-colored fur, caught on a nail in the floorboards. It came loose when I tugged it. I rolled it between my fingertips. It felt synthetic. It felt like it could have come from the Bordeaux faux-fur jacket Grey had been wearing the night we disappeared.

The nail it had been wrapped around wiggled like a baby tooth. I pulled it out of the floor with my fingertips and used Grey's knife to pry the board up. The hole beneath it was deep, dark. I put my arm in up to the elbow and felt nothing but cool air. Thoughts of needle-sharp teeth sinking into my flesh made me snatch my hand back. Gingerly, I tried again, up to my shoulder this time, until my fingertips brushed against something *furry*. I yelped and scurried back from the hole. Nothing moaned. Nothing came crawling out after me.

"Everything okay?" Tyler called from outside.

"I'm fine," I answered. "I think I've found something."

I put my hand in again, twisted my fingers around the fibers, and lifted. I pulled them out one by one: a child-size green tweed duffle. A small Bordeaux faux-fur jacket. What remained of a little red tartan coat with gold buttons. Each was stiff with dried blood. A gruesome amount of dried blood, what must have been cups and cups of it soaked through and gone dark and moldy with age.

The police had never found these items of clothing, despite extensive searches for them.

I knelt back on my haunches and held the stiff garments in my arms like children, searching, searching, *searching* my memory for what they meant.

Something terrible had happened to us here—and someone had gone to the effort of trying to hide it.

Grey, with a knife in her hand, its sharp edge dripping blood.

Grey, forehead scrunched as she concentrated on stitching the wound at my throat.

Grey, holding my hand as she led me through the forest to a door.

Grey, tucking a strand of hair behind my ear on a freezing street in Edinburgh and leaning in to whisper, "Forget this."

Forget this.

Forget what?

Forget what, forget what, forget *what?*

My mind dipped over and over again into the black depths of missing memory, each time coming back empty-handed.

I stood with the garments still in my hands and went back to the front door, my blood warm and crackling in my veins. Rosie was where we'd left her, but Tyler knelt by the gravestone, an odd expression on his face.

"I think you need to see this," he said.

I joined him in front of the overgrown grave marker by the side of the house. I used Grey's knife to cut away the lichen and vines and flowers growing rabid over the names, already suspecting what I would find there.

The first name had been scratched roughly into the stone.

GREY

"No," I said, frantically cutting more greenery away. *"No."*

A second name appeared beneath the first.

VIVI

I scrambled back across the muddy yard, a low moan coming from somewhere deep inside me, the kind of keen you make when you're trying to wake from a nightmare but can't.

"We're too late," I sobbed. "We're too late."

"That makes no sense," Tyler said. "These are old. They've been gone for a day at most."

"Time moves strangely here. It gets snagged. We must have . . . missed them somehow."

Tyler frowned at the grave and bent to pull more greenery from the headstone. There, beneath the names of my sisters, was a third name I hadn't noticed in my panic.

IRIS

"Unless you're a remarkably solid ghost, it seems there's been some kind of clerical error," Tyler said.

I crawled forwards and started digging up the soil with my bare hands. "I need to know," I said. "I need to know who's buried here."

"Look," Tyler said as he knelt beside me. "What you need is some sleep." I knew he was right, but I ignored him and kept digging. "Can't you do the magic thing?" he asked. "The energy

237

thing where you're like, 'Oh, she's definitely been here, I feel it in my bones.' Try that."

I put my hand on the earth and reached out for the thread that bound me to my sisters. "They're not here," I said. I could feel them, closer now than when we first came through the door, but still some distance away. "It's not them."

"Then maybe," Tyler said gently as he pulled me up from the dirt, "this is a mystery that can wait until after you've had a kip. There is really only space for one person on this team to freak out at a time, so I'm going to need you to pull yourself together. Okay, Little Hollow?"

"Okay."

Whoever was beneath the gravestone bearing our names, it wasn't Grey and it wasn't Vivi and it wasn't me.

So who was it?

20

WHEN MY FATHER started getting ill, I would often wake to find him standing at the foot of my bed, watching me. The first dozen times it happened, I startled awake in the darkness and yelped for my mother. Cate would come and tell Gabe to go back to bed, then hold me in her arms until I stopped shaking and fell back to sleep.

"Papa is just sleepwalking," she tried to convince me. The first few times, I believed her—but Gabe kept coming back, and each time I woke, his expression was darker, filled with more fear and loathing than the last. Eventually, I stopped screaming. I would open my eyes in the dark and find him there. I would watch, expressionless, as tears slipped down his cheeks, my tiny heart shivering inside my chest.

Sometimes, after he died, I had nightmares about him in which he stood at the end of my bed with a weapon and watched me with those cold, hate-filled eyes.

Why did someone who was supposed to love me look at me like that?

When I woke in that house in another world and saw a figure in the room, drowned in shadow, I didn't cry out. I stared at it, at *him*, the tall man who wore a bull's skull to hide his face.

I watched him as he watched me with dead black eyes and felt a flicker of recognition at the rage and hatred radiating from him.

I scrabbled back and tried to sit up. Too slow. Tyler lifted his head from where he slept, but the man was already on me. He stank of death and acrid smoke. Beneath the bone mask he wore, half shattered now by the shot Agnes took, I caught glimpses of skin, teeth, eyes: a man. Just a man. He grabbed a handful of my hair. I grunted and kicked him in the groin. The man loosened his grip and I rolled out from beneath him, my broken ribs stabbing a needle of pain that left me unable to breathe. Tyler was standing now, looking on with wide eyes.

"The gun!" I gasped as I crawled away, toward the front door. I tried to stand, but the pain in my lungs was too sharp. Tyler was yelling. Then hands twisted their way into my hair again. The man slammed me forwards. My forehead smacked against the floor and my vision shuddered. Tyler was struggling with the shotgun. I dug my fingernails into the man's skin, but it was dry and rancid, and he didn't seem to notice the pain. He yanked me up and began dragging me out of the house, toward the water. I tried to catch my breath, tried to untangle my hair from his grip.

Tyler followed behind me, still fumbling with the shotgun. The man was hauling me through the mud, toward the water's edge.

Finally, finally, Tyler pumped the shotgun and pointed it in my direction.

"Shoot him," I rasped. "Shoot him."

There was a pop of gunfire. Shots punched into the trees around me, but if they hit the man, they had no effect on him. The violence with which he handled me was horrifying. We hit the water. I thrashed, sucking in mud and water. Tyler shot again. This time, the shot hit him full in the face, entirely shattering the bone mask. For a split second, I saw the man's face, the face he'd been trying to hide from me. Then he let me go and melted into the mist. I sank beneath the surface, breathless and panicked as I swam away, sure he would come back for another go. I broke the surface and sucked in air and screamed "Help!" I wasn't far from land. Tyler was already thrashing through the water and trees toward me, and then I was in his arms, being tugged back toward the muddy bank.

"Move, move, move, move, move," he was saying. I kicked my legs hard.

"Did you kill him?" I asked—but how could you kill a man who was already dead?

"No," Tyler said as he dragged me back onto land. There was blood everywhere. My blood, I realized, slipping out of a wound on my forehead.

"You're alive, you're alive, you're alive," Tyler said as he squeezed my face, crushed me to his chest, squeezed my face again. Then he was on his feet once more, shotgun aimed into the marsh. "Where is he? Did you see where he went?"

"I don't know," I said between coughs. I was shaking. The taste of mud and marsh water lingered in my mouth, and there was an oily feeling all through me. I wanted to cry and vomit to get it out, but I could do neither. "I don't know. I just—he let me go. I saw his face. I saw his face. I know who he is."

A shadow moved between the trees, sending ripples across the water toward us.

"Fuck off!" Tyler yelled at the forest. He tried to help me stand, but the mud was slick, and I slipped backward, gasping as pain rocketed through my broken ribs again.

For a few tight breaths, it seemed as though nothing would happen. We watched and waited. I thought: *Maybe he won't come.* And then he came.

He no longer bothered with his disguise. He emerged from the water in his true form, and I saw him fully for the first time. His eyes were dark sacs and his lower jaw hung loose, at an odd angle, from where Tyler had shot him. The skin of his face was decaying to reveal stripped-bare bone and teeth. His skin was webbed with pockets of decay, and his hair was tangled with water weeds. I could see exposed tendons in each of his joints. The inside of his mouth was black as ink.

I put my hand to my lips.

"Gabe," I said quietly through my fingers.

Gabriel Hollow. My father.

He moved toward me slowly, the eyes he kept trained on me bulging from his skull. My chin was shaking. Tears slipped down my cheeks, but I didn't run, didn't look away.

"Run," Tyler whispered as he backed away, but where could I run?

I breathed steadily and kept my eyes on him. No sudden movements. Perhaps he expected me to run, to fight, and I was doing neither of those things. He was so close now I could smell the dead-flesh stench of his breath.

Then Rosie was there, in front of me. Tyler must have draped her in Vivi's old coat while I slept, because it now hung loose about her shoulders. She screamed, a defensive animal scream that kept going and going.

My father stopped to look at her, his focus on me broken.

"I have them," he said—then he backed away and was swallowed by the mist.

"What *the hell* is going on?" Tyler demanded as he helped me stand.

"We have to dig up the grave," I said to him shakily. "I want to know who's in there. I need to know."

"That's what you want to talk about right now?! The grave?! Your dead father has been trying to kill you! Your dead father kidnapped your sisters!"

"Please," I said. "My ribs are broken. I need your help."

"No. Absolutely not. I shan't." But Rosie was already tugging him toward the gravestone, and he followed her through the mud back to the side of the house.

We dug with our hands, the three of us.

It didn't take long to find them, despite Tyler's swearing and complaints. They weren't buried deep, under less than a foot of earth. I knelt by the grave and pulled damp soil back with my left hand as Tyler and Rosie dug, my broken ribs demanding to be felt.

They were wrapped in a blanket, together. We coaxed them from the earth, loosening them slowly, but the soil gave them up easily, as though it wanted them gone. As though they didn't belong in this place. We placed them gently on the earth by the hole we had dug. I unfurled one side of the blanket and then the other, my heart beating furiously as I wondered who was buried in the shallow grave marked with my sisters' names.

With my name.

There were three of them. Three small bodies, each turned mostly to forest now. Their bones were twisted roots and all of the soft parts of them—eyes, mouth—were thick with carrion flowers, but they were still in the shape of people. Still had teeth, still had fingernails. They were the bodies of children, curled up together. Each of them wore an identical heart-shaped gold locket dangling from what remained of their necks. I held the necklace of the smallest and wiped the mud away with my thumb to reveal the engraving beneath.

IRIS, it read. The body it belonged to was missing its two front baby teeth. I unclipped the locket from the dead girl's neck and held it up for Tyler to see.

"What does it mean?" Tyler asked as he watched the gold heart spin slowly in the half-light.

"It means . . ." I looked up at him. "I'm not Iris Hollow."

21

I WANDERED IN a daze back into the dark water that lapped at the wall around the house and waded in until I was hip-deep. Tyler thought I was mad—"Your father is still out there!" he shouted from where he stood by my grave—but I was covered in blood and mud and the remains of dead children and even though the water was black and cold, I lowered myself into it until I was fully submerged. I stayed under until my aching lungs urged me to the surface a minute later.

Alive. I was alive. My heart beat fast and pumped warm blood around my body. My lungs drew breath. I was alive—and Iris Hollow was not. The child that had fallen through to this place ten years ago had never left. I was sure of that now. The dark-haired girl who'd disappeared on New Year's Eve a decade ago was buried in a shallow grave a few meters away.

Something else had come back in her place.

Something that had looked almost like her, but not quite.

A changeling.

Me.

"What do you mean, 'I'm not Iris Hollow'?" Tyler asked as I made my way back to shore. I examined my own hands as I waded through the water, then touched my fingertips to the scar at my throat. The pustule had gone down, whatever angry thing that had been nesting there quiet for the moment.

"What if my father wasn't crazy?" I said. I thought of Gabe, of the morning he'd killed himself. I thought of Grey's small hand on his arm in the car and the way she'd ordered him to take us home. The air had smelled sweet and potent.

I squatted in the mud. My stomach felt wet and shuddery. I tried to keep my breathing steady. "He knew," I said. "My father knew that we weren't his daughters. He knew from the moment he saw us." I wiped my hand on my wet jeans and then pressed my fingers to my teeth. *Gabe Hollow continues to insist that all three children's eyes and teeth have changed.* "He was convinced that we were impostors. Things that looked like his children but weren't really. I think he was right."

"Are you suggesting you're not . . . human?" Tyler asked. "Then what does that make you?"

"I don't know."

"If you're not Iris Hollow, why do you look like her?"

"I don't know that either."

"Well, *try* to explain it," Tyler said.

"It's not just that I don't remember the month that we were missing. I don't remember anything from before the night we were found. It's all *gone*, the life I had before. My grandparents, my cousins, the house I grew up in, my friends at school, the TV shows I liked to watch. It all disappeared. When I came back, I was a blank slate. We all were."

Tyler looked disbelieving. "You can't not remember *any-thing*."

"I remember *nothing*. It's like I was born the night I was found. There was only darkness before that, and then someone switched on a light, and that is where my memory starts."

Tyler's expression softened. "You were seven. You were young. I hardly remember what I ate for breakfast yesterday. I mean, I don't eat breakfast, but you know what I mean."

"Do you know how my father died?"

"Yes," he said quietly. I wondered if he knew because Grey told him, or if he knew because he'd read about it on the internet.

I thought of the note Grey had pulled from his pocket when we found him, the note she'd torn into shreds so our mother wouldn't find it: *I didn't want this,* it had said.

What if Gabe really hadn't wanted to die?

What if . . . what if Grey had *made* him?

Because she knew. Of course she knew. Grey knew that she wasn't Grey.

She remembered everything.

"There are three little girls in a grave wearing necklaces with our names on them. What if, in the story Grey tells about what happened to us, we were not the three little girls?" I said. I met Tyler's eyes. "What if we were the monsters?"

☾

I fastened Iris Hollow's locket back around her neck before I reburied her with her sisters. When it was done, I put my palm against the soft dirt that entombed them. "I'm sorry," I said to all of them. "For whatever happened to you. I'm so sorry." Rosie stood statue-still at their grave, still draped in Vivi's green tweed coat, while Tyler went inside to fetch Vivi's backpack.

There would be no more tartan way markers to follow now, but that didn't matter—I knew that we were getting closer to Vivi and Grey. *My* Vivi and Grey. Whatever linked us together told me that.

"Wait," Tyler said as I set off into the marsh once more. He was close behind me, but Rosie hadn't moved from the grave.

Tyler went back and knelt in front of his sister. "Come, my darling," he said, tugging her hand gently, but Rosie shook her head. "Don't . . . you want to come home? You can see Eomma and Appa. They miss you so much. You can see Selena and Camilla. They're all grown up now. You would be so proud of them. Lena became an architect and Cammy is a pediatrician. She just had a baby girl a few weeks ago. She named her Rosie, after you. I think you'd like her. You can play together, you can go back to school, you can do all the things you—"

Rosie reached out and placed her fingers against Tyler's lips to quiet him. "Let me go, Ty," she rasped. It was the first time I'd heard her speak. Her voice was small and sweet, her throat dry from years of disuse.

Tyler shook his head, his lips mashed together to keep from breaking down. "No," he said. "No, I want you to come home."

"Let me go," she said again, still gentle, her small hands stroking the sides of his face.

Tyler's ribs were convulsing with silent sobs now. Tears tracked down his cheeks, and his jaw quaked. "I'm staying with you," he managed, his voice thick with pain. "I'm not leaving you again. I'm staying right here, like I should have the first time."

Rosie smiled and leaned in to whisper something in Tyler's ear. Then she looped her arms around his shoulders and hugged him tightly. Tyler was crying hard now, the type of crying you usually do alone in the shower when you think no one can hear you.

And then, suddenly, the green coat she had been wearing dropped to the ground and Tyler stumbled forwards, his hands sinking into the mud.

Rosie Yang's soul was untethered from her brother's grief.

Rosie Yang was gone.

☾

We walked through the Halfway for an another eternity. We rarely spoke to each other as we fell into a monotonous slog, one foot after the other. After a time, the marshland dried up and we found ourselves on solid ground again. We took off our wet shoes and slung them around our necks by their laces to dry. We inspected our darkening toenails, the way they had begun to pull away from their beds.

There were more rivers of the dead. There were more figures gathered around doors. The Halfway kept unfolding itself to us, stretching on and on and on.

I was glad for the ache in my bones, the sharpness in my chest. I was glad for each pluck of pain that would not let me sink too deep into my thoughts, because my thoughts were a well of horror.

You are not you.
Don't think that.
If you are not you, what are you?
Don't think that.

Three little girls fell through a crack in the world.
Three things that looked like little girls came back.
Don't think that.
What did Grey do to the Hollow sisters?
Don't think that.
What did you *do?*

We stopped to rest in the roots of a soft tree, its bark skin-warm and splitting with rot beneath our backs. I was exhausted. A prickle of bone-deep pain nudged against my thoughts with every movement from my ribs. I wanted to cry, but I was too tired.

Grey and Vivi were close now. They were alive, both of them, but they were weak and fading. I worried that the thin thread that tied me to them might break if I slept, but my mind was running hot with fatigue and my body yearned for rest.

I collapsed back against the tree, then sucked in a hard breath through my teeth as a rocking wave of pain battered me again and again.

"Let me see your ribs," Tyler said. It was the first time he'd spoken in hours.

"Why?" I snapped, my eyes still closed. "What are *you* going to do?"

"I'll have you know that my mother and my older sister are both doctors. I have seen a splinted bone or two in my time. Now, do you want help or not?"

I sat up and begrudgingly lifted my shirt from my chest. I felt like a fragile thing, a baby bird. I wanted to go home to my mother. I wanted to take a shower and gorge myself on hot food and let Cate braid my hair as I fell asleep.

Tyler took off his mud-spattered floral shirt and began tearing it into strips. Beneath his shirt, his arms and chest were covered in tattoos, delicate imagery of angels and flowers and a woman's face: Grey's.

"Doctor mother, hey?" I said as he worked, drinking in the way his skin stretched tight across his abs, the way his collarbones pushed through his skin in a way that made me want to press my lips to the space where they met at his throat. "She must have been really excited about your modeling career."

"She was predictably and boringly disapproving. Such a cliché. She's made her peace with it now that I'm wildly successful, but I left home when I was sixteen. Also a cliché. Part of the reason your sister and I got on so well, I think."

"It's not easy to leave everything you know and strike out on your own. You must have some guts."

"Yes, well." He began wrapping the makeshift bandages around my chest. "More than I generally get credit for. It's hard being *ridiculously* good-looking. No one takes you seriously." He tucked in the end of the bandage and put his palm against my side. "There. All better. Actually, a bandage on broken ribs does precisely nothing, but at least it made me feel useful."

"And you got to take your top off," I added. "Win-win."

Tyler laughed. We were sitting very close now. Closer than I dared to get to anyone, lest they go rabid at the scent of me. Tyler took my hand in his and studied the lines of my palm. "Strange," he said as he trailed a finger over my life line.

"What?"

"Grey taught me how to read palms. You have the exact same kind of life line as hers. Look here, where it's snapped in two, with a gap in between."

"What does that mean?"

"If you believe Grey Hollow's Guide to Palmistry, it means

something changed. There was a before and an after. A rebirth, perhaps." His eyes flicked up from my palm to my face, then back down again. A shudder ran through me. I thought of the graves, of the three little bodies buried together.

"I'm glad you're here with me, Tyler," I said. I closed my hand around his and ran my thumb in slow circles over his knuckles.

"Well, I can't say I'm *thrilled* to be here myself, but as far as company goes, you're not horrible, I suppose."

"A rousing compliment, coming from you."

"It is, actually."

There was a moment of silence and stillness between us, and then I leaned in, slowly, to kiss him. I gave him time to pull back, to stop me if he didn't want it, but Tyler did not pull back, did not stop me. I put my lips against his, hovering there to see if he would go wild, but he didn't, so I kissed him harder, faster, brought my hand up to hold his jaw as my body came to life at the closeness. I savored, for a handful of seconds, the heat and softness of a kiss that was not filled with teeth and blood and hunger. Then I felt Tyler's palm pressed gently against my sternum. Pushing me away. I pulled back from him, but only a little.

"I love your sister, Iris," he said against my lips.

"I know." I pressed my forehead against his. "So do I."

I took a deep breath, inhaling the smell of him, and then I lay back in the roots of the tree and fell swiftly to sleep.

☾

When I woke, Tyler was still sleeping—and I had to pee. I wandered away from the tree where we rested, careful to remember my path back. The sound of running water came from nearby. I followed it and came across a brook babbling with movement, but the water was dark and smelled stagnant. I picked up a moldy stone and plopped it into the stream. It disappeared with a puff of white spores, swallowed by the water.

I squatted and peed in the undergrowth, watchful of the forest. It watched me back.

On my way back, my heart jumped at the sight of splashes of red nestled among the leaves. At first, I thought they were drops of blood, but no: They were strawberries. I knelt to pluck one from its stem, but I found it mushy to the touch, its insides putrid. I pressed it with my fingers. Worms and mold squelched out. I threw it to the ground and wiped my hand on my jeans.

There was nothing good here, in this place. Nothing untainted by decay. Agnes had been trapped here for who knows how long, with nothing to eat but rancid food and nowhere to sleep but the desolate remains of knockdown houses. No shelter. No comfort. No clean water or unspoiled food to fill her aching belly.

Why were we different? The Halfway had gotten inside of us, changed us—but not as catastrophically as it had changed others. We were not rotting. We had been allowed to leave.

When I came back to our camp, it was empty.

Tyler was gone.

"Tyler?" I called, but the wood was silent. Nobody answered me. I walked through the surrounding trees looking for some sign of him. Maybe he'd also gone to pee? "Tyler!" I shouted again, but again there was nothing. No birds fluttered. The trees were still.

Something felt wrong.

I ran back to the tree where we'd slept and yanked Vivi's backpack out from where I'd hidden it in the tree roots—this was definitely our camp, definitely where I had left him sleeping no more than fifteen minutes earlier. I riffled through the bag and found the knife, then worked my way through the woods around the camp again, shouting his name, my whole body shaking. Wherever Tyler was, he had the shotgun with him. I called and called and called his name but he didn't answer. Like Grey and Vivi, he was suddenly gone.

"Shit!" I spat. I kicked a tree root and then yelped at the pain that darted into my little toe. I shouldn't have left him.

How long should I wait for him to come back? If I left him here, I had no tether to him, no way to find him the way I could my sisters. If I left him here, I might never see him again.

I thought, in that moment, of my parents. I thought of the night we had gone missing and the terrible, gut-eating panic that must have consumed them.

In the end, I waited for what felt like an hour. Until something in me stirred, certain that Tyler was not coming back. That something bad had befallen him in the short minutes I had left him here alone. I used my knife to carve a message into the flesh of the tree, almost certain that he would never see it: WAIT FOR ME HERE.

Then I left him. I left him there, alone in the woods. I left him to whatever fate had come his way because I had no other choice but to press on and do what I had come here to do: find and save my sisters.

22

I WANDERED THROUGH the forest by myself. Beads of sweat rolled down my forehead, made my eyes sting. I was alone now, with no company and nothing to mark my way except the insistent tug in my chest that, yes, my sisters were this way, that each step brought me closer to them.

I tied strips of Tyler's floral shirt around branches, hoping I would be able to find my way back to him, until I ran out of fabric and had to press on anyway.

Things followed me in the everdusk, things that moved in the corners of my eyes but disappeared when I snapped my head in their direction. Wild dogs, maybe, or something stranger. Dead things with sharp teeth waiting for me to slow, to stop, to sit down.

I kept moving, kept my knife held at my side, but nothing came close enough to try me.

There were more knotted bodies of root and bone and hair: the shapes of dead children curled with their backs against trees, turning slowly to seed; women with their arms outstretched, reaching for something the moment they became more this place than human. There were more structures, too, sloughing into rubble. A junkyard of lost people and lost things.

I kept expecting to see Tyler somewhere up ahead or trailing behind. Whenever a twig snapped or a bird fluttered into flight, I'd swivel in the direction of the sound, momentarily hopeful—but it would only ever be some strange creature, watching me as our paths crossed: deer, cats, squirrels, all of them roaming freely in the half-light of the haunted wood. All were warped, in varying degrees of severity: black-eyed, covered in lichen, little gardens of flowers sprouting from the thick moss on their backs. Creatures from a terrible fairy tale. We would lock eyes for a moment, the animals curious about the intruder who smelled of a different place—who smelled alive—and then they would continue on in the dark, undisturbed by my presence.

My lower back and legs were aching by the time I came across the shoes lying discarded on the forest floor. A pair of Nike sneakers, new enough that I could tell they hadn't been in the Halfway for long. There was no rot, no mold, no decay.

I picked them up and turned them over in my hands. They were still tied together and the fabric was still slightly damp. They were Tyler's, the new ones he'd bought in Edinburgh after he'd lost his own shoes at the hospital in London.

Tyler had come this way. Tyler had dropped them here. A bread crumb left for me, perhaps? It was both comforting and ominous—we were headed in the same direction, but I was sure now that Tyler had not come of his own free will.

I turned in a slow circle, searching the forest for any other sign of him, but there was none. I tied the shoes to Vivi's backpack. When I found him, he would need them.

I kept moving. Time kept shifting in the odd way it did here.

I was weary by the time I reached the clearing, my head smacking with dehydration and hunger. My throat and eyes were grit-dry and my tongue tasted of smoke. If I ever made it home, I was sure my hair would stink of burning wood for weeks.

The clearing was not dissimilar to the one Tyler and I had first arrived in, the ground thick with a carpet of long grass and decaying leaves, and something monstrous in the middle.

"Oh my God," I whispered when I realized what I was seeing.

Grey and Vivi were here, both gagged and bound to stakes, their wrists tied above their heads. Bundles of wood and dried moss had been stacked at their feet. A swarming garden of carrion flowers grew on them, up their legs and around their torsos and through their hair, breeding on their skin, clustering around their mouths and eyes. I could feel the bird-wing flutter of their hearts, the warmth of them, the life of them, the hot blood that still thrummed through their bodies. Vivi's was stronger, redder, more vibrant. Grey's was a faded thing now, thin and thready.

There was a third stake set up between the other two, empty and waiting.

Our father meant to burn us all—but no.

Not our father.

Gabe Hollow was the father of three children buried by a crumbling house in a halfway world. The things he meant to burn—us—were not his children, but the creatures that came back in the shape of his children. Impostors. Cuckoos.

I took my shoes off.

"Damn," I said quietly at the sight of my feet, turning them this way and that in the low light, touching the sodden, tender flesh I found beneath my damp socks. My toes had begun to blacken. When I touched the nail of my big toe, it came away easily from its bed. There was no pain. A carrion flower bud had begun to unfurl from the bed of my toenail. I plucked the flower from my skin and crushed it between my fingertips.

I shoved my shoes in Vivi's backpack and moved around the edge of the clearing barefoot, Grey's knife at my side. I was more nimble without shoes. Years of trailing Grey had taught me how to move quietly across forest floors and down creaky wooden hallways alike. I tried not to look down at my feet as I moved. I didn't want to see the dying flesh.

Vivi was awake, moving, speaking to someone I couldn't see. "Let me go!" she muffled through her gag as she threw her head back. "Let me go!" Again, she snapped her head back against the stake behind her as hard as she could. I heard a crack. Vivi fell forwards, unconscious, the whole weight of her body borne by the bonds at her wrists. The back of her skull was bleeding. Grey stirred and lifted her head. Her black eyes met mine, unblinking. At first, I wasn't sure if she could see me or could just feel my presence.

Go, her eyes pleaded. *Go. Please.*

I shook my head. Grey's nostrils flared in anger, but there was nothing she could do to make me leave. I would sooner take my place next to them on the pyre than leave knowing I hadn't done everything I could to save them.

Tyler? I mouthed to my oldest sister. Grey took a few quick breaths without blinking, then shook her head. What did that mean?

No, she didn't know where Tyler was?

Or no, Tyler was already dead?

I didn't like the way she cowered. Grey Hollow, who feared no man, who went looking for trouble because she was the thing in the dark. It was wrong to see her tremble.

Then a figure appeared from the other side of the pyre.

"Tyler?" I whispered. Tyler turned to look at me.

Alive, alive, *alive*. Somehow, he'd found his way to my sisters and made it here before me. I stepped out from my hiding place and hesitated at the edge of the wood. I wanted to run to him and throw my arms around his warm chest. The relief at not being alone—not having to face this horror by myself—washed over me.

Grey was yanking hard against her bonds, screaming silently into her gag. Tears streaked down her face as she shook her head furiously.

When I reached him, Tyler said nothing. I studied his face. There was something wrong about his eyes. All of the features were right—the skin, the lips, the smug arch in his eyebrow—but something deeper was incorrect. The bones that had been knocked out of place by the Gabe's punch back in Edinburgh had snapped back to their correct position. The tattoos on his arms were warped, as though his skin had been wet and wrung out and redraped over his bones.

And then, when his lips parted, his mouth was wrong. The gums had turned black and the teeth had started to rot.

Gabe Hollow continues to insist that all three children's eyes and teeth have changed.

I stumbled back and looked him up and down. It was a close match. A very close match. So close that, if he kept his mouth shut, you might never know.

"No," I whispered. "You're not Tyler."

"You're not Iris," he rasped in reply—but it was not his voice. It was the voice of my father.

It was the voice of Gabe Hollow, coming from Tyler's face, Tyler's mouth.

Tyler's *skin*.

Gabe took a step toward me. I took another step back.

"What did you do to him?" I asked.

"The same thing you did to my daughters," my father's voice answered.

My gaze traveled from Gabe's face to his throat. Or rather, Tyler's face to Tyler's throat. He lifted his chin a little to give me a better look. There, nestled in the crook of his collarbone, was a fresh cut stitched with silken thread. Neat work. It would heal well, as mine had.

I took another step back, my mind dipping again into the abyss where understanding dwelled just out of reach. My heart beat hard against my sternum, my skin suddenly cold with sweat. All of the little puzzle pieces were laid out, waiting for me to put them together into a picture that made sense.

I was not Iris Hollow. I looked like Iris Hollow.

My father was not Tyler, but he looked like Tyler.

Gabe Hollow continues to insist that all three children's eyes and teeth have changed.

"How could you?" my father asked. "How could you do it to *children*? To helpless *little girls*?"

I glanced at Grey, who was crying hard now.

I turned back to Gabe. "I don't understand."

Gabe searched my face. "You know what you are."

"I don't. I swear."

He drew a finger knife across his neck, then mimed sticking

the fingers of his right hand in the wound and drawing the skin up, up, up over his head. My jaw shook as he stared at me, waiting for a reaction. "That thing you call a sister is a monster," he said as he pointed at Grey, "but at least she let you forget that."

Forget this, Grey had whispered to me. "Forget *what?*"

Gabe was circling me now. I tightened my grip on my knife. "That you are a dead thing walking around wearing the skin of a murdered girl," he said, his voice shaking. "That you went home to her family—to her bed, to her parents' arms—while she decomposed in a grave in a dead place. That you slipped her warm skin over yours, and then your sister stitched you up at the throat."

"That can't be true," I whispered, because it was gruesome and terrible and impossible—but I knew, even as I said it, that it could be.

That it *was.*

Gabe had known, from the moment he saw us, that something wasn't right. That something inside of us had changed. Different eyes, different teeth. A layer of skin beneath skin.

"After that thing made me kill myself, I ended up here," Gabe said. "I searched for my children. I found them where you left them. I buried them myself."

I didn't want this, his note had read—because he'd truly had no choice. Because he could not resist the compulsion of the changeling who'd taken up residence in his nest, who had pushed out his real children and ordered him—as she'd ordered the photographer who'd attacked me—to take his own life.

Another terrible truth crystalized: "You killed Tyler," I said. "You skinned him. You're . . . *wearing* him."

"I want to go home. I want to go back to my wife. I want to go back to the life the three of you stole from me."

A sweet man. A soft man. A man who made things with his hands. That was how Gabe Hollow had been remembered at his funeral. I'd stood at the edge of his grave and thrown an iris flower on his coffin as they lowered him into the ground, so that he'd have a piece of me wherever he'd gone.

I had loved him, even though he'd scared me.

My father flicked Vivi's lighter and held the flame over the tinder. "Join your sisters."

I sobbed. I had spent years missing this man. I wanted him to pull me into his arms and comfort me the way he had when I was small. I shook my head. "I can't leave Cate all alone."

"Please don't fight." Gabe's voice cracked. "Please make it easy for me."

"This isn't you."

There were tears rolling down his cheeks. "You don't know me."

"I do. I may not be your daughter but you are my father."

"Don't."

"I know that you are kind and gentle and you wouldn't hurt me."

"Please let me have this," Gabe begged. "Please get on the pyre."

"No."

"You burn with them. Or you watch."

Gabe dropped the lighter. The pyre sparked and caught. Sour smoke began to churn in seconds. Grey started to choke, thrashing against the rising flames.

I screamed and ran toward her, but Gabe caught me by the backpack and yanked me to the ground. I lost hold of the knife. In a second he was atop my body, his knee a barbed spike against my broken ribs, his fingers around my throat. It was quick and violent and ugly.

What would Grey do? What would Grey do? I thought as I lay dying. My nails clawed at my father's hands. My heels dug into the soft ground beneath me, trying to find purchase. My eyes bulged from their sockets. My head was full of blood and a creeping darkness that seemed to be spreading from my ears toward my eyes, thinning my vision.

Grey would fight. Grey would make him bleed, somehow. Grey would scramble for the knife that had landed just beyond my reach. Grey would rend flesh and break bones and salt the earth of your life if you crossed her.

She was screaming now, more for me than for herself. "Let her go!" she howled at Gabe, her words muffled by her gag. "I will destroy you!"

A clear thought made its way through the rising shadow in my mind: *You already have.*

Grey had destroyed this man, as she had many others. Grey was a tornado in the form of a girl. She took what she wanted and left a trail of destruction in her wake, and I had always admired her for it. It took guts to be a girl in this world and live like that. She did it because she was powerful. She did it because she could.

I thought of Justine Khan and her mouth on mine, her eyes wide with fear as she bit down on my lips. I thought of my father's pale form at the end of my bed, the way he froze when I opened my eyes, the way prey freezes when it spots a stalking predator. I thought of Grey walking along dark streets at night, waiting for men to catcall her or worse, waiting for someone to give her an excuse.

Grey Hollow was the thing in the dark—but as much as I loved her, wanted to be her, I wasn't like her. I couldn't bend the world to my will, because I didn't have the stomach to hurt people the way she did. That had always made me feel weak—but perhaps that was my strength.

What would Iris do? I thought as my field of vision narrowed to a pin.

I reached out and put my hand on Gabe's cheek, the way I had when I was a child, for those few easy, early weeks he had let me love him.

I couldn't remember being dead. I couldn't remember being trapped in this place. I couldn't remember slipping into the skin of his daughter. What I could remember was this: the warmth of Gabe Hollow's chest as he carried me from the couch to my bed after I fell asleep watching TV. The scent of his shirts, always a mixture of Danish oil and the bone ash tang of his pottery glaze. The cadence of his voice as he read me bedtime stories. The iris flowers he helped me press between the pages of books. How hard I had cried at his funeral.

"Papa," I managed to gasp. Gabe's eyes in Tyler's face met mine.

I was not his daughter, but I looked like his daughter. I had her face—and I hoped that was enough. I hoped, even knowing what I was, that he couldn't stare into my face while he killed me.

Our eyes held. Gabe sobbed, gave one hard, final squeeze—and then he let me go.

I sucked in a ragged breath and lunged for the knife and scrambled out from beneath him, to the pyre, to where the flames were snapping at the heels of both my sisters. Grey was moaning, groggy from smoke inhalation. I dumped the backpack on the ground and scrambled up the burning debris toward them, picking a path through the fire. My eyelashes curled and melted in the wall of heat. There was no air to pull into my lungs. I inhaled ash and embers. The fire licked and hissed, searing my hands, my knees, my bare feet as I climbed.

I slipped Grey's blade through her leather bonds first. The moment she was free, the power shifted. I felt it. It was as if time slowed. Grey unfurled to her full height and took the knife from my hand and cut Vivi free, and then she was dragging us both through the fire as it lurched after us. Wood split and popped, sending hot embers into our hair, our clothes. The fuel beneath us burned fluorescent red and the heat was a wall, solid and impassable until Grey pulled us away and we tumbled out the other side onto the cool, sodden grass of the clearing.

"Vivi!" Grey said as she shook our sister's shoulders. "Vivi!" Then she was bent over her, her palms sinking into Vivi's chest, four, five times, until Vivi finally moaned. "Oh, thank God, thank God," Grey said as she took Vivi's ash-slicked face in her hands and bent to kiss her forehead.

I stared at my arm, where a patch of my skin had burned away and blackened at the edges. Beneath it, the truth I'd wanted to know and hadn't wanted to know: a second layer of skin, untouched by the flames.

Grey was watching me, her breaths coming in stabs.

"It's true, isn't it?" I asked her. I was shaking. The pain of my burns was beginning to gather, the singed nerve endings waking up in my toes, my hands, the tips of my fingers. "We're not us."

Grey closed her eyes. A tear squeezed from between her lashes and swept a clean line through the grime and blood on her cheek. Finally, she nodded.

True.

Then she stood and went to where Tyler's skin now lay empty and deflated on the forest floor. Gabe, like Rosie, was gone, moved on to wherever the dead went when they let go of this place, when it let go of them. What he left behind in his absence was gruesome: Tyler's skinsuit with no bones or muscle or soul to animate it. A flat sack of skin, the hair and eyelashes and fingernails still attached.

I had left Tyler alone. I had left him alone in the woods and my father had found him, taken him, done this to him.

I wondered where Tyler's flayed body was. I looked back at the pyre. The fire churned above the tree line now, the stakes that had been set up for us engulfed in flames. The smoke smelled of blistering fat, burning bone. In there. His body must be in there, hidden beneath the blaze, where we were supposed to be.

Grey was bent over his flat skin. "I'm not letting you go," she chanted. "I'm not letting you go, I'm not letting you go."

"We saw Gabe skin him," Vivi rasped as she rolled onto her side. I went to her and slid my palm under her cheek and picked leaves from the tacky wound at the back of her head. "Poor Grey."

"I'm not letting you go," Grey continued, her hands hovering over the skin that had once covered Tyler's chest. God. No one should have to see someone they loved like that. "I'm not letting you go."

"Grey," I said quietly. "We have to go home."

"I am not leaving without him," she said. "I can save him."

"How?"

"The same way I saved you. If he's stuck here, I can stitch his soul back inside his skin." She leaned down to speak to him.

"Listen to me, Tyler. I bind you with my grief. I blame myself for your death and I'm not letting you go. Come back to me."

I tried to wrap my head around all the different pieces of him. His dead body, burning unseen in the pyre. The skin from that body, laid out in front of me. His soul—or whatever it was—the leftover part of him that would pass through this place on its way to oblivion.

I might see him again. I let that small hope kindle in my chest as we waited.

And waited.

And waited.

"I don't think he's here," Vivi's cheek was hot beneath my burned hand. We couldn't linger. We had to get out of the Half-way. "I don't think he's coming."

"No," Grey breathed, her hands sinking into the forest floor. Pendants of saliva swayed from her lips as she wailed out the pain of her grief. It wrung her body of air, contorted her into a ball of ribs, fists. When she sucked in her next breath, it was the sound of a church organ: huge and long and mournful. Sobs shook her, bent her, broke her, until the despair left her spent. The most beautiful woman in the world, so used to the universe bending to her will, unable to save the life of the man she loved.

I saw a flicker of movement at the edge of the clearing. There was a figure, dark-haired and naked, staring at me from between the trees. I opened my mouth to cry out to him, but he shook his head.

Then, as quickly as he had appeared, the soul of Tyler Yang faded back into the shadows.

23

CLIMBING OUT OF the Halfway wasn't like falling into it. Falling into it had been as easy as taking a step over a threshold, like slipping down a slide. Gravity did most of the work. Coming the other way was *hard*. I had to drag my whole body through tar. I couldn't breathe, I couldn't see. I was drowning in nothingness, and then, finally, I fell backward, into a field of flowers and smoke. It was dark. The ground beneath me was hard and stank of burned wood and the chemical punch of smoking plastic. For a second, I was worried it hadn't worked. Then Grey and Vivi fell after me, on top of me. The pain of my broken ribs and the disorientation of the door forced bile from my stomach. I rolled onto my side and vomited.

I blinked. The darkness thinned to vapor. We were in a burned-out kitchen covered in a blanket of carrion flowers. Grey's kitchen. I pulled myself upright on the checkerboard floor. The backs of my arms and legs were coated in soot. The world was silent and still.

"God, it sucks even harder coming back," Vivi moaned, her voice raspy and wrong.

I helped her roll onto her side and slid her backpack under her head while Grey riffled through the books that had been strewn on the floor when we toppled the bookshelf.

"We should get her to a hospital," I said as I stroked the peach fuzz of Vivi's skull.

"Soon," Grey said. She found what she was looking for: a book that opened to reveal that it wasn't a book at all, but a secret compartment. Typical Grey. Nothing was ever simple with her, nothing was ever what it seemed. Inside was an assortment of herbs in glass vials and a small bottle of vinegar. Grey used the edge of her knife to crush the anise on her kitchen floor, then added it to the vinegar along with salt and wormwood, and then she shook. The same potion that Agnes had made.

She sank down on Vivi's other side. "Drink," she said as she put the bottle to our sister's lips.

Vivi squirmed away, her face sour. "I don't want that shit."

"*Drink it*," Grey ordered, and of course Vivi did as she was told, because Grey was in charge. Grey soothed her as she vomited the Halfway out, a slop of green dead things spilling from inside her and over the charred floor.

"You killed children," I said quietly as I watched my sister tear a strip from her hospital gown and begin to dab the tincture on the mash of broken skin at the back of Vivi's head.

Grey looked up at me, her eyes black and flat. "Yes," she answered.

"I'm not Iris Hollow."

"No. Not on the inside."

I sank my fingernails into the scar at my throat, tearing at the skin that was not mine. The skin of a dead girl encasing the body of a dead thing. The petals of a heady flower concealing something rotten and dangerous beneath.

"Stop," Grey ordered. "If you rip your skin off, you'll die."

"I'm already dead, though, aren't I?"

"Think of Cate, Iris. Think of every terrible thing that's happened to her. You are all she has left. If you die . . . you'll destroy her."

I let my hands fall to my sides and sobbed. "Tell me how it happened."

"There will be a time and a place when—"

"Tell me," I said. "*Now.*"

Grey exhaled sharply and went back to tending Vivi's wound. "I whispered to them through a door on New Year's Eve. The veil was extra thin that night, as it always is between years. The Hollow sisters heard me. They followed. When I told them I needed help, they came with me willingly. They tied red-and-black tartan way markers so they could find their way home. They were smart—but they were also too trusting. I lured them back to the hovel we were living in. They trusted me, because I was a little girl too."

"Then you cut their throats and skinned them."

Grey paused her work and closed her eyes. I felt Vivi go rigid. "Yes," Grey continued. "I helped you slip into your new skin and stitched you up at the throat. I didn't . . . enjoy what I did. I'm not a monster. I only did what was necessary to get us out of there. To give the three of us a second chance. All that was left, in the end, was a small scar at each of our throats. We followed their bread crumbs back to where they'd fallen through. We were able to crawl back through to the land of the living. We tricked the door, because we were neither alive nor dead, but something in between. Then we waited on that street in Scotland for someone to find us and give us a home."

A wolf in sheep's clothing, Agnes had called Grey. Something monstrous, draped in a disguise, something so unnatural that she confounded not only humans but the very rules of life and death. Half-dead, half-alive, and thus able to move between those states as she pleased.

"Fuck me," Vivi whispered. "We really are cuckoos?"

"You should drink too," Grey said as she handed me the draft. I took it from her. "How did you know it would work?"

"It was a guess. A hope, born from fairy tales and fables—but my intuition was right. To escape the Halfway, we had to become halfway. To leave the liminal, we had to become liminal. I don't think we're the first like us—changeling myths had to have come from somewhere, right? Old tales of fairy children left in the place of human babies, these creatures with ravenous appetites and strange abilities. Others figured it out too. Not just me. Now *drink*."

I turned the bottle around in my hands and watched suspended fragments of wormwood and anise drift in the vinegar. "The carrion flowers. The ants. Why are they everywhere?" I took a bitter, salty sip and immediately felt something move inside me, deep in my gut, and then my body was screaming to get it out. My stomach convulsed, and I vomited again, this time bringing up bile and mold and insects.

Grey held my hair back. "You're okay," she said as I retched again. "You're okay. I don't know all the secrets of the place, Iris. It smells like death and decay because everything there is dead.

271

It gets inside everything, infects everything, pulls everything apart if you let it."

Grey took the bottle back from me and took a sip herself, then gagged up what had been growing inside her. "We should get you both to a hospital."

"I'm not done yet," I said. "Why are we always hungry?"

"Because you're dead and the dead are always starving." The way she said it, so matter-of-factly. *You're dead.* "Food can never sate your hunger, can never fill the emptiness inside you."

Vivi pulled herself up. Her movements were groggy but her expression was cold stone. She looked at Grey the way I was looking at Grey: with my teeth gritted and my lips curled down in disgust.

"You made us forget," I said. "When we came back through to Scotland. You whispered something to us. 'Forget this.' You took it all away."

Grey shook her head. "I can't make you do anything, Iris, just like I couldn't make Tyler. Our power only works on the living, not on the dead, and not on those who've died briefly. I told you to forget, and you did, because you wanted to."

"Jesus. You're a monster," Vivi said.

"*No*," Grey said. "Don't call me that. I promised you I would always keep you safe—and I did. I have. I brought you back to life."

"Who is under this skin?" I pressed. "What do I look like underneath Iris Hollow's skin?"

"I don't know."

"How can you not know?"

"I know you want neat, tidy answers for everything but I don't have them. I don't remember who we were before. After we came back, I began to forget everything too. The Halfway started to feel like a dream, like something that hadn't really happened. I wasn't sure anymore whether it was a story or whether it was real. I had to know, so I tried to go back. It took me a dozen tries before I figured it out."

"In Bromley-by-Bow," Vivi said. "The week after Gabe died."

"Yes. I fell through a door. The same door Mary Byrne must have fallen through on New Year's Eve in 1955. I had no trouble coming home, though. I didn't understand, yet, that our blood was special. I didn't remember what I was or what I'd done."

"How did you figure it out?"

"Yulia Vasylyk, my first roommate when I left home. She followed me through a door. Stupid girl. I tried to bring her home but she couldn't follow me back. The doors wouldn't let her. When it became apparent that she was stuck there, she went wild. Started tearing her clothes off, biting me, scratching my face. She split my lip and I swallowed a mouthful of my own blood. Then I had an idea: If there was something in my blood that let me come and go as I pleased, maybe it could get Yulia home too. I had to knock her out, she was so hysterical. Then I smeared my blood on her, I made her drink some—nothing seemed to work. I don't know why I thought to try runes. You know I keep a copy of *A Practical Guide to the Runes* on my bedside table, I just . . . I was out of other ideas. But it worked. A simple spell. A gateway between death and life. Once we were back in London, she fought me again, ran away from me. The police found her wandering the streets naked, and she blamed me for what had happened to her, even though I saved her. I brought her back.

"It's a grim place to be trapped for eternity, but if you can come and go as you please . . . I had it all to myself to explore.

In the first year I left home, I must have gone back and forth a hundred times. It was a place of secrets, and so I started sewing secrets into my designs. People loved it. It made me even more famous. There is so much to see there. Mostly horrors, but glimpses of beauty too."

"Then something went wrong," Vivi said.

"About a year ago, someone noticed me coming and going. Someone who'd been waiting for me for a long time."

"Papa," I said.

"Yes. Gabe Hollow tracked me like an animal. Watched me. Followed me. He must have seen me bring Agnes back with blood and runes. Is she . . . ?"

"No," I said. "She didn't make it."

Grey pressed her lips together and sniffled. "I tried to make amends for what I did to those girls. I found Agnes, this living child trapped in a dead place, and I brought her home. That has to count for something, right?"

I didn't say anything. I wasn't sure it counted for anything at all. What if Grey had stumbled upon Agnes instead of the Hollow sisters? Would she have been so benevolent then?

"Gabe laid traps for me," Grey continued. "He almost caught me the first time. I got away, but he'd hurt me. He had enough of my blood to come through the doors himself. I didn't realize he'd be able to track me down, but he did. He found me in Paris. I got away again, caught a flight to London. I didn't want to involve you if I didn't have to. I didn't want him to come after you too, but I needed to leave you a message. I needed to know you'd come looking for me if I disappeared."

"You broke into our house and hid the key in your old room."

Grey nodded. "Gabe and some other dead thing ambushed me not long after, in my apartment. I got one of them. Cut his throat. If you kill them on this side of the veil, they go still. Gabe overpowered me, though. He hid the body in my ceiling and dragged me back to the Halfway. I waited. For days and days he kept me. I started to think, maybe, that you wouldn't find me, that I would die there, all alone, that I would become part of the place I had sacrificed so much to escape. I fought. I got free. But I was weak. I was lost and wandering. And then I heard your voice. I felt your heart beating in my chest. We're linked by what we did, by the lives we sacrificed. Linked by blood and death and magic. I found my way back to the door that led to my kitchen. Here. You helped lead me home."

We were sisters. We felt each other's pain. We *caused* each other's pain. We knew the smell of each other's morning breath. We made each other cry. We made each other laugh. We got angry, pinched, kicked, screamed at each other. We kissed, on the forehead, nose on nose, butterfly eyelashes swept against cheeks. We wore each other's clothes. We stole from each other, treasured objects hidden under pillows. We defended each other. We lied to each other. We pretended to be older people, other people. We played dress up. We spied on each other. We possessed each other like shiny things. We loved each other with potent, fervent fury. Animal fury. Monstrous fury.

My sisters. My blood. My skin. What a gruesome bond we shared.

"So Papa . . . knew what we were?" Vivi asked.

Grey's expression went dark. "Not your father. Not really. But yes. He knew. From the very first moment he saw us after we came back, I think he knew. It took Cate longer to believe, but she came to understand as well, after a time."

"Wait—*Cate* knows?" I asked. "How is that possible?"

"Because I told her," Grey said. "The night she threw me out. When I came home drunk, I snapped. I was angry. She was so controlling. I told her that I skinned her children and killed her husband, and if she didn't leave me alone, I'd skin her too."

"You . . . *killed* him?" Vivi said, still putting together the pieces that had fallen into place for me in the Halfway. "You killed *Papa*?"

"Like I said: I promised you I would always keep you safe, Vivi. Gabe Hollow was a threat. You know that. Papa was losing his mind. You remember the morning he put us in the car. He would have driven us off a cliff and murdered us all if I hadn't stepped in. So I . . . made a suggestion to him. I was only just starting to understand the power we had over other people. I didn't want to kill him. I didn't even mean to kill him."

I didn't want this, his note had said. Not a suicide note, after all: a last-ditch SOS to his wife.

"He wasn't losing his mind, though," Vivi said. "He was right and you punished him for it."

"I loved him," I said.

"You barely knew him," Grey said. "Besides, tell me you weren't afraid of him. Tell me you didn't breathe a sigh of relief when we found him hanging. Tell me you truly believe he wouldn't have killed you eventually."

"We deserve to die," I whispered.

"Wait," Vivi said. "Why would Cate keep us if she knows that we're not her children?"

Grey shrugged. "Who knows? My guess is that having something that resembles your children is better than having no children at all. Grief does strange things to people."

I looked my sister in the eyes and searched there for any sign of remorse for what she had done to Cate and Gabe Hollow, but I found none. I stood and made for the door.

"Iris, wait," Grey said as she snatched my arm.

"No. Don't touch me. Listen to me. I don't want to see you anymore. I don't want you in my life."

"I got you out," Grey said fiercely. "I gave you the life I promised you I would give you. I have no regrets. I want you to know that. I would do everything I did again, one hundred times over. When you are ready to talk to me, I will be waiting for you, because I am your sister.

"In this life, and in the last."

24

THE X-RAYS SHOWED that four of my ribs were fractured. There wasn't much the doctors could do for my ribs apart from pain relief, but a junior doctor was stitching the cut on my forehead by the time Cate arrived, her eyes wet and her face thin with worry.

She stood at the doorway, sniffling, looking me up and down. I knew what she was looking for this time: She wanted to make sure I was really who I said I was.

"It's me, Cate," I said as she stared at me. "It's me."

She pulled up a chair next to me and folded my free hand into hers, then bent to inhale the scent of my skin again, again, again.

"You were gone for two weeks," she said finally.

"Two *weeks*?" It had felt like two days.

"I thought . . . I thought it had happened again." Cate swallowed hard, her throat tacky with grief. "That I'd lost you again."

"I'm back. I'm here. I'm not going anywhere."

"Oh, I know. You are banned from ever leaving the house

again. Homeschooling, university by correspondence, then some kind of freelance job that doesn't require you to ever leave me again. Okay?"

I smiled a little. "Okay," I said as I patted her head.

"What happened?" she asked. I took a deep breath in. Cate could tell I was about to start lying and pressed one of her fingers to my lips. "Please. Please tell me the truth. I want to know. I can handle it."

Could she, though? Could any mother handle that terrible truth?

"All done here," said the doctor. "Let me check on how your sisters are doing, but you're all good to go."

"Thank you," Cate said as he left the room.

"I went back," I said when it was just the two of us. "I have something for you." I motioned to Vivi's backpack, on a chair across the room. Cate brought it to me. I unzipped it and took out the three strips of fabric I'd cut from our childhood coats. No—not our childhood coats. Cate's daughters' childhood coats. One of red-and-black tartan. One of green tweed. One of Bordeaux-red faux fur. There were specks of blood on each of them, though I hoped my mother would mistake them for mold or dirt.

"You found them," Cate said as she thumbed the fabric. And then she was on her knees, shaking, gasping for breath. "Where are they?"

"They're there. In the place we went. They . . . They're not . . . They were together when it happened," I continued quietly. I sank beside her, tried to comfort her. "They didn't feel any pain. They felt warm and safe. They thought they were coming home to you." I didn't know if anything I said was true, but I hoped it was. My mother was sucking sharp, painful breaths into her lungs.

279

My mother, I thought again, rolling the words around in my head. *Not my mother.* Someone else's mother. "I didn't know," I told her as she cried. "I promise. I didn't know what we were or what she did."

"I know, Iris," she said. Then she reached up and stroked my hair. "I know."

"How can you stand me?" I whispered. "How can you stand to have me in your house?"

"Because you've been my daughter for ten years. How could I not love you?"

"I'm so sorry. I'm so sorry about Grey. I'm so sorry I gave you so much grief when you kicked her out."

"You're like her, you know. My Iris. She was quiet and empathetic and whip smart."

There was a soft knock at the door. Vivi was standing in the doorway, her arms and head bandaged. She spotted the strips of fabric Cate held in her hand, then went to wrap her arms around our mother where she'd collapsed on the floor.

"I'm sorry," Vivi said as she stroked her hair. "I'm sorry. I'm sorry."

☾

Grey Hollow sat in the room across the hall, surrounded by police. Vivi escorted our mother past the doorway so she wouldn't have to see Grey, but I stopped and lingered. The light was caustic, and the air smelled thick and vile, of blood and honey and lies. Each of the half dozen people around her watched her with deep pools for eyes, drunk out of their minds on the flood of power that seeped from my sister.

A spider queen with her prey wrapped neatly in her web.

Grey leaned in to place her lips on the mouth of the lead detective, the one who'd spoken at the press conference. The man shuddered with pleasure, his bones barely able to hold up his jelly body.

"A stalker," she told him. "A crazed man, in love with me and my sisters since we were children. The same one who kidnapped us in Edinburgh. He took me and held me captive for weeks. I escaped. Tyler Yang—" Her voice trembled, a string plucked by pain. For a moment her spell wavered, but Grey was stronger than her grief. Such a human emotion was not enough to undo her. She sniffled and sat up straighter, as did every other person in the room, mirroring the enchantress who kept them rapt. "Tyler Yang tried to save me. He was killed by the stalker. It's a terrible tragedy."

"A terrible tragedy," one of the officers echoed, her fingertips trailing across my sister's thigh.

"There's no need to take statements from my sisters," Grey said, and the officers around her agreed.

"Yes, no need to put them through that," the lead detective said as he swept the back of his palm down Grey's shin.

"A stalker," one of them repeated.

"A crazed man. A monster," said another.

"What a terrible tragedy," said a third.

Grey looked up at me, as did all of the police under her spell, a sudden flood of wide irises all pinned to mine. I held my sister's gaze. The power that bound us sparked in my chest.

Then I turned and left her there on her own.

☾

My breath snagged when I saw my sister's face staring up at me from the floor.

Even when rendered as a tattoo, Grey's fine, hook-shaped scar was still the first thing you noticed about her, followed by how achingly beautiful she was. The *Vogue* magazine must have arrived in the post and landed faceup on the hall rug, smack bang, which is where I found it in the silver ghostlight of the morning.

It was not my sister on the cover this time, though, but Tyler. The tattoos on his arms and chest were exposed: Grey's portrait stood out in a sea of ink. I turned on the hall light and picked the magazine up and studied it—him—more closely.

In the photograph they'd chosen of him, he sat in a chair wearing nothing but fishnets and patent red loafers, his legs crossed, his black hair spilling around his face to his shoulders. There was no text, only the picture and the years of Tyler's birth and death. He was twenty. A year younger than Grey.

"You ready?" Vivi said as she made her way down the stairs, dressed in plum lipstick and the most un-Vivi outfit I'd seen her in since she'd stopped letting Cate dress her a decade ago: a dark, conservative dress that covered her arm tattoos and skirted her knees.

"Who are you and what have you done with my sister?" I asked.

"That's way dark, Iris."

"What, too soon for changeling jokes?"

Vivi looped her arm around my waist and rested her head on my shoulder. "I liked him," she said as she studied the *Vogue* cover. "He deserved better than what he got."

"Everyone we come into contact with deserves better than what they end up getting."

"We should go," Cate said from the top of the staircase as she tugged on a pair of low pumps, Sasha looping around her feet. "Iris, come here, I'll braid your hair."

Vivi looked at me but said nothing.

"Cate . . . ," I said as my mother made her way down the stairs. "Do you mind if I don't have my hair braided anymore?" It was a ritual she shared with her dead daughter, something to keep them tethered. It felt cruel to snatch it from her, but Vivi was right. I couldn't be everything for her all the time. I could only be myself, whatever that was. "It's just . . . I prefer it out."

Cate paused, one arm threaded through her coat. "Of course I don't mind." She shrugged her coat all the way on and took my chin in her hand. "Of course I don't mind. I do mind, however, that we're going to be disgracefully late. Come on, come on."

It was raining outside, not the usual drizzle of London, but a cold and swollen day that drove rain into our faces as we slipped into my mother's red Mini and drove toward the cemetery.

Tyler Yang's funeral was, much like the man himself, extravagant and highly Instagrammable. It was held in a church that had clearly been styled by some celebrity event planner: thousands of candles cast dim light in the shadowy space, rich floral arrangements curled up the columns and trailed down from the ceiling, and a string ensemble played mournful songs as the pews filled. We found seats at the back as a steady stream of increasingly famous celebrities filed in, most wearing dark House of Hollow creations. A British actress whose TV show had recently become an international sensation was there, as was a famous ex–pop star with her famous footballer husband. There were models, actors, directors, designers—even a few lesser-known members of the royal family. Many people were crying already.

Tyler's coffin was at the front, engulfed in an explosion of white roses and baby's breath—and closed, obviously, because it was empty. I wondered how many people Grey had had to bewitch to sell her extravagant new lie. How many careful threads of silk she'd had to weave, just so, to convince the world that Tyler Yang had been murdered by her stalker when the police would never find any evidence to corroborate her tale.

Tyler's family came in last, along with Grey.

A collective hush befell the crowd when they saw her. My sister was dressed in an elegant House of Hollow dress with a sheer black veil draped over her face. The portrait of a weeping widow from a fairy tale. Through the veil, I could tell that her eyes and nose were raw red, as though she'd been crying and had only managed to compose herself moments before. Her jaw shook as she walked down the aisle grasping the arm of a tall woman I assumed was Tyler's mother. Grey's sadness spilled out of her, rushing over the room like a wave, curling up the walls, drowning everyone. It was terrible to see something so beautiful in so much pain. Hands reached out to her as she went by, hundreds of hands jostling to touch her, hands that trailed over her veiled shoulders, her arms, soaking up some of her grief. It appeared, as she moved, as though she were a magnet moving through a field of iron filings that stood rigid and then sighed as she past.

Everyone. She would bewitch everyone to make her lie the truth.

The rest of Tyler's family followed. His father, tall and handsome like him. His two living sisters and their partners, one with a newborn slung across her chest: Rosie's namesake.

How unbearable, I thought, to lose two of your children. Then I looked at my mother, who had lost three on the same night. Who had had the living ghosts of her murdered daughters haunting her house, eating her food, siphoning her life, for a decade. I slipped my hand into hers and threaded our fingers together.

The service wasn't long. A priest led a prayer and conducted a blessing. Tyler's father gave a reading. His sisters Camilla and Selena delivered his eulogy. There was a slideshow of photographs and videos of him throughout his life. Pictures of a baby with chubby cheeks and arms that looked like bread rolls. First day of school pictures of a tiny boy in an oversized uniform. Pictures of four siblings always together, and then, after a time, only three. Pictures of him as a teenager, skinny and cute but not yet handsome and stylish. Pictures of him as I knew him, tall and angular and striking, his body decidedly masculine but his fashion sense and makeup gender nonconforming. The last photograph was of Rosie holding him on the day he was born, staring down at him while he stared right back up at her.

When it was over, five of Tyler's close friends—and Grey—served as his pallbearers. In her black Louboutin heels, she stood taller than the men around her, the image of a veiled specter from a haunting as she floated back down the aisle with an empty coffin in her hands. As she passed me, I could see her crying. I could feel that she wanted me to reach out to her, to place a hand on her shoulder, to tell her that it would be all right. My fingertips tingled, aching to comfort her. Time froze as she stood in front of me, silently begging. Then, as quickly as she came, she was gone again, the procession moving past us, toward the church doorway now glutted with press. I exhaled and unclenched my fingers. Outside on the street, police were stationed to control the roiling mass of fans who'd come to lay flowers on the steps of the church and to witness Grey's grief. They wailed as the coffin past.

There was an extravagant after-party planned, naturally—

how else would you bid farewell to Tyler Yang?—but we left after they buried the coffin. It felt wrong to linger with the people who had known him for longer than I had, better than I had. I had known him for a handful of days and only liked him for half of them. I had held his hand and led him through a doorway to another world. I had kissed him once, a clandestine kiss stolen from a man who was not mine to kiss.

We wandered across the wet lawn of the cemetery beneath our umbrellas, away from the mourners, to the grave of Gabe Hollow, beloved husband and father. Cate, who usually visited most weeks, hadn't been since Grey had gone missing. She knelt to pull the weeds that had begun to sprout at the base of his headstone, then parted the soft earth with her fingers and opened a hole, into which she placed the three strips of fabric I had brought back from the Halfway. All that remained now of Iris, Vivi, and Grey.

"They're all together," Cate said as she closed the hole and pressed her palms into the dirt.

When she stood we held her, and then we all went home.

☾

I went back to school two weeks after the Halfway let me go, when my ribs were healed enough to sit at a desk all day.

Justine Khan made a loud *ugh* sound as she caught sight of me in the hall. "Was it too much to hope she was dead?" she muttered to Jennifer and her other friends as they passed me in a giggling group. "We should be so lucky."

"Is there something you wanted to say to me, Justine?" I said. I had never confronted her directly before. Years of torment—

muttered jokes in class, dead birds slipped into my backpack, bloody *witch* smeared across my locker—and I had never once called her out to her face. *Let it go. Leave it be. It will be easier if you don't fight back.*

Justine and Jennifer both ignored me, so I followed them and said again, louder this time, "Is there something you wanted to say?"

Finally, Justine had no choice but to turn and come face-to-face with me. "Um," she stammered, searching for something witty to say and coming up empty-handed. "No."

"Are you sure? Now's your chance. You have my full attention."

"Oh, screw you, *witch*."

"Not so brave now, are you? Not when you have to look me in the eye."

Justine stared at me, lips pursed and nostrils flared, but she didn't say anything. I lunged forwards in a feint. Justine screamed and clutched at her heart and stumbled backward, landing hard on the ground behind her, taking Jennifer down with her.

"If you mess with me," I whispered as I knelt by her side and tucked a strand of her long, dark hair behind her ear, "I will make you shave your pretty head in front of the whole school again. Do you understand?"

I was not like my sister. I would not use the power that had been forced upon me through blood and violence to hurt more people, destroy more lives.

I knew this—but Justine Khan didn't need to.

Justine swallowed and nodded. I extended my hand to help her up but she scrabbled back in horror, so I stood, and I left her there, and I went to class.

I was not Grey Hollow. I was not Iris Hollow, either.

I was something stranger.

Something stronger.

For the first time, I felt the power of what I was coursing through my veins, and it didn't scare me.

It made me feel . . . alive.

EPILOGUE

"THERE HAVE BEEN mills in this area at least since Saxon times," our tour guide said. "This site has been a flour mill, a gunpowder mill, and a gin distillery in its time, among other things."

"Fascinating," I replied, for perhaps the hundredth time.

"Tell us more," Vivi said. I elbowed her in the ribs, hard. If I could tell she was being sarcastic, our guide could too.

We were walking down an interior corridor of the ancient mill complex, the same one Grey had explored the week after Gabe died. The exterior was all brickwork but here, inside, the walls were wood, warped and weathered by age.

Our guide paused. "I must say, I was delighted when you reached out to book a private tour. Not enough young people are interested in tidal mills anymore."

Vivi smiled her wicked smile. "One of the true failings of our generation."

Three Mills Island was only a short walk from Bromley-by-Bow. I'd been back at school for several weeks, but I'd been find-ing it hard to concentrate. My entire understanding of the world and my place in it had shifted—but that wasn't the only reason.

In the weeks since we came back, Grey Hollow had resumed her extraordinary life. I knew this because I continued to follow her on Instagram, saw her triumphant return to regular posting about parties and catwalks and celebrity friends, saw the announcement of her eight-figure book deal about her harrowing "kidnapping" ordeal and the equally rich movie deal to go along with it, in which she would play herself. I saw her on the cover of magazines in the grocery store and I saw her when I turned on my TV.

My sister, the stranger.

She was everywhere. She would always be everywhere.

It seemed unfair that Grey got to live and Tyler had to die and everyone just accepted that's that the way it was—but maybe it didn't have to be.

That's why I was here.

The idea that I'd missed something kept niggling at me. I came here after school sometimes and wandered the grounds, trying to find a way down to the basement. In the end, a private tour seemed like the only option to get to where I wanted to go.

I checked the time on my phone. Almost sunset. "Any chance we could see the basement?" I asked our guide.

"Oh, no. Unfortunately the basement isn't part of the tour. There are protected Saxon ruins beneath the foundations of the mill."

I sighed. It would be so easy to reach out and rest my finger on her lips and have her do exactly what I wanted her to. "That's okay. Actually, I really have to pee. Where are the toilets?"

"Back the way we came," she said. "Second right, then your first left. Do you want me to show you the—"

"No, that's fine. I'll find my way back. Vivi?"

"Oh," Vivi said. "Yeah, I'm also suddenly busting for a wee."

"Okay, I'll wait here for you both. We still have the Clock Mill and the Miller's House to get through."

"Literally cannot wait," Vivi said.

We turned and started walking. If everything went according to plan, the guide would be waiting for us for a very long time. Days. Weeks, maybe.

"I happen to think tidal mills are very interesting, I'll have you know," I said to my sister as we backtracked.

Vivi rolled her eyes. "Of course you would."

The spiral staircase that led to the basement was easy to find, tucked away behind a door that read STAFF ONLY BEYOND THIS POINT. We headed down into the dark. It was cool and damp here beneath the mill. I turned on my phone flashlight and swept the beam across the space. The walls were brick. The ground was dust. And there, in the center, was a freestanding door. A ruin leftover from Saxon times. A door that used to lead somewhere, but now lead somewhere else.

I texted my mother.

Are you sure you're okay with this? We could be gone for a while.

Her response dinged into my phone almost immediately, as was her way. **Do what you need to do to make things right. You can go anywhere you want—as long as you promise to keep coming back.**

We promise.

Okay. I'll try not to die of worry. I love you.

I love you too. See you . . . soon.

I put my palm against the stone and counted down the seconds until sunset.

On the other side of this door, in another world, I had left a message for a boy carved into a tree: WAIT FOR ME HERE.

I kept thinking back to the moment Grey had tried to put his soul back in his body, to bring him home the same way she had brought us home. How I had seen a shadow of movement at the edge of a clearing and had been certain, for half a heartbeat, that he had been there.

Maybe something of Tyler still remained in that place.

Maybe, if he was there, I could find him.

Maybe, if he was there, I could bring him back.

The seconds ticked over. Somewhere outside, the last of the sun sank below the horizon. The basement smelled suddenly of smoke and decay. The dead began to whisper.

"Ready?" I asked my sister.

"I picked a hell of a day to quit smoking," she replied.

We held hands. For a moment, a door between this world and the next opened.

We stepped through.

ACKNOWLEDGMENTS

FIRST AND FOREMOST, I owe a great debt of gratitude to my agent, Catherine Drayton. Thank you for pushing me to rewrite and rewrite and rewrite (and then rewrite some more), to tease the thread of an actual story out of a jumbled mess of ideas. Thanks are also due to the excellent Claire Friedman: Together you are an incredibly sharp (and intimidating) pair of readers. There would be no book at all without both of you being so willing to pan for gold amid the sludge.

If Catherine and Claire guided me in finding the thread, then my editor, Stacey Barney, helped me weave it into (what I hope is) a rich and vibrant tapestry. I was still discovering this story when I shared it with you. Thank you for trusting me to find the rest of it and lighting the way for me when I was stumbling through the dark. You saw the *much better* book inside the clumsy, tangled thing I first handed you.

Everyone else at Penguin Random House who worked on this book—Caitlin Tutterow in editorial, Felicity Vallence and Shannon Spann in digital marketing, Olivia Russo and Audra

Boltion in publicity, and no doubt a dozen other brilliant people behind the scenes—thank you for everything you do to bring more stories into the world (but especially everything you did for this one).

I am in awe of the cover of this book, which was designed by Theresa Evangelista from artwork created by Aykut Aydoğdu. It is the opulent, harrowing cover of my dreams/nightmares.

The whole team at Penguin Australia have been so behind this book from day one. Thank you to Amy Thomas, Laura Harris, and Tina Gumnior, especially, for your continued support and enthusiasm. Emma Matthewson from Hot Key—thank you for giving me my first publishing home in the UK and then allowing me to stick around for five years. It has been the best place to live, to grow. My film agent, Mary Pender, got my first book made into a movie without me even having to sell my soul or firstborn child to the devil—immense gratitude is due there, forever.

Melissa Albert is the godmother of this particular story. Your books and your tack-sharp feedback both have made me a better writer. I am endlessly grateful for your words and your friendship, you mad genius.

Katherine Webber, my writing soul mate, was—as always—my first reader and first cheerleader. You make me feel like a glowing literary goddess, which is not good for my ego (or is it?) but is decidedly useful to fall back on in the long, lonely stretches when the words don't come easily and you're convinced you are the human embodiment of a trash fire. Thanks for lifting me up and dusting me off countless times.

To the rest of my London writing crew—Holly Bourne, Samantha Shannon, Nina Douglas, Alwyn Hamilton, and Laure Eve—it has been a delight discovering you all, my coven of literary witches. Thank you for giving me a home in London, for keeping me (semi) sane during the pandemic, and for manifesting by candlelight. You're all magic.

I have warm feelings of appreciation also toward Kiran Millwood Hargrave, Anna James, Katherine Rundell, and Louise O'Neill. What a treat it has been to arrive in the UK and find such searingly brilliant women (some of you within walking distance!).

I have spent much of the past year enamored of the sparkly brilliance of my Luminaries, Harriet Constable and Anna Russell. Thank you for the costumes, the glitter, the festivities (and—very occasionally—the writing).

Thank you to Amie Kaufman, my lifeline across the seas.

I owe thanks to two great writing residencies: Firstly to Varuna, The National Writers' House, where the first chapter of this book was written in the Blue Mountains outside Sydney. Secondly to Studio Faire in Nérac, France, run by Colin Usher and Julia Douglas, where the closing chapters of this book were laid down in March 2020, in the final days before borders began closing and the world held its breath.

There are women from my hometown who have nourished my writing dreams for over a decade now: Cara Faagutu, Renee Martin, Alysha Morgan, Kirra Moke, Sarah Maddox. Thank you for celebrating each small win as though it is a grand victory.

I hope, despite its darkness, that at its heart this book captures something of the deep bond between sisters. I am the eldest of three girls and many of the sweeter moments (and some of the feistier ones too) between Iris and her sisters were inspired by growing up alongside my own two brilliant, maddening, magnificent sisters. Emily, Chelsea: As Iris said, I love you both with potent, fervent fury.

My parents, Sophie and Phillip, and my grandmother Diane continue to be my greatest champions. You built me from the ground up. I cannot thank you enough for your unfailing enthusiasm and belief in me.

I am also grateful for the encouragement from my Seneviratne family, who have embraced me and supported me with fervor from day one. Thank you to Lisbeth, Aruna, Tom, and Lauren, but thank you especially, this time, to Archa: The kernel of this book was born in Sri Lanka, on the morning you took us to Anuradhapura and I found the broken doors.

The greatest lashings of appreciation must be reserved for Martin Seneviratne, my inexhaustible fount of daily encouragement. No one has cheered louder, celebrated harder, or consoled more than you. You are on every page of this book. Thank you. I love you.

KRYSTAL SUTHERLAND
READERS' CLUB

Did you know you can now join the Krystal Sutherland Readers' Club? You'll be the first to hear about Krystal Sutherland news, upcoming books, projects and more.

Sign up today to get exclusive instant access to a bonus chapter from House of Hollow...

To join, scan the QR code or use the URL below:

http://bit.ly/krystalsutherland

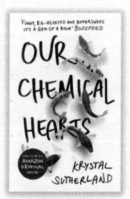

HOT KEY BOOKS

Thank you for choosing a Hot Key book.

If you want to know more about our authors
and what we publish, you can find us online.

You can start at our website

www.hotkeybooks.com

And you can also find us on:

We hope to see you soon!